BILLY AND
THE DEVIL

BILLY AND
THE DEVIL

by
DEAN LILLEYMAN

Publications

urbanepublications.com

First published in Great Britain in 2015
by Urbane Publications Ltd
Suite 3, Brown Europe House, 33/34 Gleamingwood Drive,
Chatham, Kent ME5 8RZ
Copyright © Dean Lilleyman, 2015

A CIP catalogue record for this book is available
from the British Library.

ISBN 978-1-910692-33-2

Design and Typeset by Julie Martin

Cover by The Invisible Man

Printed in Great Britain by
CPI Group (UK) Ltd,
Croydon, CR0 4YY

urbanepublications.com

The publisher supports the Forest Stewardship Council® (FSC®) (FSC®), the leading international forest-certification
organisation. This book is made from acid-free paper from an FSC®-certified provider. FSC is the only forest-
certification scheme supported by the leading environmental organisations, including Greenpeace.

CHAPTER AND VERSE

In the middle of my journey through life, I woke to find myself in a dark wood.

Dante

There is no fate that cannot be surmounted by scorn.

Camus

You wake to a soundless house...

And the knowingness that they're not here anymore seeps slow-creep inwards, that dark weight that makes you blur, yourself falling away from yourself, that shadow-hook-tug that pulls from deep.

You keep your eyes closed, bringing your knees up to your chest, wrapping your arms around your legs until you're a tight ball in the womb of your bed. You lie there, your head under the stale-ale fug of bed-sheets, damp from night-sweats of whatever dark dreams took you.

And yet, you wish for a return to this sleep, a sleep that takes this waking away.

A lurch of lead-heavy gut makes you free an arm to pull the sheets from your face, and eyes closed tight, you breathe.

In. Out. In.

And then you can hold it no longer. The daylight snaps and burns as you retch that brown-yellow water onto the green lino below, again, again, feeling that bitter string of saliva hanging from your lips as you see the empty Guinness bottles skittled, that black scuffed shoe by the dirty skirting board, that spatter of black shit in the seat of your crumpled trousers.

The room tilts.

You remember walking the burning fields with her. She wore that long blue dress, those little red roses dancing over her breasts, her behind. You had her in the woods by the stream, her eyes catching the sun that glittered through the leaves.

There's a three-quarters-drunk bottle of Watney's Pale Ale on the mantelpiece. That light lights itself inside of you. You knock the sour booze back. A salty tang makes your tongue spasm. **PISS?**

In the dusty gold-rimmed mirror is your thin mottled face. You reach for the half-toothed comb from your inside jacket-pocket, then tug it through your oily matted hair.

Behind you is the living room you shared with your wife and your children.

They left the red settee and the table. They left the cupboard and two yellow plates. They left a picture of a crying clown and a blue teacup. They left a coal bucket and this mirror.

You wash your face in cold water from the kitchen tap, and then you piss into the sink.

By the sink is a dirty blue teacup. By the dirty blue teacup is a solicitor's letter saying you can't go near her, or the kids.

You zip yourself up and leave by the backdoor. You don't lock up.

———

There is four pounds in your pocket and change. You finger the coins as the bus nears town. Through the window you see the Crooked Spire. The lead slates catch the sunlight in a dull glint. A swirl of pigeons twists like backwards smoke over rooftops to your left. A mother with a shopping basket walks the pavement holding her small daughter's hand. They are laughing at a joke you will never hear.

When Ena and the kids left, they didn't tell you where they'd gone. When you came back from the pub and read the note, you sat on the red settee and cried. Then you threw the two yellow plates against the wall. No one would tell you where they'd gone. The whole street pretended not to know. Then you went to the council offices pretending you were Ena's brother just out the army, and that you'd been to her old address and she wasn't there anymore. And of course the woman from the council told you.

She was stupid, like all women are.

———

The first pub you go to is The Fox's Vault. You're not barred from here but the landlord gives you that look as he pours your pint.

Behave now, he says.

You smile, and say, Of course.

The first pint is beautiful. You neck it in three. That light lights itself inside of you.

You ask for another. The landlord gives you that look again, says, Last one, Walter.

You nod, say Yes, go sit by the jukebox with your drink.

You drink, light your first fag of the day. It too, is beautiful. Remember the first fag you ever had? The one Dad gave you? Both of you sat in front of the hearth, the firelight dancing on his face. How old were you? Ten? Eleven?

Dad never said much, did he. Unless he was pissed. Mam saying, Don't Frank, don't.

He broke her wrist once, didn't he. Her telling you and your brothers and sisters that she fell making the fire. None of you believed her. But then, none of you said anything, did you.

You finish your pint and walk out into the sunshine. So bloody what if she's gone and took the kids with her? So bloody fucking what?

In The Queen's Head, the landlord says No, so you flick him the jacks and head to the Fleece. You're not barred from there.

You drink three pints of Brampton Bitter, three double Bell's. You're on your fourth when Gerry Jones walks in so you sup up unseen in the snug, walk out by the side-door. You owe Gerry money.

You already know he's been looking for you.

The Welbeck, you think.

As you head out onto Knifesmithgate, a Salvation Army band is playing. A woman in a stupid black hat shakes a collection box in front of you. You tell her, Go sell your fat fuckin tits for pork.

She stops shaking her tin and looks at you, her lips parted as though to say something, but she doesn't. The Co-op clock says two-thirty. Half-an-hour till closing. You quicken your pace.

When you leave the Welbeck, the town gets in your way. You push the stupid chuffs from out of your path. Somewhere the Salvation Army band is still playing. Onward, you weave your way past the market, and that gobshite fruit and veg bloke has parked his stupid fucking horse and cart by his stupid fucking stall. You slap the horse's arse with the flat of your hand and it jumps a little, the cart's wooden wheels rattling across the cobbles. The gobshite fruit and veg bloke stops shouting about apples and says Hey! Hey! What the bloody hell d'yer think you're doing? his scraggy lad grabbing the reins, Eeeasy Samson, eeeasy.

You spin on your heel and point a finger.

SHUT. YOUR BLEEDIN'. TRAP.

And off you walk, too much on your plate to be bothered by stupid little chuffs like him, pushing past a stupid long-hair busker on the corner of Clark's, his guitar clanging against the lamppost, **SHIFT PUFFTER**, knowing you need space, space from these stupid chuffs and their stupid fucking faces.

You head to the Regal Picture House. You don't care what's showing. You just need space.

The film is called The Reptile. People are dying of what they think is the plague in a little village on the moors. A darkie with black staring eyes seems to be at the bottom of it.

You fall into sleep, and you see her eyes catching the sun, a sun that glitters through leaves, your fingers that move through her soft hair, the cool hush of the stream and the woodpigeon's lullaby, the warm breath of September soft hustling the trees, and I love you Ena Black with all my heart I do, and I will...

And you will wake, and a mansion will be burning, a reptile man-creature screaming in the flames, and you will leave the dark of the picture house, walking back out into the late afternoon sun, through the thinning streets to Woolworth's, where you will find that long aisle of plates and bowls and cutlery, take that silver ten-inch breadknife from the shelf, leaving with it pocketed and unpaid for, that blade nestled beside your oily half-toothed comb, and that piece of paper, with that house number on it, that street name, that place where they went.

CHAPTER 1

Halfway up the street

She stops to light a fag, watches some sparrows fight over batter-bits, left by a slow-blown chip-paper that tumbleweeds across the Courthouse grass. From the pavement she squints to make out the headline exclaiming Sandie Shaw a winner.

She drags deep on her fag, exhales, puts both hands back on the pram and starts walking, steering around a curled mound of dog muck.

Jean and her sisters watched the Eurovision on their new second-hand black and white TV on Saturday night, bought by her mam the weekend before from a woman at work. Jean and her sisters gasped when Sandie's microphone didn't work at first, and then moved as one to the edge of the new second-hand settee when Sandie's voice came through loud and clear.

Jean would like her hair cut like Sandie's, but for now she wears it in a beehive.

She stoops by the cenotaph to pull the backs of her

sandals up, and to stop her heart beating fast she sings the first line of Sandie's chorus, almost breathing it into the mouth of the pram. Say you love me madly, I'll gladly, be there.

She frowns, drags on her fag, then starts reading the blackened names on the cenotaph.

For those who fell.

She gets as far as Evans G, then understands these names mean nothing to her, and placing one hand on the pram she moves on in slow measured steps, fag in mouth, using her free hand to check her hair.

In the mirror this morning she thought she looked older. This is something she wants, and has been practising an older face. The older face doesn't smile.

She takes her fag out and glances down to her belly and legs as she walks. In her brown suede miniskirt her belly has lost its little pudding, and she thinks her legs have gained nothing after the birth.

In the distance, the Post Office clock looks like it reads a quarter-to-one, but she can't be sure without her glasses.

Jean puts the brake on the big old pram and moves around to the side of it, peering into the flaky chrome struts that hold the hood up. Her black eyeliner is thick today, and her slate-grey eyes stare back between curls of peeling silver. She rubs the loose flakes off and wishes she had a new pram. When the woman from the Social came to tell her someone had donated a used pram and did she want it, Jean felt happy. She walked all the way across town to a big old house to collect it. The woman who was donating the pram smiled at Jean, but she could tell the woman was judging her.

Jean's mam warned her people would be like this when she came home with the baby.

Jean knew this anyway.

Lifting the brake with the toe of her sandal, Jean and the pram move off slowly. She still has quarter of an hour until she meets Mick, and Mick is always late.

Her heart starts beating faster again when she thinks of him, and she hates herself for not being strong and calm like an older woman would.

She parks the pram by the bench and sits down, pulling her skirt down lower.

Stamping her fag out, she remembers Mick's face when she told him she was pregnant. She remembers the flicker of shock in his eyes, the blink, then the grin, the Oh well I suppose we'd best get married then. Typical Mick. But there was to be no wedding, white or otherwise, Jean's mam forbidding her to ever see Mick again.

He's bad like your dad, Jean's mam had said. And you can't make the same mistake I made.

No.

Jean cried when she found out she was pregnant. She didn't tell her mam at first, not until she started to show. Jean's mam was still poorly anyway, so it would have done no good to tell her.

Jean remembers standing up in the courtroom to tell the judge what she saw her dad do to her mother, all the time knowing that inside her belly a new life was growing, and would keep on growing until she could hide it no longer.

Her dad stared at her in the courtroom as she told what she saw, so she looked down at her black sandals while she said it. Jean had promised herself that she wouldn't cry when she told it, but she did. The judge gave him six years, which made Jean cry again.

She wanted him to go away forever.

She wanted him to come home and be her dad.

Jean watched the policeman put the handcuffs on him, and then take her dad down some steps that led to a heavy door. He glanced over his shoulder at Jean, and she thought he smiled at her.

She lights another fag, standing up to look at the Post Office clock again. In her letter she told Mick one o'clock at the Town Hall steps. She picked there because it was far enough from home for her mam not to see, but close enough to get home quick if she needed to.

She won't let Mick see her cry. She can't cry. She's too old for that now.

Rocking the pram as she walks, the squeak squeak of the springs measuring her stride, Jean checks her beehive again with her free hand, pulls her skirt down a little, then looks up to see a single white cloud shaped like a fish. In all the blue sky this is the only cloud, and Jean imagines herself laying across the back of the cloudfish, high above the world and the people in it, looking down on everything and no one knowing she was there.

She stops at the street corner that turns towards the Town Hall, takes another drag on her fag, then with both hands firmly on the pram she moves on, around the corner to where she can see the Town Hall steps, long slow-breathing like when she had the baby.

Typical.

Mick is late, but Jean is almost happy at this. This gives her time to sit and think what she's going to say to him.

She parks the pram and sits three steps up with her feet on the pavement, careful not to show her knickers. She imagines Mick stood in front of her, and she thinks that she will stay sitting, she will stay sitting and she will tell him that the baby in the pram is his son.

When Jean's mam made her not see Mick anymore, Jean wrote him a letter to tell him. She said she would always love him, but she couldn't be with him. She told him she was going away to a Magdalene house in Sheffield and someone would adopt the baby. She imagined herself older in the letter, and had used words like fate and responsibility.

Jean was crying when she wrote the letter. She had to rewrite it twice because some tears had fallen onto the page and that was no good. That was the kind of thing that girls did in films and books, crying onto letters to be sent to far-away lovers, and this wasn't a film, or a book.

Jean drags on her fag, stamps it out, then looks up again to the cloudfish. Its tail has broken away from its body and she imagines herself falling through the gap, rushing towards the earth and its people, all of them looking up and pointing.

Hello Jean.

She blinks, turning her gaze across the face of the sun towards the voice.

There stands Mick, grinning. He is wearing the same leather jacket he always wore, and his hair is still long like it always was. He is holding hands with a blonde girl in a short red dress who is also grinning. Her lipstick is a brighter red than her dress and Jean thinks the girl looks like a slag.

Jean stands up quickly and points to the pram where the baby lies sleeping, its little fists slow-clenching by its tiny mouth.

This is Billy, says Jean in a voice that sounds older, stronger, And I'm keeping him.

Mick and the girl have stopped grinning as Jean turns on her heel, pushing the pram back towards home, where she will make up the baby's bottle, feed his eager mouth by the backyard daffodils, his dark eyes watching the yellow heads nod in the first breath of summer, the world underneath them slow-turning, a tiny hand gripping a little finger, mine, these things will say...

...mine.

Two things have happened

Nannan's dog Sandie keeps being sick, and my aunty's gotten married.

This means two other things. Nannan has to keep washing the lino, and I've moved into the attic. The attic was Aunty Belinda's room, and still has pictures of George Best on the wall. George sometimes has a beard in the pictures and sometimes not. In the pictures where he has a beard he looks like Chris. Chris is Mum's boyfriend. Mum and Chris have gone to see Joe Cocker sing in Sheffield.

Nannan says there's a Dracula film on later. I like watching horror films with Nannan. When they get scary and someone has been bitten and fallen over, Nannan says things like Ooh, go and help her up, Billy, and Ooh, go and take her a plaster, Billy.

This makes them not as scary, and makes me laugh.

Nannan always makes bread and dripping and Marmite for the films, and sometimes we have crisps covered in red sauce. She makes shandy for us too, and sometimes I make them. Nannan showed me how to do them with half a glass of beer and half a glass of lemonade. You have to pour the lemonade in really slow, because if you don't, it goes all frothy and tumbles over the sides.

Before the film, Kojak is on. Nannan likes Kojak, and says one day she's going to marry him. He has a bald shiny head and sucks lollypops all the time. Sometimes, Nannan says things to me that Kojak says, like Who luvs ya, baby? Nannan likes Christopher Lee too. He's Dracula, and she says he can bite her any day of the week.

After tea we watch It's a Knockout, which is really funny when they play football in big costumes with giant heads, but then Sandie is sick under Nannan's chair. The sick is bright yellow and smells like our dustbin when it's sunny. Then Sandie goes around the room bending his back like he's folding himself in half, making burping noises in his belly. More little bits of sick keep coming out so Nannan shoos him outside into the yard. I don't like the smell of Sandie's sick so I go upstairs till it's gone.

Walking up our stairs I can still hear Nannan saying Bloody dog. Mum said Sandie should go to the vet, but Nannan said Where's the money coming from?

Upstairs in my new bedroom, I move the little desk from the side of Aunty Belinda's old bed, which is now my bed, and I put it under the window. The window is high up on the slanty ceiling so I have to stand on the desk to see out. I open the window and look down into the yard to try and see Sandie but I can't because it's too dark. The yard has an oblong of yellowy light from our window and a darker one from next-door's. We did about oblongs at school, so I know they aren't squares.

All I can see is the washing line with some pegs on it like a cannibal necklace made of teeth, and the girl next-door's bike leaning against their wall. I don't think the boy has a bike.

Sometimes, when me and Nannan are watching the Saturday night horror film, they start shouting next-door, and sometimes Nannan puts her ear to the wall to listen. Sometimes she doesn't need to put her ear to the wall because they're so loud. When this happens Nannan shakes her head and says Bloody booze.

Out of my window I can see across Chesterfield. It's all lit up, and I can see the Post Office clock, the Crooked Spire, and a double-decker bus moving quietly to where the park is. This is the best thing about my new bedroom. Sometimes at night I play spaceships, and I pretend the streetlamps are stars, and I'm in a spaceship, and the arm thing that holds the window open is the steering lever, the holes in it the buttons for speed, and Captain Billy zooms through the universe, where no man has been before, and I laser alien spaceships to bits with just one shot, sometimes two.

I get down from my new desk and move it back to my bed. I look at the pictures of George Best, and I think about Mum. She was wearing her best dress and hat tonight and she smelt like flowers. I miss sleeping with Mum now I'm in the attic. She used to give me little presents to open while I turned to the wall so she could put her pyjamas on. My favourite present was a green plastic ray-gun with a silver trigger. When you pulled it, little yellow sparks lit up inside the gun and it made a revving sound like a little motorbike. I took it to school one day and Kelvin Oldfield stamped on it and broke it. I hate Kelvin Oldfield. He's fat, and has a nose like a pig. He smells of sour milk and he says things like You don't have a dad.

I look up at George Best and I don't want him there. This is my room now, and Aunty Belinda doesn't live here anymore so she won't tell me off. I stand on the desk and start pulling the drawing pins out with my fingernails. In this picture, George is smiling. He's got a beard and he's wearing a Man U shirt with a little devil on it. I hold the other pins in my hand while I push my nails under the last pin. It's stiff but it comes out with a hard pull. George slides down the wall and I fall backwards. I hit the floor with a bump, landing on my bum. Inside my head is a little flash, and in my hands a sting. I stand up and open my hands to see red blood marks where the pins have stuck in. I put the pins on the desk and look at the tiny holes in the middle of each hand. I stop myself from crying, and the sound of Sandie howling outside makes me look up to the window where one star shines brighter than all the rest.

CHAPTER 3

While five grown-ups sit at the scratched dinner table

The three kids sit cross-legged on the rug, the cheap Formica coffee table between them and the telly, mouths full and forks paused, their eyes fixed on the screen where Tonto is in heap big trouble.

Six tins of Co-op baked beans and two loaves of medium-sliced white are shared between them all, on this, their usual Saturday afternoon family gathering.

At the table, Jean and her older sisters, Belinda and Julie, are listening to their mam, Ena, tell a story about a woman at work who slipped on the ice and broke her ankle. Belinda's husband, George, isn't listening. He's thinking about two horses in the three-thirty, the handicap weight, the heavy going, the jockeys.

Belinda also drifts from the story, and thinks how annoying the sound is that her husband makes when he eats. She wonders if she'll ever get used to it. She wonders too if her sisters or her mam notice the sound. She watches him a moment as he shovels another heaped forkful in, slurps, smacks, breathes in and out through the open-shut mouthful of mashed toast and beans, watches as his oversized Adam's apple rises then falls with the swallow.

She hopes his bad acne goes away. She hopes his constant sweating stops. She hopes he becomes more considerate in bed. She hopes they have children. Soon. Belinda looks to her younger sister, and wonders why it was so easy for Jean to get pregnant. Then she looks to her older sister Julie and thinks how easily she got pregnant too, just weeks after she married Gerry. Maybe it's George, Belinda thinks.

Ena finishes her story about the broken ankle by shouting at the whining dog to get out from under the table. She asks if anyone else can still smell dog sick, and the grown-ups nod and pull faces. Ena sighs as she mops up the last of her bean-juice with a piece of burnt crust.

Her daughter Julie drinks the dregs of her sweet strong tea and thinks about her husband Gerry. She thinks how tight money is, how Barry and Daniel need new shoes, and how Gerry can still afford to go to the football with a bellyful of ale.

Jean breaks her sisters' thoughts by saying she saw Shirley Mackison in town yesterday. Jean says Shirley Mackison asked how their dad was getting on in prison.

Ena puts her knife and fork onto her plate with a clatter and says Shirley Mackison is a nosey **OLD COW**.

The kids look up as one from the telly and Ena smiles at them, blowing a raspberry and crossing her eyes. The kids laugh. Nannan is funny.

—

While the grown-ups wash the pots and get sorted for their shopping trip, Ena takes the kids to the park. She tells Billy, Barry and Daniel to be careful as they take the Courthouse steps down onto West Bars. The morning frost clings stubbornly to the ground, and Ena tells the boys to go steady, or they might slip and snap their legs off, **CRICK CRACK**.

Daniel, the youngest of the three, looks up to his Nannan with frightened eyes. Ena laughs, bends down to hug him, and tells him it was only a joke. Billy and Barry tease Daniel all the way across the Queen's Park bridge, grabbing their knees and going **SNAP! SNAP!** Ena telling Daniel to ignore them, holding his hand all the way to the swings.

From the park bench, Ena watches the boys play. She lights a fag and thinks about what Shirley Mackison said about Walter. Ena imagines him in a dirty little cell, a rusty bucket for a toilet, a murderer or a rapist for a roommate. She is surprised at how sorry she feels for Walter, despite the times she hid behind a door from him, the times he found her.

Billy pushes a swing towards Daniel's face and Ena shouts **CAREFUL!** Billy holds the swing still for a moment and helps Daniel climb on.

Ena thinks again of Walter. Strange how things work out. Who would she have married if Ethel hadn't arranged that blind date for her and Walter at that dance? Ena remembers the dress she was wearing when she met Walter. A long blue cotton dress with its swirling pattern of little red roses. That night, when she danced with Walter she felt something like sunlight inside of her, that the hard life she'd lived was behind her, and that with Walter there would always be dancing.

Ena stubs her fag out and watches the three boys run to the merry-go-round. She smiles as Billy and Barry help Daniel onto the middle, patting his hands onto the rail as though to say hold tight. She remembers her older sister Mabel doing the same to her as she showed Ena how to hold the rolling pin so it spun in her grip. Mabel, with her horrible flaky eczema so she couldn't bake, which meant Ena had to do it, as well as all the cooking, the cleaning.

How she grew to hate Mabel.

She thinks how different her life might have been if her mam hadn't died so young, if her dad hadn't deserted them, disappearing back to Ireland never to be heard of again. How can anyone turn their back on eleven kids?

Ena remembers the arguments she had with Mabel and her husband, Eric, the way their kids would fight with Ena, and how if Ena hit back she would cop it, the sting of the strap, the look on Eric's face as he swung his belt down onto her backside, the way her dress billowed as it was held over her head...

Daniel's screams pull Ena out of her daydream. **SLOW DOWN** she shouts to Billy and Barry, who dutifully start dragging their weight back against the merry-go-round as though pulling back a stubborn horse.

Good lads.

She lights another fag, watches the three boys troop in a line to the climbing frame, then calls out for them to be careful, to look out for one another.

Ena remembers when she was a child, passed from one relative to the next, until her eldest sister Mabel took her in. She remembers the ever-returning pain in her ears, the times at school where the teacher's lips would move but the words were nothing but a muffled sound, like a newsreader on a badly-tuned radio.

Ena wishes she were clever.

Maybe then she wouldn't have had the life she'd had.

Maybe then she could have had a good job and protected herself, her kids.

How she hated that job Mabel made her take.

Gutting chickens for eight-and-six, Mabel and Eric taking the eight shillings, her left with only sixpence. But at least she got into the pictures for half-price because of how small she was, even at sixteen. But how guilty she felt pretending to be younger. Ena had always felt guilty about one thing or another. She remembers how she used to feel having to wear her dress inside-out when it got dirty because Mabel told her wash powder cost money, and of how guilty she felt when Walter used to shout at her, accusing her of the dirty things, the things she would never do.

She watches the three boys waving to her from the top of the climbing frame and she waves back, feeling the smile spread across her face. Stay together, she says to no one but herself, remembering how alone she felt when she went into service, living with that sad old woman in that big empty house in Nottingham, how she had to sleep with her under that steel sheet in the cellar during air-raids, the bits of brick that fell from the cellar roof and rattled the sheet above them as the house shuddered from the bombs. It was awful back then, having no friends, in a big city knowing no one, going to the pictures on your own, only to return to that big house with no one in it but that sad, lonely old woman.

Strange, she thinks, the only time she had proper friends was when she came back after the war and went to work at the pottery, going on bike rides with the girls, going dancing, and then…And then she started courting Walter and she wasn't allowed to see her friends anymore.

Why didn't she see it then?

And then that big row with Mabel and Eric, and her now eighteen, and so it was decided, and off she went to live with Walter's family.

How she hated sleeping with his three sisters, all of them cramped up in that little bed with no space, no space at all.

CAREFUL! shouts Ena again, as Billy holds Daniel by the arms from the top of the climbing frame. Billy calls back that he is being careful, and that it's okay, because Daniel is a monkey. Ena tells Billy that he's a little bloody monkey, and Billy laughs.

She remembers the shock when Jean told her she was pregnant. Thank God Jean listened to her, and had nothing more to do with that Mick. Just like Walter he was. Nothing but trouble.

Ena stubs her fag out and looks up to the sky. The wind feels sharper and it looks like rain. Or maybe even snow. She looks at her hands that are red from the cold and she slips them inside her coat pockets. She remembers how cold the bombs were in the factory, how her hands would get sore from the grease, how Walter would hit her when he got stupid jealous about the men she worked with.

Then she remembers how thankful she was when

they put him in the army because he'd lost that job at the box factory. How many jobs did he lose? God, she can't even remember. Too many to even count.

A woman walks-by pushing a pram and she smiles and nods. Ena smiles back and thinks of her first baby. How when they took it out of her its skin was blue, its face, hands and feet, all perfectly still. Why didn't she see it as a sign?

She watches as the boys run over to the seesaw horse. Thank God they're happy, she thinks, thank God.

She remembers his so-called job at the foundry when he came out the army, her pregnant with Jean, him supposed to be out at work when all along he was in the pub, using his demob money as a pretend pay-packet, handing her a little each Friday for several weeks from the same tatty brown envelope, and her finally left with nothing for the kids. Again.

She thinks about all the places she used to hide money. Inside the clock, the vase, her knicker drawer, behind the clown picture on the wall, sometimes even up the chimney in an Oxo tin.

And just when she thought he was as big a bastard as he could ever get, he just got worse, and everyone telling her to leave him, to get out, and her with nowhere to go, no parents to turn to, and no relatives that would take her and the three kids in, and then, she broke.

Ena lights another fag and watches the three

boys laughing and yeehawing on the seesaw horse. Daniel is in the middle, and Billy and Barry are front and behind. She watches as they stop their pretend galloping to let a little girl get on. Good lads.

She remembers when that tight feeling snapped inside her. The hands she wrapped around Belinda's throat when she'd lost that ten-bob note on her way to the shop and returned empty-handed and tearful, the way Ena shook her beautiful daughter against the larder door until her dark eyes flickered upwards, the way Jean and Julie cried as they tried to pull Ena's hands from their sister's throat.

The institute in Sheffield was clean and white.

She remembers how much she slept. For days. And then when that man from the Social came, to tell her Walter hadn't given that money to the neighbours who were looking after the kids while Ena got better, and that the neighbours said they couldn't look after the kids without any money, the man from the Social saying they'd have to go to a kids' home, for a while at least.

Ena had always felt guilty about one thing or another, but this was the worst.

She remembers pleading with the doctor to allow her home again. Thank God he did. Funny how things work out though. If the kids had been sent away then Jean might not have met Mick and got pregnant, but then again there'd be no Billy. And if Ethel hadn't have arranged that blind date then maybe she wouldn't have met Walter, but then again there wouldn't have been a Julie, a Belinda, or a Jean.

Funny.

She remembers when they finally got away from him, the letter from the council about that house, him out at the pub, and them packing a neighbour's van with everything they could fit in, saying Hurry hurry, leaving the curtains and the coal, the beds and a settee, the table and that picture of a crying clown, and when they got there, the new house bare-floorboarded and empty, heaven, all four of them sitting on boxes and eating fish and chips, drinking cheap sherry and toasting to a new start, no more doors banging, no more yelling, no more heavy footsteps thumping the stairs in the dead of night, and then when he found them again, thumping the backdoor wide open and walking in, pulling that breadknife out of his pocket, You hate me, he said, You hate me and I love you.

Ena looks up to see Billy and Barry and Daniel stood in front of her. Daniel has his trouser leg pulled up, and with bottom lip quivering he points to a graze on his knee. Billy is waving a crumpled pound note in the air.

Look! he says, Look what I found near the bin, Nannan! And then, Why are you crying, Nannan?

It's just the cold making my eyes run, she says, ruffling his hair.

They start walking back as the first flakes of snow begin to soft-spiral down from the grey sky. They talk of the Lone Ranger, and Billy makes his hands into a mask telling Barry he can be Tonto. Barry says he doesn't want to be Tonto, and that it's not fair that Billy found a pound note and he didn't.

Ena tells Barry that's how things are sometimes, that sometimes people are lucky, and then sometimes not.

When they get back, Belinda watches Julie put a plaster on Daniel's knee as she tells Barry that they're all going out to buy new shoes for him and his brother. Ena asks Jean if she has the Christmas list, and Jean says Yes, Mam, exchanging a quick grin with Billy. Ena looks into her purse, nods, then turns to the mirror that hangs over the fireplace, dragging cherry-red lipstick over her thin lips. They all put on woolly hats and scarves and bustle out into the backyard, leaving Billy with his Uncle George. George wants to watch Grandstand and World of Sport. George likes sport, and sometimes plays games with Billy.

CHAPTER 4

My uncle explains how it works

And because I found a pound note on the park, I pick a horse called Merry-Go-Round, which at ten to one to win means you get eleven back. And when he's back from the bookies we watch World of Sport, my uncle yelling his horse on, invisible whip flashing the arm of Nannan's chair, me shouting GO MERRY-GO-ROUND! GO! And my uncle now on all fours, bum pushing against the invisible saddle, his face now a neck from the screen. GO ON, RED HAND! GO ON! But Merry-Go-Round pushes out in front, beats Red Hand by the length of our backyard, me jumping up and down on the settee, my uncle drooping his face to the rug like his horse needs a drink or something, and now we have to wrestle, which my uncle always wins at, me with my knees pressed back to my chest, him riding me across the carpet like Red Hand, me feeling the hard change in his pocket.

CHAPTER 5

He'd only ever seen them on the telly before

But as soon as Billy crawled through the bushes into the den behind the cenotaph, he knew what it was. And by the time Barry and Daniel had followed, Billy was already pressing down the lettered keys.

Tap tap. Tap tap.

Wow, said Barry, as Billy pulled at the silver lever, sending the roller sliding to the left.

DING!

Buh. Ih. Luh. Luh. Yuh.

DING!

Barry squatted close beside Billy, a look on the older boy's face somewhere between joy and grim intent, his right hand now pushing Billy down onto his backside.

Buh. Ah. Ruh. Yuh.

DING!

This tit for tat escalated quickly, and within half a minute saw Billy and Barry scuffling on the sandy soil, the cast shadow of the crucifix a grey X across the wriggling bodies of the two boys, Barry now on top holding down the arms of his younger cousin, until a swift rise of Billy's knee into his cousin's spine toppled Barry with an **OOF!**

BASTID! yelped Barry, now kicking out at Billy, who stepping back, stumbled over both typewriter and Daniel, who had taken the opportunity to tap tap in ignorant marvel while his older cousins fought.

AAAARRRRHUH! AAAARRRR! screamed Daniel, thin drips rolling down his cheeks, the sun's glint under the armpit of the cross giving his tears the sheen of a slug-trail, **BAS-TIDS!**

And so it was decided. The treasure would be carried home as a shared find, much to the simmering anger of Billy, with each of the three cousins having a single hand upon the typewriter as they trooped across the Courthouse grass to Billy's home, where their gathered relatives were doing what they normally did at this point of the week, which was to have a dinner of beans on toast, drink tea and talk about their lives, telling and retelling their stories, with parts added or changed for the want of a better tale, actuality distorted over two sugars and a splash of milk.

Ena was just finishing a tale about *him*, whose name had now devolved into that emphasised pronoun, a tale that saw its narrative sidestep the yelling of a cruel and threatening crudity, when in walked Billy, Barry and Daniel, a six-legged swarm of whining and tugging and **IT'S MINE!/NO IT'S NOT IT'S/IT IS!/NO IT'S/I FOUND IT FIRST!/ NO YOU DIDN'T IT'S/LIAR!** to which Jean and Julie and Ena and Belinda rose as one from the table **HEY!/HEY HEY!/PACK IT IN!** seeing Ena wrench the typewriter from the three boys, placing it with a **KUNK** on the scratched dinner table in front of George, whose Adam's apple rose then sank as he took in and swallowed another tea-dunked bourbon in one.

What the bloody hell's going on? Ena demanded, a restraining hand on a shoulder each of both Billy and Barry, with a quiver-lipped Daniel shivering between them like a fly-bothered pony, wiping an exclamation mark of snot onto the back of his hand and staring down into the lino.

And where the hell did you get this from? sang Julie, pointing to the typewriter that sat beneath the blemished nose of George.

I found it behind the cenotaph, said Billy.

I FOUND IT TOO! yelled Barry, pushing Billy in the back.

AAAARRRRHUH! AAAARRRR! IT'S MINE TOO NANNAN! whined Daniel.

And with this, the push and shove crackled to life yet again, whereupon Ena and her daughters saw fit to separate the three cousins into three separate rooms while the boys calmed down.

This left George alone with the focus of all

this strife, who turned the machine around, and tentatively brought a hand to the keys.

Ghee. Ghee. **DING!**

Meanwhile, a decision had to be made. And reminded of a story that involved a wise man and baby, Ena despatched George to solve the unsolvable by dividing the typewriter three ways, the hatchet delivering the roller to Barry, who saw it as a policeman's truncheon for two consecutive Saturdays then threw it into the River Rother, the keys going to Daniel, who saw them as two fistfuls of monster claws, which ended up in the dustbin after three days because the Q cut a little slit between his thumb and forefinger, then finally, the machine's hollowed-out body, emptied of clacking keys and a dinging roller, was given to Billy, who used it for nothing.

CHAPTER 6

You press play

And watch as the reels turn, the thin brown tape feeding from one reel to the other, the crickle-crackle sound of little autumn leaves being trod on by little feet, and the reels turn like robot eyes, and you see a robot's face in the tape machine, its big white buttons toothing an evil robot grin, and then you hear your mum's voice singing from inside the robot's head.

Yummy yummy yummy, I got luv in my tummy, and I feel like luving you.

You watch the robot eyes turn and listen to the baby laughing and the mother laughing and you understand that this baby is you.

Billy bay-bee, Billy bay-bee.

Say Mumumum.

And then there you are again, a soft-curled gurgle, a word that isn't a word, your baby voice sounding back to your mum.

This seems strange because you don't remember this. It's like it never happened, but you understand that it did happen because you're hearing it from the tape machine, and yet this still doesn't make sense because you just don't remember it.

You press stop, and lie back on your bed, looking up at the moon peeping its big white eye through the attic window.

How can something have happened if you don't remember it?

And now you remember feeling this way before, when you looked at those photographs with Nannan, her saying Look Billy, there's you in your pram, and Look Billy, that's you having a bath, and you remember feeling strange, like you didn't believe it was you in the photographs because you didn't remember being there, and looking like that, and someone taking your picture there, but at the same time you had to believe it was you, because Nannan told you it was, and besides, why would Nannan fib?

There was something else you felt too when you looked at these photographs. You remember feeling like you wanted to cover them up, to hide yourself, to put something over your bare body, and you wanted to tell whoever it was that took these photographs that they were naughty, and that they shouldn't have done it, and you remember feeling that the whole world was looking at you.

You remember it was the same kind of funny tummy feeling you had when you came back from cousin Raymond's house when he'd played that game with you, where he was Batman and you were a baddy, and he had to catch you and trap you on the floor, saying he was good at catching baddies which is why he was going to be a policeman.

You sit up, and pull the eyes off the robot's head. The thin brown tape squeaks then crickle-crackles as you snap and stretch and pull and break until there is no more tape left in the robot's eyes.

You look at the curly brown pile on your bed and you remember the hairs on the girl next-door as Nannan shouts up that the film's on.

You like films.

It's like you're in a place where bad things can happen but when the film ends they're gone.

CHAPTER 7

Their mum and dad would scream at each other

The tinny clank of her eff words, the dagger in his every jaggy shout, and my mum and Nannan, ears pressed to the thin wall that splits us from next-door, whose yard I always daren't go in, with its ghost-grey shadow hanging like a sticky spider-web from wall-end to backdoor always, and that smell of sour baked beans and vinegar.

And when I saw the girl she was by the dustbins, that same smell coming off her, us going over the road to the Courthouse grass, her snogging me and me tasting that smell, then behind the cenotaph under bushes touching, her taking her pants down but I say Turn around, looking up at the black names as I rub it against her, and we don't play again.

Nannan says she went to live with another mum and dad. I never did play with the boy. He never played out then fell under a train.

CHAPTER 8

When Mum said I do

Me and Nannan started giggling. Nannan was crying a bit too. Then we had a party. I'm tired now.

Chris's car makes a funny whirring noise as we stop at some traffic lights. Chris shakes his head and pats the steering wheel with his hand. Mum turns around to look at me. She's smiling, and she still has her hat on.

I saw you laughing, she says, You little devil you.

Chris pushes the gear-stick forwards and we move on. The windscreen wipers squeak a bit of rain across the glass. I look at Chris's big curly sideburns and wonder if I'll have them when I grow up. Mum puts her hand on Chris's hand as he rests it on the gear-stick.

On the radio the DJ says this is his favourite Slade song of last year and plays How Does It Feel. I listen to it as I look out the window. This side of town looks different at night. I watch people come out of a pub laughing. Some people are snogging. I like Slade. This song is sad but I still like it.

Chris's car is called an MG. It's orange. There isn't much room in the back but it's okay. Noddy Holder has big sideburns too.

Mum asks me if I'm excited and I say I am. It feels strange leaving home though. My tummy hurts a little. I felt sad saying goodbye to Nannan at the party.

I see Chris's eyes in the mirror looking at me and I smile at him. He smiles back and his sideburns move on his face. Mum said to me yesterday that today Chris will be my dad. Then she said they're doing something special for me, and instead of going on honeymoon like normal married people do, we were all going to our new house together after the party. She said that her and Chris thought it was important that we did this together as a family. I said I didn't mind, but she said it was the right thing to do because we're a family now.

At the party I heard Uncle George say to Aunty Belinda that he thought it was daft taking a kid on honeymoon. He said something else too but Aunty Belinda saw me behind him and she told him to shush.

I haven't seen the new house yet. It's meant to be a surprise. I'm excited a bit because the house is on a farm. Chris told me there are pigs and cows and a big wood I can play in. He says I can ride on tractors too. My mum asked me what I thought and I said I won't have any friends there. She said that I'd make some friends.

My new grandma said the same thing at the party. She's Chris's mum. They live in a big house so the party was there. I heard her telling one of her friends in the kitchen that she was sad the wedding wasn't in a church, but she understood why. Then she saw me and said Look! Here's my lovely new grandson!

Outside the car, everything is dark. There are no streetlamps here. Chris said the farm is in the country but near a village. At the party he came and sat with me on the stairs and he talked about how I'd be able to play in the fields. I asked him what I could play, and he said anything I wanted.

Chris's car slows down quick and Mum says Look! In the headlights, a hedgehog is crossing the road. Mum turns around and smiles at me. I feel tired but the hedgehog wakes me up. The hedgehog has stopped moving now. It puts its head under itself and stays still. Mum and Chris are laughing.

Chris gets out the car, pulls his seat forward, and says Come on Billy, come and have a look.

I get out of the car and walk over to the hedgehog with Chris. It's really cold and I want a wee. I must be really tired because I feel a bit wobbly. Chris says hedgehogs curl up like this because it's how they protect themselves. He looks up at the car and says he doesn't fancy its chances against the MG though. I watch as he picks the hedgehog up carefully in both hands. He holds it out for me to look at, and

I look at where its face is. Its little brown eye goes orangey-red as Chris turns it towards the headlights. Then a car comes up behind us so we have to put the hedgehog under the hedge. We get back into the car and Mum looks really happy.

On the radio, the newsman is talking about a bomb going off in London. I look up at the tall hedges as we drive down a twisty lane. The newsman says an eyewitness said there was a loud bang and a lot of smoke in the street. Chris says Bloody paddies, then tells Mum about how he keeps getting pulled over by the police because the MG has an Irish number plate.

I close my eyes and listen to the radio. The DJ is playing Evil Woman by ELO.

ELO stands for Electric Light Orchestra. I know this because Uncle George likes ELO.

At the party, Uncle George kept making me and Barry shandies. Twice Uncle Gerry poured some of his beer into my glass until it was full. I think that's why I keep wanting to wee.

My belly hurts.

Chris says if I can stay awake we'll be at the farm soon. Mum asks me if I'm excited about my new school. I open my eyes and say Yes. She's smiling at me again, and she says I'll make lots of new friends.

There is nothing to see outside. It's dark, so I close my eyes again.

Sailing by Rod Stewart comes on and I hear

Mum say to Chris that she loves this song. I think about the farm. Mum and Chris said that from my window I'll be able to see the woods.

My bedroom at home has been nearly empty for a week. There was only my bed and my wardrobe left. Mum says Chris has bought me new ones. I'm glad I have a new wardrobe. I used to have bad dreams about a wolf in a top hat coming out of my old one. I feel sad about not sleeping in my old room anymore though.

I'm a bit scared about living on a farm. A few weeks ago, me and Nannan watched a horror film called Blood On Satan's Claw, and there was a farm on that. This girl was locked in an attic because she'd been scratched by the claw and she was turning into a devil. Her arm went all hairy and her fingers turned into claws. Lots of horror films are in the country. Dracula. Wolfman. Frankenstein. When something's after you, there's nobody around to help you in the country. You have to fight the monster yourself.

Mum is singing and Chris is laughing at her. Mum makes her voice go funny and Chris laughs more. Mum said yesterday that I can call him Dad whenever I want to.

My eyes feel hot and itchy. It seems a long way from town to the farm.

When I wake up everything is wrong. This is not my

room. My head hurts. This is not my bed. My legs are cold and they sting a bit, and when I put my hand down under the covers I've wet myself. I get up quick and take my trousers and pants off. I go over to the window and open the curtains just enough to see out. I feel sick. Outside are tractors and barns and a wood that stretches down to some fields. There are no houses anywhere. I don't remember getting here. My tummy feels heavy. Then the door opens behind me and it's Mum. She's smiling and sings Morning sleepyhead! Then she says Well, what do you think? Isn't it brill!

I cover myself with the curtain and shout **GET OUT!**

Oh Billy, Mum says, and she closes the door.

CHAPTER 9

That first summer on the farm

Billy's new stepfather was fixing a hole in a barn roof when he fell through it and broke his ankle. Billy was in the woods when it happened, and when he got back, his mother was making a cup of tea and crying a little. She told Billy what'd happened through sniffles and sips of tea, that they'd taken him to hospital, and that it was high time Billy called him Dad.

Upstairs in his new bedroom, Billy took Queen's Night at the Opera LP out of its sleeve, blew a few specks of dust off side one and placed it carefully onto the turntable. His new stereo was a gift from his stepfather, given with the smallest of fuss, such was his way. Billy would play his records loud, imagining he was Freddie Mercury, and would stride about his bedroom in long graceful steps like he'd seen Freddie do on telly. At Billy's new school, Grant Cooper with his big rabbit teeth said that Freddie Mercury was a bum-snogging homo. Billy punched him, and was losing the fight when a teacher split them up. Billy didn't feel like being Freddie today, and just listened while he looked out of his window.

The sun was low over the woods, casting long thin shadows of barns and trees across the farmyard. Billy watched as Ernie the pigman slouched heavy-footed across the yard to his dirty blue car. Yesterday, Billy had watched Ernie cutting open a cyst on the back leg of a sow. The farm was a great place to play, but some things made Billy feel sick.

—

Billy's stepfather hobbled in on crutches just before bedtime. Billy's mum helped Chris into a chair at the kitchen table.

Sit down, poor luv, she said, and once certain he was comfortable, she busied herself making him a cup of tea and a bacon sandwich.

Billy looked under the table at the bright white plaster cast and said, Does it hurt, Chris?

—

The next day, Billy played football in the yard with Carl Partridge. Carl lived up the lane, and his dad worked at the farm in charge of the cows. Billy's mum said that Carl's mum was a bit funny with her because they got to live on the farm and she didn't. The farm belonged to a man called Trout who had a long twisty moustache and wore shiny brown boots. Trout had lots of farms, and once, when visiting Billy's mum, told Billy the importance of taking your shoes off so as not to muddy the carpets. Trout said it showed respect. Billy was looking at Trout's shiny booted feet as he said all this, sat sipping his tea in the living room rocking chair, little cubes of dried mud peppering the rug around his shiny boots.

Afterwards, Billy's mum said it was okay for Trout to say such things and not do them himself because he owned everything. Billy said this was crap and Billy's mum told him not to swear.

As Billy toe-ended one past Carl to make it nine-all, they heard shouts coming from the hay barn, so Billy and Carl ran across the yard to see what all the noise was about. The farmhands and Ernie had found a mouse nest and were stamping on the mice. When they'd gone, Billy and Carl looked at the brown-red mush on the concrete floor of the barn. Under the corner of a bale was a tiny quivering mouse the farmhands had missed. It cowered with its nose twitching and its big black eyes closing then opening. Billy picked it up, cupping it in his two hands. He took it to Chris to ask what to do.

Chris was sat in the garden on a deckchair. His broken ankle was raised up onto another deckchair and he was reading a book called Great Walks of the Peak District. He smiled when he saw Billy and Carl. Chris suggested that they put the mouse back, because it would do better in its natural environment. Billy thought about this, then went inside the house while Carl held the mouse, Billy returning with a shoebox filled with ripped-up toilet paper. Billy carefully placed the mouse into the box, where it sat hunched-up under the pink tissue, trembling its whiskers. Billy decided to call it Grand-Smart-Lucky because it was all those things.

That night, Billy sat in bed with the shoebox on his lap. The mouse had touched none of the cheese, and as far as he could see, none of the milk in the saucer. He dipped his finger into the milk and slowly put it to the mouse's nose. Grand-Smart-Lucky shrank further into the corner of his box, turning his head away. The bedroom door opened and in hobbled Chris, smiling. Chris said Billy's mum wouldn't be happy with a mouse in the house, and if it escaped it would live under the floorboards and chew the electricity cables. Billy said it wouldn't escape and put the lid back on the box, getting out of bed and placing it on top of the stereo. Chris smiled again and said that maybe Billy ought to put some holes in the lid. Billy used his stepfather's penknife, carefully twisting the tip of the blade to make a row of holes, then handing back the folded knife said, Thanks Chris.

The next morning when Billy awoke he watched two sparrows fighting on the telephone wire outside his window. The noise of a tractor rattled by and the sparrows flew off. Billy got out of bed, and lifting the box lid, looked into the shoebox. Grand-Smart-Lucky was still in the same corner, its big black eyes staring dully out at Billy. He still hadn't touched the cheese, and as far as Billy could see, the yellowed milk was also untouched. Billy prodded the mouse with his finger. It felt baggy and cold, and didn't twitch, blink, or move away. Billy got dressed, then went downstairs for breakfast, where Carl's dad was in the kitchen talking to Billy's mum. The kitchen smelled of cow dung, and as Billy poured Sugar Puffs into a bowl, Carl's dad said a smiley goodbye to Billy's mum. Billy watched as Carl's dad walked past the window towards the back garden. Billy poured cold milk onto his Sugar Puffs and asked his mum if she loved Carl's dad. Billy's mum dropped a spoon into the sink, and closed her eyes as a tractor shook by.

CHAPTER 10

In the woods

It's more quiet when it snows. My wellies make a grunch-grunch sound as I walk. A rook scraws, and then another. Rooks sound nasty and it makes me feel funny when I hear them. I see them in my head as little old black men in cloaks, with big black hooknoses, red eyes and little pointy teeth. I stop and write my name in a drift. I use my stick that I sometimes use as a gun.

Be. Eye. Ell. Ell. Why.

A few weeks ago I carved a snake into my stick with my penknife. The snake twists all the way up, its forky tongue hissing up to the fat bit at the top. The fat bit fits into my shoulder when my stick is a gun. Chris has real guns. I like it when we go ratting. That rat we found in a corn bin the other week was as big as a cat. I've dreamt about it a few times since. Me holding the torch as we look down, its eyes red in the torchlight, hissing and scrattling as it tries to climb up the shiny corn bin but can't, Chris firing pellet after pellet into it, and still it keeps trying to climb.

Sometimes we find rats that have taken the blue bait. They're easy to kill. They move like they're drunk, all slow and stumbly. I feel a bit sorry for the small ones though. The old ones don't matter. Once, me and Carl saw a load of them eating grain off the barn floor. We went to fetch Chris and he got his shotgun out. It's a twelve-bore and makes a massive bang when it goes off. Chris shot under the barn door at them. There were big ones and little ones. After both barrels went off most of them were dead. The ones that weren't we stamped on.

I look up at my climbing tree. It looks too icy to climb today. A woodpigeon clapflaps through the branches so I shoot it with my stick gun. Carl said there's no such word as clapflaps. I told him I know, but I like to make up words that sound like what something does.

The farm gate skranks when you shut it.

Piglets snork when they feed off their mum.

My trumps sometimes floof.

Carl calls them SBDs when they come out like that. SBD stands for Silent But Deadly, but I like floof better.

—

When I get to the den, the corrugated sheet is invisible under the snow. A bird has hopped over it because I can see its footprints. I put my hand into the snow and it sinks up to my coat sleeve. It must have been a small bird like a sparrow or a robin or a chaffinch, not a bigger bird like a blackbird or a thrush or a starling.

I look at my wellie prints in the snow behind me. It's funny seeing where you've been. I look at each footmark and try and remember being there and how I felt, but I can't. I see if it works to think about what I was thinking when I got here. I say floof out loud but I still can't remember how I felt.

At school Mr Dilks said that everything always goes forward, never back, and this is how the universe works.

I sit in the den for a bit because the roof has kept the snow out. I have a log for a settee. It feels cold on my bum but I stay sitting. One of my favourite films is The Time Machine and sometimes I play that I'm George. I pretend to twist the dial on my time machine and go back in time to where I was walking up to the den. I watch myself walking, and thinking about floof. If I could really go back in time I'd change some things. Like that time at the bus stop when Grant Cooper moshed up that cake I'd made at school, digging his hands into it and licking them, going **OOOOOH OOOOOH**, then saying only bummers made cakes.

If I could go back in time I'd put rat poison in it so he'd die.

A real time machine would be brill. Every time

something went wrong you could go back and change it into something good. In the film though, George finds monsters. I know real monsters didn't exist back in olden times, unless of course you count dinosaurs. Stegosaurus. Brontosaurus. Diplodocus. Tyrannosaurus. Brachiosaurus. Iguanodon. Triceratops.

In the film, the Morlocks keep the humans happy by feeding them fruit so they never have to do work, but the bad thing is that the Morlocks eat the humans, so even though everything seemed good, things were actually very bad.

I get out of the den and go over to the fly-tip. I like the fly-tip because if you dig around in it you sometimes find things. My stick is good for digging things up. It's not as easy today though because the ground is stiff. Last week I found a nudie book. There were some pictures of girls holding their fannies open so you could see right inside them. Me and Carl looked at the pictures, and he kept pretending to kiss where their holes were. It made me feel sick but Carl said in real life that's what you have to do. I told him he was being stupid, but Carl said his brother had told him, so it was true.

My stick gets stuck underneath something so I push then pull my stick to one side, lifting the ground up. There is a bent old tin that says Oxo, and an old bottle with bumpy glass writing on it.

Asmodeus Elixir.

The bottle is green and has something dark in the bottom of it. There is a rubbery stopper that I twist then pull out. The dark stuff is sticky-stiff in the bottom of the bottle. I know it's dangerous to drink old medicines so I put my nose over the opening and sniff it instead. The bottle smells like burning. I pretend there's a genie in it and I make a wish for a time machine.

A rook scraws.

It seems dark, so I go home.

CHAPTER 11

You're playing war

Running through a hail of Nazi bullets to the barn, climbing up crates of spuds and you and Carl arming yourselves with soil-pocked grenades and **GO!** Through the red-lit pig room past hot pockets of soft grunting P.O.W.'s and **GO!** Out the back to lob bombs that crack and splatter on the corn silo missile base that **BOOMS** and **GO!** To the waste heap sticking sharp sticks into jelly glass eyes of dead runts that pop and ooze, now **GO!** To the dust-humming corn-hold to kick the fuck from flat maggoty rats and **THERE**, staggering drunk from a dose of blue bait, now **GO!** Brick it till its brain splits and **GO!** Pelt the Massey-Fergy Nazi tractor tank, **BOOM**, and **THERE!** Gaz and Glen them bummers from up the lane and **GO!** Lob fuck off spud grenades and **DIE BUMMERS DIE!** And they run, straight out the gate into the lane when **BOOM!** Gaz's uncle hits Glen head-on with his red car, Glen's white plimsoll arcing up into the air, Glen twisting up after it, falling bent and wrong, shinbone sticking out through a mouth in his leg, and all you can do is stare at it.

CHAPTER 12

Listen

There's that sound like a dog whimpering. Billy's having a bad dream again.

Chris turns over and grunts. I get out of bed, walk soft down the hall, listen in at Billy's door. I'm worried about him. Since that man came to sort the papers out to change Billy's last name, Billy's been … I don't know. It's like there's something underneath. Billy still doesn't call Chris Dad. It hurts when I think about it.

I used to think would we'd always be on our own, me and Billy.

I step quiet to the bathroom.

I love this house, this life that Chris has given us. What boy wouldn't want to grow up on a farm?

There's that noise again. I wipe myself, wash my hands, go back to listening at Billy's door. Why can't we all just be happy?

I go into Billy's room, pull the covers over him, touch his hair. He's definitely dreaming.

That poor boy from up the lane. He was in agony.

My stomach still feels heavy from it.

After the police had asked their questions I sent Billy his room. I could see in their eyes they blamed him.

Chris took me inside and made me a cup of tea. Told me not to cry. That it was just an accident. That Billy wouldn't have made that boy run out in front of that car on purpose. They were just playing, he said.

Why does everything seem to happen around Billy though? All I want is for us to be happy.

I walk soft back to bed, take my dressing gown off, slip under the covers careful not to wake Chris.

Please God, make everything alright.

I wanted the floor to swallow me up at parents evening last week, Billy's teacher telling me how Billy made those girls cry by blowing his nose into that hanky then wiping it all over their desk. Disgusting. Chris just said, Boys will be boys. The teacher said Billy could do really well if he stopped messing about. Why does he do that, always showing off?

Listen. The tawny owl is calling. And now the female calls back. I love it when me and Chris lay awake together and listen to them. Chris has shown me so much. He told me it wasn't my fault the way things are, and that Billy is troubled but we can be there for him, make him happy.

I didn't know what to say when Billy told me about the things last week. I don't even want to think about it. Chris said it's just kids being kids. Doctors and nurses. Games. I didn't understand what Billy was talking about. I didn't know what to say. My stomach twisted into a knot when Billy said he'd got something to tell me.

I knew it'd be something bad. I sat down on his bed, his head under the covers while he told me. What could I tell him? That it's alright to play such games? Why would he want to play games like that anyway? I asked him that much and he cried. Said it was the Devil that made him. He said it over and over. I think he got it from a film or something.

When I told Chris about some of the things, Chris said not to worry, that Billy sometimes makes things up, pretends, that I shouldn't worry myself over it. But I do. How could I not?

Listen. The male is calling again. And now the female replies. It's beautiful. It sounds so sad.

Please God help us. Help me and Billy and Chris be happy. Jesus please we've hurt enough. Our Father, who art in Heaven, hallowed be Thy name, Thy kingdom come, Thy will be done, on Earth, as it is in Heaven, please Jesus please, lead Billy from temptation, and deliver him from evil, for Thine is the kingdom, the power and the glory, for ever and ever, Amen.

CHAPTER 13

In the barn

You put a shotgun cartridge into the vice, lay it lengthways then tighten, jaws locking hard around the red plastic tube, flat brass end offering itself to the six-inch nail and the hammer, then the ear-whining crack of it, the smoke and the smell of it, and now into the oily drawer for a Razzle, now up the ladders to the bare floorboarded hayloft, lying down sideways on dry dusty wood with jeans and pants around knees, turning the page to see her surprised at you being there, the red O of her mouth, her uniform falling from freckled bony shoulders, nipples half-peeking through cheat hide and seek hands, now opening herself with red fingernailed fingers, eyes closed under slipped down nurse's cap as you rub it up against her, avoiding staple and spilt milk swelling of someone else's doing that comets across the page from her elbow to her red-brown glisten when underneath, the noise of boots and squealing, and through a gap in the floor you see Ernie the pigman, carrying a newborn runt by the back legs, its brothers and sisters now suckling their mother somewhere in the red-lit pig room, caged and laid on her side unknowing that her lesser-made son is smashed against the wall, again, again, slow dripping the soft straw floor as your mum calls tea.

CHAPTER 14

She sips her tea and thinks about this mystery

Then placing the white china teacup on the left arm of her chair, she rises in two steady movements, a hand on the right arm of the Shackleton supporting her first rise, a little push with the second, then with the merest hint of a shuffle in her gait, she moves towards the mantelpiece.

The tableau of Christmas cards is ordered methodically. Her son and daughter-in-law's taking the right centre stage. To Mother, with all our love, Chris and Jean. Her daughter's taking the left of centre. To Mum, Merry Christmas, love Deirdre. And dead centre, in the prime placing of all, stands the smallest card of this hierarchy of near-relations, a glitter-strewn snowy rooftop where stands a cartoon Rudolph, clown-like nose sparkle-red and slightly flaking, thought-bubble thinking He's been a long time, and underneath, in the X-rayed insides of a terraced house, a fat ruddy Santa snoozing on the sofa, brandy glass in hand, nose aglow, **ZZZ**.

For the third time today she takes all this in, and with a smile spreading soft across her pale lined face, she picks the card up from the mantelpiece, with care not to dislodge the others from their carefully orchestrated standing, up and open in a slow near-perfect right angle beneath her still smiling face, her nose tilting up to give her field of vision a pathway through her bifocals.

To Grandma, love and hugs, Billy XXX.

She replaces the card on the mantelpiece with the same near-perfect right angle and returns to her chair, her still unsolved mystery soft-footing itself back into her thoughts, back down into the still warm Shackleton, one eased movement into her comfort, the teacup to her lips, a sip, then another, and still the mystery remains unsolved.

Where did it all go?

She thinks about the Christmas day tea of salmon and turkey, the trifle, the cake, Schweppes lemonade and white wine. The cracker she pulled with Billy, his elbow jagging back to knock Deirdre's wine glass onto the floor. Jean saying Oh Billy! and her saying Oh it's alright Jean, it's only a splash, and then the smile her grandson gave her for sticking up for him, the red paper crown she placed on his head, the cracker-birthed bottle opener he attached to his belt loop.

She thinks how quickly he's grown these last three years. That big eyed, lank-haired skinny puppy that regarded her nervously on that first meeting, this ten-year-old boy that she knew would be her grandson within months, her son to be a father to a full-grown boy, a boy made by another man and this woman that her son loved. And how he loved her. She could see this from the very first.

She drinks deeper of her tea, lifting her legs from the carpet just enough to view her new slippers. Red, with a black-ribboned bow. Not what she might have chosen herself. No. But she will wear them, wear them until they tire, and thin.

Merry Xmas Grandma! Love from Billy XXX.

She puts her feet to the floor, looks to the tree with its white angel twinkling at its peak, its flicker-creep lights slow-travelling crimson through the branches, and she thinks again about the mystery.

After Christmas tea they watched the Morecambe and Wise repeat. What did they drink? Deirdre had more white wine. Jean had white wine too. Chris had beer. She had one gin and tonic.

Then after Morecambe and Wise they all had crackers and cheese and played charades. Oh how funny it was. Billy pretending to be seven cowboys riding seven horses one at a time, holding his fingers up to count One cowboy, two cowboys, three…
What a sweet, funny boy.

Through the window she sees Dolly Faversham walking her old Labrador. She thinks about what Dolly told her about Jill Baker's son. Sent to prison for robbery. How the news shocked her. She remembers Martin Baker when he was a young man. Jill telling everyone how well he was doing at university training to be an architect. Dolly told her she'd heard that Martin had gotten into drugs. Why do people do such things? All that promise burnt up for what? To make their head all stupid that's what. Poor Jill.

And after charades she remembers Billy putting a record on. What was it? Was it that Abba record? Billy likes that one, doesn't he. Such a sweet boy. She thinks how proud she felt when he played waiter for them all. Chris laughing at how much head was on his beer, Deirdre and Jean laughing at the little umbrellas Billy had placed into their wine glasses, and the tea towel draped over his arm when he brought the tray of drinks through.

Just like a real waiter, Grandma! he'd said.

And oh the six cherries he put into her gin and tonic. How they all laughed. She didn't have the heart to tell him about her drink being too strong, stronger than she would've liked, but still, there's no way she drank half a bottle of gin to herself. Is there?

CHAPTER 15

YES!

Billy is having the best night of his life. Everyone will love him, and his girlfriend Anna will change her mind and let him finger her for sure.

Life feels fucking great, Billy's usual self-conscious restraints falling onto the pavement with each step, with each empty miniature Gordon's gin cast under hedges, thrown into bus stops, back gardens, shop doorways, post-boxes, schoolyards, shopping trolleys, playgrounds, graveyards.

YES! Billy is more alive than he has ever been, colours and movement, sound and sense, everything is different, better, new and improved. By the time the staggering Billy reaches the Church Hall doorway he has already decided that this is how he wants to stay, from this thirteen to forever. He smiles at the old lady who collects the entrance money, telling her how beautiful she looks.

Love you, says Billy with a nonchalant flick of the wrist, swinging back the dull thump-thump-thump doors to the sound of Selector, that mod band that a headbanger like Billy cannot dance to, cannot admit to liking amongst his headbanger friends, and yet, tonight, Billy the Incredible is crossing boundaries, squeezing the juice from the gonads of life, and jumping straight in amongst the trilby-headed, narrow-tied, two-tone knees-up of the bum-boy mods.

YES! Billy cries, pogoing dead centre of the enemy, like a brick dropped into a bowl of milk, the ripple of astonishment stopping the running-on-the-spot suited dancers around the epicentre of Billy.

WHAT THE FUCK YOU DOING? yells fat Johnny into Billy's ear as Billy the Wonderful lands from a deer-like spring through the air. Billy fixes fat Johnny with a bozz-eyed grin. **YES!** he shouts into fat Johnny's face, but by now the modboys and beatgirls have all stopped their jag-kneed dancing to gawp. This will not do! But before they can decide on how to react to Billy's crime of dance, the opening flourish of No More Heroes by The Stranglers causes a spiky tide of punks and punkettes to wash across the dancefloor, studs and white paint on leather, tartan and straps and green-laced Doc Mart's send the mods scattering to their corner of the Church Hall, and the grinning Billy does the only thing he can do to celebrate this life, this wondrous gift of existence, and that is to do The Twist.

And this, is where things take a turn towards the ugly. The punk boys and girls doing what they have to do too, which is to hurt Billy in the form of dance, by hurling their pogoing spit and boot into the twisting, laughing fool that has the audacity not to dance the dance that has to be, stubbing their fags out on Billy's face, which now hails a call to Billy's headbanger friends, who up to now have been watching goggle-eyed and gob-smacked from their corner of the Church Hall, and can hesitate no longer as one of their own is kicked and spat on and used as an ashtray.

The music stops.

And the elderly ladies and gentlemen of the Church Committee attempt to quell the push and the shove as best they can, and as the yellow light of fluorescence fills the hall, the white-haired reverend leads Billy by the wrist to the fire exit, the bloody-lipped three-minute hero of the hour, grinning at the adoring crowd, knowing full well that he is now champion of the world, a new god, a name that will be passed from classmate to stranger, throughout the whole village to the town. Billy, the boy who danced against the grain, the boy who everyone will want to be, want to be with, to fuck and to worship, the boy who started a revolution.

———

Outside his bedroom window, the birds are singing to Billy. Billy wishes they'd shut up and leave him alone. He doesn't want to remember pissing his jeans at the top of the slide, standing open-armed and crucified like a pissy Jesus, all the faces looking up and laughing as he tells everyone to piss themselves because it's the only way. He doesn't want to remember the broken chip shop window, the cut hand, the same cut hand that smeared Anna's face with a slap when she called him a stupid cunt. He doesn't want to remember his mum and dad when the police brought him home, the same mum and dad that are now sat downstairs waiting to talk to him, to cry and to shout, to tell him there is something wrong with him, to tell him that he's breaking their hearts, and to ask in the name of good-God-all-bloody-chuffing-mighty: **WHY?**

CHAPTER 16

30-second punch

Take one two-thirds-done bottle of orange squash, lose half. Take one two-thirds-full elderberry 1980, pour half in. Take one decanter, probably sherry, two tilts remember where it stood. Take one just-opened whisky, Happy Christmas from all of us at Jackson Animal Feeds, one good pour maybe two, close cabinet doors, shake mixture, put in schoolbag, go.

CHAPTER 17

Now we are looking at

A secondary school classroom, the late May sun casting a grapefruit light through dirty glass, onto ragtag blue/grey/white uniforms, slouched and fidget-bored pupils listening to their dull-drone RE teacher, as one might listen to the shipping forecast's monotone Dogger on a Sunday afternoon at Granddad's, that tickling sense of summer's footfall a soft static crackle of promised freedom and cavort, like ten-stretch prisoners blank-staring those last few imagined dashes scratched onto grey cell walls, and ever-on the frump drone of the overweight RE teacher paper-combs as Billy's thoughts ebb and tide, head tilted into crooked palm, gazing to his left at the occupant of the desk two desks down, tracing the small of her back, the bump of a bra strap then around to her budding breasts, the soft but insistent pressure upon her white school shirt, then back again to the snug hoop of her grey waistband, the curve down to her arse, now flattened by the press of the seat, and still the frump drone of the overweight RE teacher paper-combs, paper-combs...

MISS JENKINS (*off screen*): There was a man in the land of Uz whose name was Job, and that man was blameless and upright, one who feared God and turned away from evil.

BILLY (*voice over*): Jesus.

Billy turns his gaze to Miss Jenkins.

MISS JENKINS (*Bible in hand*): And the Lord said to Satan, Have you considered my servant Job? There is none like him on Earth.

BILLY (*voice over*): Jowwwb.

Billy turns his gaze back to the girl. The girl turns her head slightly towards Billy, makes brief eye-contact, smiles.

BILLY (*voice over*): I should ask Rache out.

MISS JENKINS (*off screen*): And the fire of God fell from Heaven and burned up all the sheep and servants.

Billy looks to Miss Jenkins.

BILLY (*voice over*): This don't make sense. This gadge is one of God's bum-chums, yet God sends the Devil to fuck him over?

MISS JENKINS: And Satan made a raid upon the

camels and took them.

Billy rolls his eyes then looks to the window. He watches as a woodpigeon lands heavy in a nearby tree.

BILLY (*voice over*): How can anyone believe this shit?

The woodpigeon lifts a wing and starts preening itself with its beak.

MISS JENKINS (*off screen*): Your sons and your daughters were eating and drinking wine in their eldest brother's house...

The woodpigeon flies off. Billy returns his gaze to the girl.

MISS JENKINS (*off screen*): When behold! A great wind came across the wilderness...

The girl turns her head slightly to Billy. She briefly smiles again before turning her attention back to her Bible. Billy looks to his lap. We see the pronounced outline of an erection through his grey school trousers.

MISS JENKINS (*off screen*): And struck the four corners of the house.

Billy slides further under his desk. He looks back to the tree. The woodpigeon is back. It sits scrunched up, with its feathers plumped out.

MISS JENKINS (*off screen*): And it fell upon the young people, and they are dead.

Billy narrows his eyes and looks back to Miss Jenkins, who pushes her glasses back up her nose then leans back against her desk, turning a page of her Bible. She sniffs, then rubs the back of an index finger across her nostrils. She sniffs again.

BILLY (*voice over*): This is fucking ridiculous. All that bollocks about how God is love. Utter shite.

MISS JENKINS (*raising her voice*): Then Job arose and took off his robes and shaved his head. Then he fell down upon the ground (*speaks softly*) and worshipped.

BILLY (*voice over*): What? (*shaking his head*) God sends Satan to shit death all over your farm, kills your servants, your animals and your kids? And what do you do? Strip off, shave your head and say Ta God? What. A fucking. Mong.

MISS JENKINS (*her voice raising again, lifting her free hand into the air*): Naked I came from my mother's womb! And naked I shall return!

Billy sniggers, as do several others.

MISS JENKINS (*looking to the ceiling, her raised free hand clutching at something unseen*): The Lord giveth! And the Lord taketh away! (*nearly shouting*) BLESSED BE THE LORD!

Stifled laughter ripples around the room. Miss Jenkins snaps her gaze from the ceiling and glares angrily at the pupils.

MISS JENKINS (*her nostrils flaring*): **SHUT! UP!**

Miss Jenkins breathes heavily for a moment and surveys the classroom. The sniggers subside. Billy looks to the tree again. The woodpigeon seems to be sleeping.

MISS JENKINS (*off screen*): And so God said to Satan, See! Job still worships me despite these trials! To which Satan hissed, Skin for skin! And to prove Satan wrong, the Lord then afflicted Job with terrible sores.

Billy looks to Miss Jenkins and shakes his head.

BILLY (*voice over*): What? (*frowns*) I've just killed your kids but keep worshipping me so I can fuck you over again?

Billy sighs, and returns to looking out the window. The woodpigeon has been joined by another.

MISS JENKINS (*off screen*): And yes, I know what you're all thinking, but Job was as confused by this as I'm sure you all are, but his wise friends gathered around him and tried to help him understand God's mysterious ways...

The newly-arrived woodpigeon waddles along the branch towards the other. They regard each other,

*their necks moving this way and that. Billy looks
to the girl again.*

BILLY (*voice over*): How shall I ask her out?

MISS JENKINS (*off screen*): Man that is born of
woman is of a few days, and full of trouble. He
comes forth like a flower (*speaks softly*) and then
withers.

BILLY (*voice over*): Ask her to the disco this
Friday?

*Billy looks back to the window as the
woodpigeons fly off together. Billy stares at the
empty branch.*

MISS JENKINS (*off screen*): But of course, the
Jewish scriptures tell the story of Job's trials a little
differently, and feature a curious tale about Job's
wife.

*Billy looks to Miss Jenkins, who places her Bible
gently onto her desk, exchanging it for another
book, and turning the pages roughly, she rolls her
eyes and sighs.*

BILLY (*voice over*): Jesus. Nazi much?

MISS JENKINS (*clearing her throat*): So. This is a
bit the Jews have added on when Job and his wife
have lost their farm and their livelihoods through
God's test of faith (*she clears her throat again*).
And then Satan took the guise of a bread-seller

at the market, and when Job's wife tried to buy bread, she found she had no money, and they were starving...

Billy returns to staring at the empty branch.

MISS JENKINS (*off screen*): So Satan told her he would give her three loaves of bread for her hair...

On the playing field beyond the tree, Billy sees two mongrels approach each other under the goalposts. They circle each other, the bigger of the two sniffing the behind of the smaller.

MISS JENKINS (*off screen*): But. For the purpose of your exam, we should focus on...

The bigger mongrel suddenly mounts the smaller dog. The mongrel on top fucks faster and faster, its tongue lolling from its mouth.

MISS JENKINS (*off screen*): Because it's a difficult concept that has puzzled many Christians, but considering...

The smaller mongrel underneath looks to be trying to escape.

MISS JENKINS (*off screen*): A question of faith in God's...

The mongrel on top clamps its jaws around the other's neck and keeps thrusting. Billy watches as it finally unclamps its jaws and dismounts. And as the bitch mongrel runs off across the playing field, the male sits licking its genitals in the six-yard box.

MISS JENKINS (*off screen*): **BILLY! ANSWER THE QUESTION!**

Billy jumps in his seat and looks to the red-faced Miss Jenkins.

MISS JENKINS (*angrily*): **WHY!** Do you **THINK!** That **JOB! NEVER! SPOKE OUT!** Against **GOD! DESPITE!** The **TRIALS!** He **PUT** him **THROUGH?**

Billy smiles.

BILLY: I don't know, Miss, but I know this much. God's like that bully in that video we watched last week in Miss Tanner's class, where the bully gets his mate to beat that spacky kid up so he doesn't take the blame.

The class erupts with laughter. Rache smiles at Billy. Billy smiles back.

MISS JENKINS (*furious*): **GET OUT! GET OUT AND STAND IN THE HALLWAY!**

And so Billy gets to his feet, red Adidas sports bag hiding his stiff as a crucifix erection, walking tall through the admiring crowd, collecting the sweet smile of the flowering Rache Bradwell, swinging the classroom door wide-open, now taking a bow.

MISS JENKINS (*off screen*): **GET! OUT!**

And does he stand in the hallway as directed? Of course not. Billy swaggers the squeaky-floored labyrinth to the boys toilet, secreting himself into a cubicle to masturbate, the vision of Rache Bradwell's imagined bare arse a kite in the up-draught of his coming as the dinner bell rings, his penis now dabbed dry on crinkle-crisp toilet paper, and from his bag, a swig from the plastic bottle of orange squash (sherry, whisky, elderberry 80) and now feeling the courage of love's lust swim his adolescent veins, he smokes a quick fag behind the physics lab before moving on, finding the girl by the bike sheds, who faced with such a heroic figure backlit by the grapefruit sun, how could she say no?

CHAPTER 18

At the kitchen table

You sit, picking your nose whilst flicking through the latest copy of Kerrang! See how your grey school trousers are cut off at the knee, and how big-stitched onto the pocket of your black school blazer is a patch that says AC/DC. Canted, it half-hides that bigger blue castle behind. On your head sits a red baseball cap, onto which someone has rough-sewn the horns of a devil. They are over-stuffed and cow-like.

You open cheese and onion, then salt and vinegar crisps, pouring both into a black china bowl.

You turn a page of Kerrang! eat a crisp, get up, then bend down to a nearby kitchen cupboard.

From your backside hangs the tail of a devil, over-stuffed and dog-like, now wagging you back to the table, Labrador-happy at finding the brown sauce.

What the bloody hell are you dressed as? your mum says, dropping her workbag onto the table. And what have you done to your school trousers?

She blinks.

You look down at the HP, sit, shuffle, and with an understated sweep of your free hand, you dress the devil's tail to the left.

Your mum mutters Beyond, and Belief. Why? she says.

You shrug. Say, Disco.

What? she says, Fancy dress?

You pull the peak of your cap down. Your horns twitch like fat divining rods. No, you say, Just the Church Hall disco.

Brown sauce runs down your chin. You scoop it with a finger then suck it clean.

So why are you going dressed as...Her hand becomes an emulsion brush.

You drink some dandelion and burdock pop, then mumble something about Angus and For a laugh.

Your mum does a little hop, landing wide-eyed and open-palmed like a minstrel.

I KNOW WHO YOU'RE SUPPOSED TO BE! she says. YOU'RE THAT BLOODY ANGUS WHATZIZNAME FROM THAT STUPID BLOODY POP GROUP AND YOU'VE GONE AND CUT THE LEGS OFF YOUR BEST BLOODY SCHOOL TROUSERS TO DO IT!

You go over to the sink, rinse the black china bowl, place it face down on the draining board. You say, Can I have my pocket money? Please.

Your mum looks up at the ceiling.

JESUS! YOU'RE CHEEKY DAFT, LAD! YOU'VE JUST COST ME ANOTHER PAIR OF BLOODY SCHOOL TROUSERS! AND YOU KNOW WHAT ME AND YOUR DAD SAID LAST WEEK! IT'S TIME YOU LEARNED A LESSON BY HAVING TO EARN YOUR MONEY! THEN MAYBE YOU WOULDN'T WASTE IT ON MAKING YOURSELF BLOODY SICK ALL OVER YOUR BEDROOM FLOOR!

I did the logs, you tell her.

OHHH NO! she says, THERE'S STILL THAT PILE BY THE PIGGERY! I'VE GOT EYES IN ME HEAD, YOU KNOW!

She slides a chair out from under the kitchen table.

What about half now, half tomorrow? you say.

She prods the air between you and her. Sit, she says.

Her green workbag falls over on the table, a yellow Tupperware box and a red purse spilling from its mouth.

Your mother stares at you. Listen. We're trying to teach you something here. If you end up like... Are you listening to me? If you end up like...

She stands up and moves over to the worktop, rips off a piece of kitchen roll, blows her nose, flicks a switch on the kettle. You pull at your baseball cap, slide lower into your seat. Your mum puts a teabag into a cup, straightens a tea towel on the oven door, puts the crisp bags into the bin, stands her workbag up, opens her purse.

Here, she says.

Three pound notes lay across Gene Simmons' tongue, leering wet from front page of Kerrang!

I'm doing steak and chips for tea, she says.

I'm off out in a bit, you say.

She sighs, and fifty pence joins the three pound notes, balancing silver on the tip of the hideous tongue.

For chips, she says.

—

In the kitchen, that muffled rumble from upstairs is the sound of the shower washing your mum's workday away. Your hands move quickly. Green workbag, red purse, blue fiver... disco.

CHAPTER 19

Two tens then last week a twenty

I bet that Marge Partridge is rubbing her bloody hands together with glee. I knew something was wrong when Trout came round. All that talk of how well the farm shop's been doing then Oh by the way Jean, Mrs Partridge says the money's been down a few times of late. Are you careful counting the change out? Do you leave the bag lying around?

Bloody Marge Partridge. She's had it in for me since we first moved here. Always breaking her bloody neck to tell me how well their bloody Carl's doing at school, and then that stupid bloody pretend sympathy face she pulls and Ooh, Carl tells me your Billy's in a bit of bother at school, or, Tell me Jean, how's your Billy doing? Has he settled down a bit?

At least my husband sleeps in the same bloody bed as me.

I wouldn't be surprised if she weren't bloody diddling the takings herself, just to make me look bad. Or to pay for her bloody Ooh did I tell you Jean, me and the boys are going to Spain again next month, well, you can't take it with you can you Jean?

Stupid woman looks like a tangerine with legs six months of the year. A great fat horse chestnut the other six. Ooh Jean, you ought to come round and try our sun-bed. It'd do wonders for your complexion. Cheeky cow. She doesn't even have a complexion. An inch of foundation sees to that.

God. It's so bloody embarrassing. I'm sure it's just a slip-up somewhere, Trout said. Don't worry about it Jean. Just double-check the change you give out. And make sure you put all the takings in the bag with the float. I felt so ashamed. I couldn't even look him in the eye. How can I tell Chris?

Funny how some things never go away. Mam asking Dad where the rent money had gone from the Oxo tin, Shirley Mackison telling me how Dad got sacked from the knicker factory for pinching the tea-money, Jenny Sanders telling me how Dad had been to her house, cadged a fiver off her Mum, to pay for shoes for me he'd said, the lying...

I'm always careful with the change. I do count it out. No one touches it until her highness calls round for it. It stays locked up in the drinks cabinet the rest of the time. No one even goes in there unless it's a Saturday night. Who's going to touch it anyway? There's only us three in the bloody house.

I'm always careful with the change.

Bloody Marge Partridge is wrong. Or making it up. Or it's her.

CHAPTER 20

You're at the bottom of Castle Lane

Orange lamplights snaking uphill to the bend. Rose Cottage 1910 gate open. Nip in, tip bottle up, two fifties and a ten. Soft-down steady don't chink. Put note back in neck saying No milk today. Stop, look and listen. Under a black belly of laburnum tree. Number thirty-three, four blue tokens, useless. Thirty-one, ten bob and a dog barking. Go on, quick up the road soft-shoe close to the wall. Slow down, look normal, headlights on treetops so tie shoelace. Let Big D's taxi go down slow. Gone. Thinking how close tonight, Rache Bradwell's tits over bra behind disco. Twenty-five, twenty-three, nothing. And next week you're going under and she'll let you you know. Dun Roamin, six bottles, which one? And there, right at the back, two quid ten, Get in, and **CHINK**, Stupid! Soft-shoe over gravel back out past stupid pot cherubs and run. Up past the bend to the lamp-lit bench and stop, and look, and listen, motorway hum from beyond the estate and coal-black fields as a bat skit-flickers this arc of orange-lit trees, remembering last Mischief when you dangled that suicide body of tights and scrunched-up news from the crook of that streetlamp, letting it swing out from the trees to shit the passing traffic, then later, when you lifted that window in the blackened-brick church, did a pint-pot Ouija board below the feet of a dirty Jesus, Is there anybody there? Like fuck. So you lobbed big books of God, crack-snapped half-burnt candles, gargle sang Strongbow then pissed in the font. And from the castle gates now, the town as quiet as corn, remembering when you jimmied that lock to the keep, ghost-hunting the Grey Lady up spiral steps to that murder room with no window, slow closing the coal-dark door, sitting quiet as corn in the coal-dark cold, your breath unbraiding back from unseen walls, and nothing, and in all your life you've never seen a ghost, except, when sometimes you talk about it, you might say you have.

CHAPTER 21

We are now looking at

A farmhouse at dusk. Long shadows from the last of the day's sun stretch trees, tractors and barns across the quiet farmyard. A yellow car enters from the lane and parks up by the farmhouse. A short middle-aged woman gets out the passenger side. A tall older man gets out the driver's side. They both look up at the house.

We are now looking in at the front room of that farmhouse. Jean and Chris are drinking tea. The television is on, and the newsreader is talking about Thatcher and the Falklands. Chris looks up from his Derbyshire Times and cocks an ear.

CHRIS: Did you hear that?

JEAN: No. What?

A knock at the door. We see Jean followed by Chris come through into the kitchen and head towards the backdoor. Through the patterned glass we see the wobbly outline of two people. Jean opens the door. The short woman smiles at Jean then Chris. The tall man does likewise.

SHORT WOMAN (*still smiling*): Sorry to intrude. We're Jake's mum and dad. We were just passing through and thought we'd pop by and say hello.

Jean frowns for a moment, and then a smile lights across her face.

JEAN (*touching the short woman on the arm*): Oh! You mean Jake Jake! Billy's friend Jake! Come in! Come in!

The short woman and the tall man enter, and they all shake hands. The tall man introduces himself as Derek and the short woman introduces herself as Daphne. After a little small-talk, Jean nervously makes a pot of tea before they all move into the front room, Daphne and Derek sitting on the settee, Jean and Chris taking a chair each. They chat about the weather, the Hawkwind concert that Billy and Jake have gone to see in Sheffield tonight, and then, a pregnant pause.

DAPHNE (*clearing her throat*): Derek and I wondered if we could have a little chat with you about your Billy?

Jean and Chris look at each other for a second. Jean puts a hand to her forehead.

JEAN (*closing her eyes*): God. What's he done now?

DEREK (*light-heartedly*): Nothing Jean, it's just that, well, don't get us wrong, we think your Billy is a lovely lad, lovely, and honestly, we have absolutely no problem at all with him hanging around with our Jake, but...

DAPHNE (*cutting in*): But me and Derek are a little, well, worried about your Billy.

JEAN (*anxiously*): What's he...

DEREK (*cutting in*): Nothing, Jean, honestly. We're just a little worried about his... it's when he stops over at our house, he...

DAPHNE (*cutting in*): We're worried about your Billy's drinking, Jean.

A pause. Jean blinks. Chris reaches over and pats her arm.

CHRIS (*softly*): It's okay, Jean. (*to Derek and Daphne*) Yes, we're concerned too.

JEAN (*shakily*): What's he done?

DAPHNE (*softly*): Nothing, Jean. It's just when he gets back to ours, he...

DEREK (*cutting in*): He's always really pissed. Pardon the French. I mean, our Jake's no angel, but Billy always seems totally hammered, and, well...

DAPHNE (*cutting in*): Last weekend he threw up all down the landing.

JEAN (*putting her hands over her face*): Jesus.

DEREK: The week before that, all over the spare room.

DAPHNE (*sighing*): All over the pots in the kitchen sink.

A pause. Jean still has her hands over her face. Chris sighs, rubs the top of his head.

DEREK (*light-heartedly*): To his credit he always says sorry. It's quite funny really. We all laugh about it, pull his leg and that.

Derek laughs, but no one joins in. Daphne frowns at him for a moment.

DAPHNE (*shaking her head*): It's not just the being sick though. It's some of the things he says when him and Jake get back. I mean, our Jake's no angel, but…

DEREK (*cutting in*): Your Billy just seems really depressed when he's…

DAPHNE (*cutting in*): And angry, and his language is sometimes quite…

JEAN (*taking her hands from her face*): Nasty?

DEREK (*chuckling*): Well, no, not really. He's just a lad, isn't he, and his language is sometimes a bit…

DAPHNE (*cutting in*): Rich.

A pause. Jean reaches beside her chair to a box of tissues. She blows her nose. Derek smiles.

DEREK: He's a lovely lad when he's not had a drink. Always laughing and joking around.

A pause.

CHRIS (*clearing his throat*): We've been thinking of taking him to a doctor. Or someone we could talk to. To try and sort his head out.

JEAN (*wiping her nose with the tissue*): He worries us so much. He doesn't seem to be able to find in-between. He's always way up, or else he's way down. And his mouth, his mouth can be so bloody hurtful.

DAPHNE (*sympathetically*): We're sorry, Jean. But we felt we had to come and…

JEAN (*cutting in*): It's as though he hates us sometimes. We don't understand. We've done everything we can to make him happy.

DEREK (*sympathetically*): It's a difficult age, Jean. God knows the problems we've had with our eldest.

Unseen by Derek, Daphne shoots him a stern glance.

DEREK (*shaking his head*): He's twenty-four now,

but he went through a right old phase around your Billy's age where he…

DAPHNE (*cutting in*): Exactly. A phase. It'll soon pass. These things do.

Chris shakes his head, scratches at an oil stain on his sleeve. Jean blows her nose again, saying she's sorry, she's so very sorry.

We are now looking at Derek and Daphne driving home. Daphne says they were right not to tell Chris and Jean about their other suspicions. Of who stole the peach schnapps that Aunt Teresa brought them back from Tenerife. Or of who drank from Derek's expensive single malt whisky then watered the bottle down to make it look untouched. Yes, they had said more than enough to Jean and Chris tonight. There was, after all, only so much a parent could take. And next time he comes, they will lock the drinks cabinet and drop the key into the teapot, and to make sure, above all things, they slow-turn their son away from that no good little drunken bastard called Billy, because he's bad, and is certain to do something terrible one day, end of story.

CHAPTER 22

Proper mester's beer this

Not like that puff piss you're supping, says Pete. He takes a swag from his can of Tennent's Super, eyes swinging left then right at Tony and Jake, who grin at the fat bastard to show their bum-chum yeses. I wish the bus would hurry up. I wish Jake hadn't told Tony and Pete about the Hawkwind gig. I wish it were just me and Jake. But then again, I wish it were just me now. Jake's a cunt for siding with Pete. Tony might as well be wearing a sheep-fleece too.

I take a swag from my squash bottle, feeling the glow of whisky, sherry, elderberry wine, gin, brandy, and cherry liqueur going down my throat, the flat tang of orange squash dry on my tongue, the booze humming the walls of my mouth. Pete makes a hacking sound in his throat then gobs a greenie at my feet. I take a step back and lean against the bus shelter. Jake and Tony laugh as Pete hacks another up. He gobs again. This time it hits the toe of my trainer. Creamy green slime bubbles slow off my foot towards the pavement and Jake and Tony laugh like girls, all high-pitched and squeaky.

I wipe my trainer on the grass verge, feeling sick and angry. Pete drinks, deadeyes me over his can, black pit eyeliner circling his arrogant-fuck eyeballs. I swag at my stuff as the 83 makes its way down the hill.

I am fifteen and skinny. Pete is nineteen and built like a fat-fuck brick-shithouse.

This is why.

—

When we get to Sheff we have a couple in the Howard Hotel. I'm not talking anymore. Them three cunts sit at a table by the door. I'm playing pinball, drinking my barley wine, smoking a Number Six. It's been non-stop shit since the bus stop. All led by fat bastard Pete. The other thing is, I know he fancies Rache. This is another reason why. He's got no chance anyway. She's fit and he's a fuckarsed swamp-donkey.

On our way up to The Sportsman, Jake asks me what's up. I tell him nothing's up, but in my head I hear myself shouting Fuck You.

I put Stone Free by Hendrix on the jukebox while they're at the bar. Pete's patches on his denim jacket are pathetic. Stupid glittery Quo and Motorhead. A really wank AC/DC patch that says Back in

Black under a crap Angus Young head that looks like a cow wearing a mong's face. You can always tell the placcy DC fans. They only know the new stuff. Anyone that's real knows the early stuff with Bon Scott pisses all over the Brian Johnson stuff. I put Cream's White Room on too, then I notice an old Quo song from the Sixties. I punch in the letter and number and make a bet with myself. I go over to the bar, smiling, happy the cunts haven't got me one in. I order another barley. Pete calls it a woman's drink. I light a Number Six and tell him Actually, it's stronger than yours, turning the bottle around to show him. He doesn't even look, turning to Tony and saying Did you hear something queer then? Tony looks up to the ceiling pretending to listen, cocking his head one way then the other. Jake laughs. Pictures of Matchstick Men comes on the jukebox. I neck the barley, order another, and as the barmaid takes the top off it I ask Pete if he's heard this track before. Pete says no because he doesn't listen to shite. I drink, feeling the glow. Them three go and play darts, Pete's Status Quo patch glittering under the dartboard spotlight. Twat.

In the Frog And Parrot, Pete, Tony and Jake order Roger and Out. Pete bets Tony and Jake he can sup more than they can. I go to the pisser. When I get back they haven't got me one in. Strongest beer in the World, says Pete, bringing a glass of treacly shit to his fat-fuck lips. He downs it in one then clanks the empty glass to the bar. Fifteen fuckin percent, he says, wiping his gobshite gob on the back of his hand.

I order two more barleys, not saying a word as Pete talks more shite. The more I listen, the more I realise it's Pete that does all the talking while the other two just play noddy-dog.

I drink and think.

Jake asks me again What's up? and again I say Nothing. He turns to listen to Pete telling a story about how some gadge down the pit kept nicking some bloke's sarnies, so one day the bloke shat onto some bread to make a shit sandwich and put it into his snap tin.

Pete says That stopped the cunt.

Jake and Tony laugh like girls. I don't believe the story. Surely you'd smell shit before you put it into your mouth?

Sometimes I don't know how I feel about people. I like having mates but then I see things for what they are. Jake doesn't give a shit about me when Pete and Tony are around. When it's just me and him he's totally different. Like that time a few weeks ago. Why be like that with someone then behave like you're ashamed of them when you're with other people?

I drink and think. Am I?

I look at Jake as Pete tells another hard-man story about the pit. I don't feel that way towards

Jake today. At all. I fancy Rache all the time. I don't really understand why I feel like I do about certain people. Jake went all weird after that thing a few weeks ago. I didn't see him for a fortnight. Maybe he told people? I remember that time with Carl Partridge's sister at that party when we were kids. She said if I showed her my cock then she'd show me her fanny. I showed her my cock. She ran off and told her mum.

I go over to the jukebox. Three songs for twenty pence. My Sharona by The Knack, Money by Flying Lizards, Hong Kong Garden by Siouxsie And The Banshees. Back at the bar them three have got them in again. No one got me one in. I buy myself a barley, pretend to go to the bog, take myself to the City Hall.

When I get there I realise I have all the tickets. Then I realise them three haven't paid me for them yet. I sell three to a tout on the steps for half of what they cost me, finish my barley and go inside.

When Hawkwind come on I realise how happy I feel. I look up at the television screens flashing with nuclear explosions and think how beautiful the end of things are.

I like people sometimes, but usually I don't.

People lie, use you for what they can get, talk shite about what you mean to them.

I stand among a thousand people smelling of sweat and fags and booze. Their bodies press against mine.

No one looks at anyone else other than at the band.

I'm with a thousand others, but I'm totally alone. Beautiful, as my right hand is wedged against the curve of an arse.

Girl or boy, I don't even look.

CHAPTER 23

Babysitting

And the kid's in bed, so Rache pierces my ear with a sewing needle, puts one of her earrings in my ear, tells me it looks cool, squeezes the blackheads on my back, says she likes me in my new blue Adidas tee-shirt, lets me finger her on the front room carpet, then rub my cock on her cunt and up between her arse cheeks, and when I spunk it spits through the air, over the back of her head onto the red settee, which she cleans off with a wet tea towel quick, says What if I'm pregnant? So I tell her don't be stupid, and she says she's not stupid, so I tell her she is, her saying Fuck off, so I do, down the road to The Blue Bell, sink seven quick ciders with Kingy and Skinner, then back babysitting to sort stuff out, but she won't let me in, says I'm pissed. And when I throw up by the backdoor the kid's fat mum and dad pull up onto the drive, him getting out the car saying What the fuck's going on? And Rache's crying, and I'm saying nothing, the kid's fat mum saying Go now and don't come back, me wiping my mouth on my new blue Adidas tee-shirt, throwing them all a two-fingered fuck-it, walking home down the lane under a blue-black blanket of stars, full moon silvering the woods, singing Highway to Hell and not giving a fuck, making a promise to myself that I never will, the stink of wild garlic heavy in the hollow as a low-slung fox cuts across to the fly-tip, and I can't decide whether this is good luck or bad luck, so I piss my name into a pothole, howl moon-mad like a cunt-hungry mongrel at the sky, shout God to go fuck himself, no echo returning.

CHAPTER 24

My schoolbag chink-chinks

So I stop by the fly-tip, swing my bag off my back, sliding a big bottle of Woodpecker out. The white sun glints through the trees, making me squint as I tip the bottle, the bubbles popping on my tongue.

The birds sing as I drink. Somewhere a tractor buzzes. The midges hang in twitching clouds low to the lane.

I tip again. I don't stop until half the bottle is gone. Then I tip again. I keep tipping till I've done the whole bottle then I chuck it down the bank, satisfied by the smash it makes somewhere down below.

The stink of wild garlic makes me feel pukey. I shoulder my schoolbag and head on through the yellow morning, feeling my insides rise and rise, flickering like a midge cloud.

My watch blinks a red 7:23. I punch the dry heat. Last day at school. **EVER.** Let's fuckin have it.

The lads are already waiting at the rec as I turn onto the field.

8:09.

I launch an empty Woodpecker towards the goalposts as I walk. A cheer goes up as it lands in the six-yard box, popping like a little bomb of brown shards. Big grins all round.

Skinner's on Carling. Jag's on Heineken. Kingy's on Harvey's Bristol Cream, the twat.

I open my third bottle of Woodpecker with a *pishhh*. A cheer goes up as I start necking it, cider running down my chin onto my blazer.

We smoke Bensons, then make a little fire out of our school ties. Through the wobble of heat the school shimmers across the rec.

Skinner pulls a marker pen out of his blazer pocket and we take turns writing on the back of each other's blazers.

Kingy's says PUSSY FUCKER. Skinner's says TITTY SUCKER. Jag's says SPUNK CHUCKER.

They won't tell me what mine says.

Everything supped, we cause fuckery by the school gates. Skinner bangs Andy Baxter in the face, because. I make myself useful by grabbing lasses' arses as they walk past. Some like it and laugh. Some don't. Lindsay Nolan says she's going to tell her brother Mickey. I say to her, Tell the cunt, I'm ready. Mickey is a big fucker but I don't care. Let him fuckin try it. Kingy takes a piss on the school sign and shouts **FUCK MOORFIELD** as Miss Bacon's car goes by. She sees him and he sees her, so he turns around still pissing. She speeds up.

We seem to be attracting a lot of attention. We're the lads, and we sing it, arms locked around each other.

Outside Mr Graves's office window, we stop to have a fag. He looks up from his desk but doesn't come out to us. Jag grabs Sharon Tolly's bag as she walks by and he starts rifling through it. She starts crying when he lobs her Tampax at her one by one, singing We're jammin, we're jammin, we're jammin from a fanny hole.

I feel a bit sorry for her. I think it's cos she's fit.

The bell goes and we decide to forget registration and go lie down at the back of the hall. Some teachers go by and look at us but no one says anything. The first-years start coming in for assembly so we all drop moonies.

Everyone's looking at us. We're the lads.

The hymn is Glad That I Live Am I, but we just fuck about, singing as loud and as out of tune as we can. Jag starts singing like a spack, tapping spacky Freddy Lester on the back of his head. Spacky Freddy turns around and tells Jag to Fuck off. Freddy has spit on his chin so Jag starts drooling spit out of his then wipes it off with a pretend spacky hand. Miss Cartwright comes stomping down the line and drags Jag out by the arm. Jag laughs and cops a feel of her arse as she pulls him to the side of the hall. From where I'm standing he looks really pissed.

I watch as she says something red-faced into his ear. On the stage Mr Graves is saying something to Mr Brown. Mr Brown is a proper hard bastard. Before the hymn is done he disappears off the stage and appears like a gnarled genie by Skinner. He drags Skinner out by the ear. The hymn finishes and the sound of the main doors slamming dull-thumps into the hall. Mr Brown then drags Jag out the same way.

Mr Graves is talking on the stage about how proud he is of the school's achievements this year. Kingy is grinning at me but I start to feel flat. Kingy's grin disappears as Mr Brown bustles his way down the line and drags him out like the others. I feel shit now. Everyone is turning around and looking at me. I nod as Mr Brown beckons me with a curling finger from the end of the line. I walk slow towards him. My lion has left me.

From Mr Graves's office I can see the lads messing about by the gates. Skinner and Kingy are trying to pull the arms off Jag's blazer. The office door opens and Mr Graves comes in, looking stern and angry. He tells me to **SIT!** then walks a line from his filing cabinets to his desk and back again.

I'm very disappointed in you Billy, he says.

He points at the window to where the lads are now doing a Space Invaders dance across the school entrance. I stop a grin. Mr Graves clears his throat.

That lot, he says, I expect it from. They're a lost

bloody cause. But you... He pauses, stops walking to and fro and sits down opposite me.

You have two choices Billy, he says, and it's as simple as this. You let that lot go and you stay on for the sixth form, or, you just piss your life away.

He looks straight into my eyes for a moment then smiles.

Listen, he says, putting his hand on my shoulder, You have every chance of doing something with your life. Stay on. Surprise yourself. Surprise others. Miss Cant's always saying how much she likes the things you've written in her class, and I know she's told you the same, but Billy, it's always the same old story with you isn't it? Miss Cant's one of half a dozen teachers who've told me the same thing over and over again about you. If you stopped pissing about and got stuck in you could actually do something for yourself.

He smiles again and takes his hand off my shoulder. Thank fuck. I look out the window to where the lads are whistling and mooning. I look at Mr Graves.

Sorry, Mr Graves. I can't stop on. I have a job to go to. I'm on a YOP Scheme at a dry-cleaners in town. Twenty-six quid a week.

Mr Graves shakes his head. He looks disappointed. I feel a little sick. My head dull-thumps.

And where will that take you exactly? he says, tilting his head.

I shrug.

He sighs and writes something on a scrap of paper. He hands it to me.

This is my number, he says. Ring me if you change your mind. You have two months to decide. Now please go straight home, Billy, you stink like a pissing brewery.

It's funny hearing a teacher swear.

When I get home, Mum and Dad are out. I get all my school books and start a fire in the old dustbin Dad uses to burn garden rubbish. Then I go into their bedroom and get the stuff Mum keeps in a box under her bed. There's things in there from way back. Some of it even has my old last name on it. Pictures, stories, school reports, and even a photograph from my old junior school in Chesterfield. In this photo I've got no front teeth and a feather cut. My shirt collar is nearly as wide as my shoulders. Funny.

I throw most of these things into the fire, but I decide to put some things back. Some crayon drawings and a card that says Happy Birthday Mummy. I think Mum would be mad if I burnt everything. The last thing I burn is my school blazer. It says **CHICKEN PLUCKER** on the back. I don't even know what they mean by that.

CHAPTER 25

The Bottle by Billy Slaney class 3

One day, when David was playing in the woods, he found an old bottle in a crack that was in the trunk of an old tree. David was surprised. He'd never noticed it before. David had walked down this path in the woods lots of times and had never seen the bottle in the crack before. He looked at it for a moment and wondered how it got there. Then he pulled it out. The bottle was very old and had something in it. David looked closer and he saw that it was a scroll of paper. He picked up a twig from the floor and used it to poke the scroll of paper out. When he got it out he unrolled it and there was writing on it. David couldn't quite read it at first, and then after a while he could. It said "Ask a devil many things and some of these come true, make a wish that pleases you and a devil will come and do". At first David was too scared to try it, but after a while he wasn't so he read it out and he made a wish to be invisible. Suddenly a big black rook appeared on a branch in front of David and made a loud scrawing sound. Then there was a sound like wood cracking and when David looked down to the scroll of paper it looked like it was floating! David couldn't see his hands or feet or anything! David became very scared and cried "Oh no what have I done?" and then he threw the scroll of paper to the ground and he ran home.

On his way home he saw his friends Jimmy and Steve. They were sat on the farm gate talking. As David got closer he heard Jimmy say "I think David is an idiot and I don't really like him" and Steve said "Yes me too". Jimmy then said "The only reason I pretend to be his friend is because he lives on a farm and that means if we're his friends then we can play on the farm" and Steve said "Yes that's right". This made David stop still. He felt very bad and was going to shout something at Jimmy and Steve when he stopped and thought of something. "Wait a minute! I'm invisible and I can get my revenge on Jimmy and Steve without them knowing!" So David crept up and hid behind a hedge and he called "Jimmy! Steve! Come and look what I've found!" This made Jimmy and Steve get off the gate and follow the sound of David's voice who they thought was calling them from far away. David repeated this four times, each time taking them deeper and deeper into the woods until he had lured Jimmy and Steve under the big old tree. "Where are you

David?" cried Jimmy and Steve, and then lifting the old bottle into the air, the invisible David smashed it over their heads until they were dead. From then on, the invisible David never had any more friends, and living on his own he always felt happy because he could do whatever he liked and no one was ever untrue to him again.

CHAPTER 26

You forgot your handbag, she says

And as the 83 moves off with a jerk, you look up at the brown-haired woman from the bus stop, your carrier bag swaying from her outstretched hand. Her breasts bob twice as the 83 finds then leaves the kerb. You like her smile. Her name is Carol.

It's Friday. Payday. You masturbate in the works toilet, arrive five minutes late to the steam-press, get given the hospital contract basket, spend the morning in a cloud of piss from old man's trousers.

You think of Carol. One o'clock at The Golden Fleece, she said.

You're there at one minute past.

Carol is a secretary at a bank. She has a crooked front tooth. She has brown eyes and a small mouth. She has a husband who works for British Telecom. In Scotland. She has freckles. Steak and ale pie. Two halves of Carling and Why don't you call by if you're out tonight? I'm opposite The Bull number 23b just above the fruit shop I won't bite ha ha.

You drink, and under the table Carol's foot rests on yours.

You put an arm across your lap.
Well? she says.

———

Tonight you smell of Old Spice. You're happy that your mum washed your best jeans. You knock twice at number 23b opposite The Bull. Carol opens the door not long from the bath or the shower. She wears a red dressing gown and black eyeliner that's smudged a little. She has an Alsatian called Ralph. Ralph sniffs at your crotch then backs you up against the kitchen sink. Carol says Ralph is a big softie really. Ralph belongs to Roger. Roger is back on Tuesday.

The wine is from Australia. The glasses are like blue fishbowls on stalks. Carol puts Roxy Music on.

Do you like these? she says.

You're watching Ralph, who is laid on the rug watching you.

They're okay, you say.

Carol sits down next to you on the settee. She turns to face you and curls her legs underneath her. Carol's lips are cherry red. She's 25 or 26, maybe even 30, and when she smiles her crooked front tooth shows through.

Another? she says.

Ralph closes his eyes. You hold your glass out.

You can sleep in here, she says, opening the door to the spare bedroom. She turns the bedside light on. Next to this is a clock that blinks a red 01:20.

The room is small and blue with a single bed and a double wardrobe. Carol pats the duvet.

You say Ta.

Carol says she'll leave you to get sorted.

You say Ta.

You leave your pants on and the bed smells of lemons. You turn the lamp off and the room moves a little. You consider masturbating into your sock. You should have tried to kiss her at least.

Idiot.

The bedroom door opens in a soft arc of landing light. Carol wears a short red nightdress through which you can see each dark O of her nipples. She holds a blue plastic bowl filled with water. She has a small blue towel over her arm.

I thought you might want to wash, she says.

You feel yourself frown.

Carol tells you to get out of bed, to take your pants off.

Look! she says, pointing.

You both look.

All ready to be washed! she says.

Carol says it would be wrong to do it in her and Roger's bed. She sucks on you then turns around on knees and elbows.

Like this, she says.

No, they untie at the sides, she says.

Smack me and fuck me, she says.

So you do.

CHAPTER 27

They didn't believe you at first

But then when you're crossing the road to The Swan, Unfuckingbelievable! It's her! Eating crisps and walking towards you with a brick-shithouse, Grady and Blue saying Fuck off and No chance, you saying Don't say owt, shurrup that's her husband, Newt saying Yeah right, just as they walk past, Carol giving you the quickest smile, throwing that screwed-up crisp bag behind her in your direction, glancing over her shoulder and smiling again, her husband not seeing, thank fuck, Grady, Blue and Newt now laughing and you saying See, see, I fuckin told you didn't I?

It's Grady's round in The Swan and it's a pint of Merrydown and There you go shagger. It's a good night. You like being out with the mesters. All old enough to be your dad but so fucking what? Friday night and wage-packet fuelled, two in The Bell, one in The Anchor, The Angel, The Crown, The Cross Keys, and now here. Nine-thirty and you're feeling it proper. It's like schooling, yeah? Fuck all the lightweights. Out with the mesters and no one fucks with you. Tell it how it is, and how it was with that bird Carol. The mesters laughing as you talk little stringy knickers that untie at the sides, Slap my arse slap my arse now fuck me from behind. And of course you don't tell them how you shot your load in two minutes flat, how Carol said Don't worry about it, then went off all sulky leaving you alone in the spare room, Ralph sniff-sniffing under the door-crack all night, you leaving early before she woke up, running tiptoe down the stairs, Ralph slobbering after you, Carol's stringy knickers still fanny-damp in your jacket pocket.

The barmaid gives you a slitty-eyed stare from behind the Heineken pump.

Wouldn't touch her with yours, Grady. And now Grady scowls, says Steady lad, and then to the barmaid, Ignore him Beryl, he's been trying to keep up wi' mesters, and the barmaid now laughing, singing Some-one's gonna be sufferin' tomorrow.

And then in The Bull it's your round, and just to show the mesters you're real it's three barleys in a pint pot, and the landlord telling you to Keep your language down, and in the bog you spew brown water, and on your way back to The Bell you piss in the bus shelter, and in The Bell taproom they all laugh because you've pissed down your leg and you feel a bit alone but that's alright, you now telling some woman to Fuck off but you don't know why, this bloke now telling you he's Gonna smack yer one, but Newt telling him to Leave it because blah blah blah, you now singing Subterranean Homesick Blues stood on a stool pulling a moonie, Shirley the landlady yelling **GET DOWN AND PULL YOUR TROUSERS UP BILLY-BOY OR YOU'RE OUT!** Smile. And now you're telling someone called Tom that you Don't take shit from no one as you button up, now sticking twenty p in the box for Stones and Yardbirds and Kingsmen. **I WAS BORRRN IN A CROSSFIRE HURRI-CANE.** Grady now prodding some gadge in the chest, telling him he's a **DIRTY FUCKIN SCAB BASTARD,** lots of pushing, shit on the verge of kicking off, **I WAS SCHOOOLED WITH A STRAP RIGHT ACROSS MAH BACK,** the gadge getting pushed towards the door, people shouting **SCAB! SCAB! SCAB!** Shirley the landlady shouting **ALRIGHT LADS! ENOUGH NOW! ENOUGH!** You telling Tom you Don't take shit, Not from **ANY** fucker **COS IT'S ALLL-RIIIGHT NOW, INFACT IT'SA GAAAS,** Tom handing you another barley and kissing you on the cheek ha ha with a Get that down you Billy-boy, and you saying No shit, Tom, Don't take none from no fucking fucker, *chink*, **LAST ORDERS PLEASE! LAST ORDERS!** Barley fucking wine, Tom, proper mester's drink, **I WAS CROWWWNED WITH A SPIKE RIGHT THROUGH MAH,** Yeh, get the fuckers in, **LAST ORDERS PLEASE!** Love is a fuckin lie. A. Fuckin.

Lie. Just fucking is fucking. Know worramean, Tom? Blah blah blah. Cheers. To fuckin fucking. Don't take shit. Right?

You put your fag out in the palm of your right hand. You and Tom look at the damage done.

It's funny.

CHAPTER 28

You think Billy's funny when he's drunk

You've watched him for a couple of weeks now, ever since you and Bruce started going to The Bell. You'd heard the jukebox was good. That's how you and Billy started talking. He'd just put a song on and you made yourself brave and went over to ask him who it was. He grinned at you, told you it was The Yardbirds, Jimmy Page on guitar. You liked Led Zep, and you told him so. He asked you what your favourite album was. You said Zep Four and he smiled, said Yeh, me too. Billy then said him and his mates were going for a mooch around the village. He asked if you wanted to come. He smiled when he said Come, and you laughed.

Bruce didn't feel comfortable with Billy and his mates. He told you this as he walked you home that night. He said they were trouble. You told him that you thought they were a good laugh. Bruce just said, Idiot piss-heads more like. Then he said something about Billy. You could feel Bruce looking at you when he said Billy's name. You kept your eyes on the street ahead, then said something about not looking forward to work tomorrow.

The Wednesday after the Friday night, Billy called into the estate agents where you work. Your heart started beating faster when he walked in. The shop was empty so you both went and sat in the back. You made a pot of tea and you listened to the new ZZ Top album on your tape player. Billy said he preferred their older stuff, and asked you if you'd heard Tush. You said you hadn't and Billy said it was a song about girl's bits. You laughed. Then you kissed. Billy started touching your breasts over your blouse. Pretty soon he was under your bra but you didn't stop him. It excited you to think that the shop doorbell could ring at any moment. He put his hand up your skirt and touched you over your pants. Things were moving too fast but you told yourself to relax. He put a finger inside you, and you unzipped him, wrapping your fingers around him. It was only four-thirty but you closed the shop. You made love in the back. You didn't come.

You showed Billy how to touch you right two weeks later, that first night when he stopped over. You'd finished with Bruce the Friday before, but you and Billy were still keeping things quiet. It was too soon after, and you didn't want to hurt Bruce any more than you already had. Bruce cried when you told him. He kept saying Why, Sarah? and you kept saying that you wanted to have a break for a while, that you didn't want to be tied down, that at twenty-two you were too young to be engaged. Bruce said Please, and Let's just be boyfriend and girlfriend again and not be engaged. You said No, that you needed space to think, and that you were sorry. Bruce stopped crying then. He just said Fair enough. You looked at him for a moment and thought how pathetic he looked. His moustache too neatly trimmed. His hair too tidy with its nice side-parting. His jeans too new and blue and clean. His tee-shirt from a Def Leppard tour he never went to see.

Back then, you were still living at Janice's. Renting a room in her house, and you knew Janice wouldn't have liked Billy. Janice was good to you when you needed to leave home. You didn't want a scene with her. You felt you owed her.

You and Billy took each step of the creaky stairs together so it sounded like it was just you. You showed Billy to your room and sat him on the bed, put a finger to your lips in a shush, whispered to him to wait while you had a few minutes with Janice in the front room. Janice was blind in one eye, but you still thought she looked at you funny when you said Goodnight.

When you opened your door, Billy was already

in your bed, grinning like a devil. You lit a candle, took your clothes off slow, got in beside him. You kissed and touched each other for a while, and then you sat him at the end of the bed and told him to watch. You played with yourself, showing him the little circles. He shuffled forward on his knees, wanking himself. You both kept on, not touching each other. You came quite hard and felt his come hit your legs and belly. You'd never done anything like this before, but it felt right with Billy, didn't it. He laid on top of you, wriggling about, his semen all slippy between you. You giggled, trying not to in case Janice heard.

You both smoked a cigarette then Billy got hard again. You made love, Billy sliding his hand between you both, making the little circles like you'd shown him. You both came together. Then Billy whispered in your ear that it was great to be with an older woman to show him the ropes. You play-slapped him on the bum, whispered Hey, it's only four years.

You both moved into this terraced house in July. You'd only been going out with Billy for six weeks but it felt right. The rent was cheap and you did the place up for next to nothing, everything painted Co-op magnolia. Then Billy painted a big black star on the floorboards of the spare bedroom, and all these weird words on the wall. He told you he got the words from a book on witches, and that this would be the party room. You thought it was a bit nuts but you just laughed and said Okay, because Billy is funny, isn't he.

The first party you had was a house-warming. You invited some people back from The Bell. You lit candles in the party room and listened to Zeppelin and Hawkwind, The Doors and Black Sabbath. At midnight, Billy took all his clothes off and sat cross-legged on a beanbag in the middle of the star. His mates laughed but some people left. Billy put some of his clothes back on. He said it was the best way to sort the wheat from the chaff. Before too long there was only you, Billy, Tom, and Karen left. You smoked some resin and danced to Bachman Turner Overdrive, you and Billy yelling **B-B-B-BABY YOU AIN'T SEEN NOTHIN YET!** and Tom and Karen laughing, and everything felt great and you knew that life would always be a dance with Billy, and there would always be laughing, and there was nothing to feel bad about anymore because all the bad stuff had gone, and then Billy put Tush on, and was shouting **SEE! SEE! IT'S ALL ABOUT FANNY!** Then you and Billy made love on the floorboards and so did Tom and Karen, and it was fun and exciting watching them do it while you and Billy were doing it, and you'd never imagined yourself doing such a thing but you did it, didn't you.

Then Billy said you should swap.

This made you feel awkward. You didn't want to

do it with Tom. You told Billy as much, and then he yanked himself out of you real quick, and said if you didn't fuck Tom then you were **JUST NORMAL AND FUCKING BORING LIKE EVERY FUCKER ELSE!** He sounded really spiteful, and you felt your belly go heavy like you were falling from somewhere high up to somewhere under the floor. Tom and Karen had stopped what they were doing, and they were watching you. The music had stopped too, and you remember the needle on the record player going *chk chk chk* at the end of the record, the arm not lifting to go back to its resting place, just that static tap of little commas.

Billy stood up, and you watched as Karen watched Billy walk towards the record player, still stiff, now lifting the arm off the record, leaving nothing but the sound of Tom and Karen moving against each other, and you remember how cold you suddenly felt as you rolled over onto your side to face the wall, the words that made no sense flickering in the candlelight to the sound of soft guitar like spots of rain on a pond, Billy now back beside you, warm against your back, whispering Crosby Stills Nash and Young into your ear, and I'm sorry, Sarah, I'm an idiot sometimes, and now he's back inside you, soft kissing your neck, moving gentle, careful, now some joke about having the Devil in him, and Tom and Karen laughing, now stepping over you and filling the gap between the words on the wall and you, and even though you don't really want to, you kiss with Karen, touching her breasts while Billy and Tom tell you what to do, your dad's whisky breath still burning behind your closed eyelids as he breathes Sarah, Sarah, do you love me?

CHAPTER 29

I load the machine with hospital contract stuff

Pissy trousers, pissy pyjamas, pissy shirts. I turn the dial, press start. I watch the clothes turning and tumbling through the little round window for a minute then I get the sense I'm being watched. I turn around and the gaffer's glaring at me.

Billy! I thought I told you not to mix darks with lights?

I look again to the little round window, watching black trousers and pale green pyjamas wrestle with each other. I look back at the gaffer. His knackered baggy face is red and blotchy and he huffs and puffs as he leans against the contract basket. Poor cunt is sixty-summat going on ninety. Years of dry-cleaning fumes have fucked him up right good and proper.

I didn't think it mattered with the hospital stuff, Mr Gilly.

IT MATTERS WITH EVERYTHING! he barks, turning on his knackered Hush Puppy heels and heading back to the steam-press. **DON'T DO IT**

AGAIN! he sputters, hobbling huff-puff into the steam and slamming the door behind him.

I mutter Cunt under my breath and push the basket out of the way of the clothes bins. There are four bins, these big wooden boxes, and my job is to sort out the loads, grouping them by colour and material, applying pre-clean where needed, then loading the machines. It's boring work but it's better than working the steam-press, which is what I have to do some days, but not today thank fuck.

I start dragging all the dark nylons out, mainly suits and trousers, and start checking each item for stains. Mostly it's sweat under the armpits and ink in top pockets. Then I make a pile in front of the other machine and start checking through the pockets as I load it. You have to be careful, because a lot of these clothes are from office workers and the like, and you're really in the shit if you dry-clean a jacket with a leaky pen in it. Even tissues are trouble. They disintegrate into a thousand tiny shreds and cover everything in the machine with little pale flecks.

I check the pockets of a black jacket and my fingers touch something cold. It's a big silver badge with a clip on it. I close my hand and take a quick look over my shoulder. All clear, so I open my hand to look.

Derbyshire Constabulary. Funny. I drop it into my overall pocket. I dip again and my fingers touch something else hard and cold. I know what it is without even looking. I push the jacket into the machine and quickly open and close my right hand to flash a thick gold wedding ring. A dirty copper on the pull.

The morning drags fuckarse slow. At dinner I head into town, my finger slipping in and out of the pocketed ring as I walk. The pawnshop gives me fifteen quid after some half-hearted questions about the ring's history.

It were my Uncle George's, I say. He's dead. Brain cancer.

I order pie and chips at The Fleece and a pint of Carling. I sit near the pool table and wait for my food. It feels great to be drinking cold lager at dinner. I never have the money usually. I get another in just as the food arrives. It tastes great. A woman comes in with her arm around an old biddy, sits her at a table then fetches a menu from the bar. I think about my mum as I drag a chip through gravy. We haven't really talked since I moved in with Sarah.

When I left home it was quick, my dad putting my stuff into the back of his van with nothing much said. My mum didn't try to stop me either. She didn't say anything really. But then again, she hadn't said much to me for weeks. Maybe we just outgrew each other. Maybe this is how it is for everyone. I'm not a boy anymore.

I finish my pint and get another in. The clock on the wall says twelve-forty. Twenty minutes left.

I call at Hudson's record shop on my way back to work and buy Sarah the new Whitesnake album. She has a thing for David Coverdale. I feel good. The sun is shining.

LOOK AT THIS! barks baggy-faced Mr Gilly, holding up a pink dress with a blue-black streak across the tit.

Oops.

WHAT DID I TELL YOU ABOUT MIXING LIGHTS AND DARKS! HOW COULD YOU MISS THIS! IT'S BRIGHT BLOODY PINK FOR GOD'S SAKE! YOU DON'T MIX A PINK DRESS WITH DARK SUITS YOU IDIOT!

I take a breath. I don't like being called an idiot.

LAST CHANCE! ONE MORE AND YOU'RE OUT!

He leans into my face and sniffs. Have you been drinking, lad? Have you **BEEN DRINKING?**

I shrug, a smile breaking across my face, unstoppable.

IT'S NOT FUNNY, YOU IDIOT! WHAT HAPPENS IF THERE'S AN ACCIDENT? HEY? WHAT DO YOU THINK THE INSURERS WOULD SAY IF THEY FOUND OUT THE CAUSE OF THE ACCIDENT WAS PISSED?

I'm not pissed, Mr Gilly.

He huffs and shakes his baggy head. Well my lad, the cost of this is coming out of your wages, make no mistake. He shakes the dress in my face, throws it back into the clothes bin, then turns and hobbles huff-puff back into the steam room.

Idiot, he says, closing the door with a bang.

I lean the Hudson's carrier bag against the machine. I take the copper's badge out my denim jacket pocket and slide it onto my lapel. I open the machine door and ram anything and everything into it. Half-a-dozen white shirts, a purple dress, a green suit, black trousers, a red coat, a yellow dress, a blue overall, a cream suit, that pink dress, again, and then I turn the dial up to the hottest wash possible. And then, unzipping my fly, I piss into the mouth of the machine. It's a long and happy piss, disturbed only by Madge the counter-lass pushing a barrow of clothes down the alley towards the machine room.

I zip myself up, close the little window and press start, the hundred degree light flashing on/off/on/off as I pass her on my way out, swinging my carrier bag, singing Highway to Hell, walking out the shop door into the clean bright sunlight, the change in my pocket saying poppers from the porn shop, a quick pint, then home.

CHAPTER 30

So where's the money coming from?

She doesn't answer him because he's got that edge to his voice again. She looks out the kitchen window and listens to the sound of him pouring another Merrydown. She thinks about Zep the cat, and how the house stinks of cat, of the three other kittens that are now grown-up cats that they can't find a home for, of the cat-basket full of Zep's new kittens in the front room, of the twenty-six fucking quid to get Zep spayed, of the three other twenty-six quids to get the kittens that are now cats spayed, of the other twenty-six quids to come if they can't find homes for the new kittens.

After a minute, she says, So if we've got no money, then where's that lot come from? From the sink, she turns and points to the carrier bag of bottles by his chair.

He drinks, then puts his glass on the table. Tick, he says, smiling.

She thinks about this for a minute. After two and a half years of living together, they owe three hundred and twenty quid on the overdraft, ninety quid in missed loan payments, a hundred and thirty on the catalogue, and her with two hundred and fifty five quid's worth of IOUs hidden in the safe at work, which somehow needs sorting before the auditors come next month, and him with no job, no sign of getting a job, and now tick at the corner shop for ale.

Great.

What if Zep gets pregnant again? she says.

I got you this, he says, lifting a big bottle of Riesling from the carrier bag by his chair. Have a drink. Relax. Let's talk about it, he says.

When he gets back from the corner shop, he puts the two carrier bags on the table with a chink, then kisses her.

This is a great idea, he says.

Last big one, she says, last big one before we get sorted. You get on that job scheme and we'll stay in, watch what we're doing. Get the debts cleared in six months or so. Easy.

He puts another record on. They dance to Subterranean Homesick Blues then kiss again. They fuck on the settee and she watches his face as he comes into her.

Why hadn't you told me about that job scheme? she says.

They finish the cider and the wine. Then they open the Bell's and sit looking at the kittens. Some are asleep. Some are feeding off Zep.

I love cats, she says.

CHAPTER 31

When Billy said But Grace I love you

I knew things were going to happen. I was seeing Martin at the time, but I didn't love him. I'd been seeing him for about a year, and I always knew he was more serious about it than I was.

It happened like this. Martin said he'd been asked through a friend of a friend if he wanted to play bass in a band. I could see he was excited about something. The covers band Martin was in had packed up a couple of weeks before. He asked me what I thought, if it was worth another go. He'd said when the covers band had packed up he'd had enough of it all, that it was too much hassle, that they were dickheads and he wouldn't want to go through all that again. I told him lightning never strikes twice, and how would he know if it was a good thing or not if he didn't give it a try.

Strange how life works out.

This is how I met Billy.

We went to meet them that Friday night. The house looked a bit scruffy from the outside. Martin knocked on the door, and when it opened the first thing was the smell of cat wee. The second thing was this skinny lad with a cheeky smile.

Hello, I'm Billy, he said.

I liked him straight away. I sometimes joke with Billy that when I smell cat wee I always think of that first time we met.

He introduced us to his girlfriend Sarah and his friend Tom. Sarah seemed nice. Tom looked a bit dodgy to be honest. Loads of bad tattoos and a sly grin. Billy and Tom were already half-drunk. We all sat round drinking and talking, listening to music. Billy made me laugh, dancing stupid to this weird hippy music. Then Billy, Tom and Martin got the guitars out and played for a bit. To be fair, it wasn't very good, but it was fun all the same. We got drunk on cheap wine and vodka. Me and Billy talked to each other loads. Sarah kept giving me these funny looks. By midnight I was really drunk and felt sick. Billy helped me outside and held my hair as I threw up in his front garden. He told me he liked me, and then we kissed.

Things happened quickly. Within a few weeks me and Billy were living together. A bedsit in town. Martin kept coming into work, bugging me about Billy, telling me I needed to be careful.

It didn't matter though, Billy told me he'd done some iffy stuff in the past, but I told him, I said, Billy, what's gone is gone, and what matters now is now.

Mum wasn't very happy. She fell out with me a bit for moving in with Billy. She said I hardly knew him, and that I ought to take my time. I said But Mum, you and Dad only knew each other three months before you got married. Mum said, Yes, and look what happened there. I told her she needed to get over all that, that it was years ago when Dad left, and that she ought to get herself another man. She told me I was being stupid, that she was too old for such stuff, and anyway, this wasn't about her, this was about me and Billy. Then she said there was something about Billy she didn't trust.

This is where we fell out. We're okay now though, and she's even started seeing a widower called Frank. My sister and brother aren't crazy about it all, but I'm working on them.

It was tough at first in the bedsit. But fun. We didn't have much money so we used to stay in, watch telly, listen to records and play board games. Billy said he was sick of all the mad stuff, and he wanted to settle down. He got a job at Halfords selling bikes. I knew he hated it, but he stuck at it to help pay the bills. He still played guitar a bit, just for fun, but he didn't see Tom anymore, which I was quite happy about. Not that I'd choose Billy's friends for him, but there was something about Tom I didn't like. I think he was a bad influence on Billy.

We stayed at the bedsit for about six months, saved up a little money, and put it towards a deposit on a house. We found a little two-up two-down we liked on the outskirts of Chesterfield, so we went to the bank and sorted a mortgage out. I'd started working as a secretary at a legal firm, and the money was better so we were doing alright. We got the legal fees a little cheaper too, which helped. We moved in on the first of September 1988. Mum was okay with me by then, but Billy still wasn't getting on with his mum and dad. They'd had another big fall out and Billy had said some angry things to them on the phone one night. I know he can have a temper about him, but he's always sorry afterwards. Billy said he used to drink too much too often, and it didn't suit him. He said that any big problems he'd had in his life were when he drank too much. Sure, we have a drink now and then, like on Friday nights when we buy some wine and watch the comedy shows on Channel Four, but Billy doesn't get drunk that much.

There are times when we fall out a little though. We always make up pretty quickly, and making up is always good.

The worst I saw Billy was last New Year's Eve when he phoned his mum and dad up. Billy was shouting at his dad saying **TELL ME YOU LOVE ME** and he kept shouting **SAY IT SAY IT**, which his dad did do in the end. And then Billy's mum got on the phone and Billy started shouting that she'd never loved him either, that he was a just a complication to her, a mistake, that she didn't really want him in the first place.

Billy was really down the next day. He often is when he's had too much to drink the night before. I think he drinks too much sometimes because he's hurting somewhere. I think he hurts because he doesn't know his real dad. He's said as much to me some nights when we talk.

Yesterday when I came home from work Billy had made a settee for us. The second-hand one that we'd bought when we first moved in had broken and we couldn't afford a new one. Billy used the cushions off the old one, built a base out of scrubbed-up bricks from the backyard and covered it all in an old blanket with little elephants on it. It looked beautiful. I cried when I saw it. His mum and dad don't seem to see this side of him. Billy can be really sweet when he wants to be.

One night last week, I came downstairs to see what he was doing. It was late and he hadn't come to bed. He was looking through the phone book. I asked him what he was doing and he said he was looking for his father. He looked empty. When he's like that he has this look in his eyes like he can't actually see me.

I'm going to make Billy better. I'm going to love him and look after him. I think I want to marry him, have kids with him. He's not a bad person like some people think. He just gets lost sometimes.

That's all.

CHAPTER 32

By the time I get through the shop door

That fuckarsed wall of car radio clocks blink a seventeen/nineteen/fifteen minutes past nine as though to say late late late. Rob stands at the till, frowning at his watch, tilting his wrist as though trying to catch the light.

Well, good afternoon Mr Billy, how nice of you to give us the pleasure of your company.

I flick him the fingers, quick-foot towards the stairs, sidestepping a tracksuited cripple in a sporty wheelchair, a tin of Turtle Wax sat in his thin-legged lap. Fuck, how I hate Saturdays.

As I get to the bottom of the stairs and turn onto the cycle-floor my arse winks.

Let me get that down for you sir, smarms Norris, eyeing me over the customer's shoulder as he levers a BMX off the rack.

Cue knotted scowl, cue daggers, cue woopdi-fuckingdoo.

In the staff-room I slide my stupid blue-grey overalls on. I look at my name badge. Fuck, how I hate this job. The staff-room stinks of Norris's cheap cigars. My head hurts and my knob itches like fuck. I scratch it through my overalls and my ears crackle. I make a quick coffee and head upstairs to the cycle-floor. Great. Eight hours of fuckarse shoppers.

You are kidding, right? says Norris as I pull the curtain back and walk onto the shop-floor.

What? I say, taking a sip of coffee.

Norris walks towards me like one of those mongy speed-walkers, his elbows nearly level with his shoulders. He looks like a fucking cartoon. The man with the BMX looks up just as Norris grabs the coffee from my hand, some of it slopping onto the floor, my leg, my trainer. Norris makes an angry blowing sound.

IF YOU THINK YOU CAN TURN UP HALF AN HOUR LATE THEN HAVE A BLOODY TEA BREAK YOU MUST BE THICKER THAN YOU LOOK, BILLY-BOY!

God, how I hate this cunt.

I don't feel very well, Mr Norris. The coffee's for my throat. It's sore.

Norris pulls a sarky face, then says Oh deary dear, Saturday flu again is it?

Behind him, the man leans the BMX against the till and starts walking up the stairs.

Norris spins around.

WE CAN PUT IT ON ONE SIDE FOR CHRISTMAS, SIR! ONLY A POUND DEPOSIT!

Norris shakes his head and makes that blowing sound again, points to the floor where little puddles of coffee glint like chocolate piss.

GET THAT MOPPED UP! AND YOU CAN FORGET ABOUT HAVING A DINNER BREAK! YOU OWE ME TIME! AGAIN! CONSIDER THIS A VERBAL! AND GET THAT PROMO STUFF SORTED! TODAY!

He speed-walks up the stairs, elbows pumping, head jut-jutting like a fuckarsed chicken. Cunt.

I look at the pile of posters and price labels by the till, then run downstairs, make another coffee and get the mop.

Thankfully, the first hour is fairly quiet. I put Abbey Road on the tape player and stick some Christmas posters up. CHRISTMAS CRACKERS AT HALFORDS! 10% OFF ALL BIKES! Cue behind-the-hand shifty whisper, *When purchased on a Halfords credit card only four-hundred percent APR ha-ha-ha.*

I hear footsteps on the stairs. I look up and it's Grace. She smiles and holds a carrier bag out to me.

Bought you something, she says.

It's some sarnies wrapped in cellophane. A bag of Wotsits. Two cans of Fanta. A Mars bar. And what looks like a chicken leg wrapped in tinfoil.

I tell her she's just saved my life because I haven't got a dinner break today. She shakes her head.

They can't do that, she says, It's illegal.

I stroke her arse with my hand and tell her what we did last night was probably illegal too. She giggles.

HEY!

Me and Grace look up to see Norris hanging over the stair-rail.

THIS ISN'T A BLOODY SOCIAL CLUB! GET THOSE POSTERS UP! YOU CAN SEE YOUR GIRLFRIEND AFTER WORK!

He turns and jogs back up the stairs.

Grace looks at me and shakes her head. She tickles me under the chin. Take no notice, she whispers.

—

Later on that morning, Rob comes downstairs on his way to the staff-room for a tea break. He grins at me as he makes his way past a fat mum and dad stood around their little fat daughter trying to get her fat leg over a trike saddle.

Rob's alright. We've been out for a beer a couple of times. He's the assistant manager but he's not a jumped-up knobhead.

Got a minute? he says.

We go behind the curtain.

Listen, he says, pushing his glasses back up his nose, I shouldn't be telling you this, but Norris is shafting you.

I ask him what he means.

He tells me he's just been doing the timesheets, and Norris won't pay me for the overtime I worked last month. Rob tells me I can't say anything because he'd get into trouble.

I stare at my feet.

He pats me on the shoulder.

Soz Billy, he says.

I go back onto the shop-floor with a fire in my belly that licks my chest, my throat, my brain. I want to run upstairs and kick Norris's fuckarsed face in. Fat mum and dad ask me if I have any other trikes that'd be right for their daughter. I tell them they don't make them in her size and they fuck off tut-tutting and shaking their fat stupid heads.

I scratch my knob.

Something has to be done.

I eat the chicken leg, put John Lee Hooker on the tape player, and think about the problem.

The phone rings. I push the rest of the Christmas promo shit to the floor and answer it.

It's Grace. She asks if I'm okay. I tell her in a low voice what Rob has just told me.

She says Norris can't do that, that I should see him about it.

I tell her I can't, because I've promised Rob.

She sighs, says not to worry, that we can talk about it later, that she loves me. You too, I say.

For the rest of the day I do everything I can to not

sell a bike. By four o'clock I up my game. I spike bike tyres with a staple gun, enjoying the slow-soft hiss as I lift the staple out with a flat-end screwdriver. I jab scissors into spare inner tubes. I take cogs out of bells so they won't ring. Then I take a pair of pliers and twist the gear changers of the most expensive racers until they won't work.

Then, at five to five, I run downstairs to the staff-room, take Norris's tin of Café Crème cigars from the table, go into the toilet, take my overalls off, pull my foreskin back to a hot stink of thrush, roll the gob-end of each cigar around the underside of my bell-end, holding each cigar under the blow-dryer until all the thrush smears have dried into the leaf, nipping back into the staff-room to grab my coat, putting the Café Crèmes back onto the table for Norris to stick in his fuckarsed gob, leaving the shop without a word, walking home to my girlfriend Grace, who's laid a table of cheap steak and curly fries, a big bottle of Liebfraumilch, wearing a look on her face that says it all, the pots waiting to be washed as we fuck on the floor, looking into each other's eyes as we come, a drag-rush of star, brown eyes deep as mineshafts, forever as I arc back to pump my come deep inside her, that comes and keeps coming, her thrush, my thrush, our thrush, the meat of each tit slipping from my grip as I arc back, until all I have is her nipples between my tightening fingertips, her rising moan as she comes again, again, my skin burning near-tearing as I push deeper into her, all this pain and come, one, the same, and the voices echo from the throats of a thousand brick-built jennels, when all is done we have suffered, and we fall, and we keep falling... enough.

CHAPTER 33

Let your yes be yes and your no be no

It's what the Bible tells us, John the vicar says, his curly eyebrows rising up his mottled forehead, And that's the best piece of advice I can give you, he adds, smiling.

Grace looks across to me from where she's sat, leaning forward slightly to see past the little face-high wings either side of the high-backed chair.

Well, my yes is definitely yes, she says, reaching across the small space between her chair and mine to hold my hand.

John leans over the little three-legged table that seats our three tea cups, the engraved crucifix on the table-top forming a four-way divide between them, a small blue and white plate taking the fourth space, a single digestive biscuit left uneaten, me smiling back at Grace, saying It's a yes from me too, John's hairy hand now patting the back of mine as I hold Grace's, me avoiding a joke on how it looks like one of those stupid things Americans do before a basketball game, the thought of all three of us now lifting our hands skyward and shouting **GO WEDDING!**

Thankfully, vicar John moves his hand and so do I.

There's a moment's pause. A grandfather clock in the corner ticks.

Outside the window, sparrows flicker about on a bird table.

A bus rattles by. The clock ticks.

You know, says John, folding his arms and sliding back into his chair, The main thing is to accept each other's faults, the idea of in sickness and health being a much wider concept than what it would seem.

I look to the digestive biscuit. John continues.

You see, marriage is a support network where you both have this shared concern, which is your love, that somethingness that reaches far beyond the physical, that divine glue that holds you both together.

I stare harder at the digestive biscuit.

Does that make sense? John says, and me and Grace both say Yes. I often crack a couple of little jokes during these things, John says, chuckling the words out, And they're both from the cheeky quill of Lord Byron.

I have no idea what the fuck he's on about but I hear myself say Oh yeh?

Yes, chuckles John. The first is, All tragedies are

finished by a death, but all comedies are ended by a marriage.

John unfolds his arms and grabs his knees as he wheezes forward, his spine visible through his thin chequered shirt as he laughs like a cat coughing up a head-sized hairball. Grace leans forward a little and does that pretend laugh that always ends with a sung Ohhh dear. John looks up at me so I pretend I've just finished laughing.

What the fuck is he on about?

And the other, he says slapping his knees with his palms, Is... marriage from love, is like vinegar from wine. He wheezes forward again, singing Ohhh Byron.

I look at Grace who does the Ohhh dear thing again.

I do that thing where I blow air down my nostrils like this is how I laugh.

Ohhh Byron, sings John again, folding his arms and soft wheezing himself back into his chair. This bloke should have his own show.

But of course, John says suddenly, releasing one of his folded arms to rub his forehead with his palm, Perhaps we shouldn't take him too seriously. After all, the devilish Mr Byron did have an affair with his half-sister.

I laugh for real now, a short pop of a laugh, and say Good man, before I realise what I've just said.

John raises his curly eyebrows a little, then leans

forward and slides the last digestive from the blue and white plate.

He takes a bite, then sputters dryly Oh sorry, did either of you want this? Me and Grace both say no thanks and I watch John chew thoughtfully, before reaching for his cup, knocking back the last of his hour-old tea. He licks his lips. His curly eyebrows dip a little, making a slight V towards his nose.

But seriously, he says in a serious voice, I think good old Shakespeare said it best when he wrote, God, the best maker of all marriages, who combines your hearts in one. And if you also consider what Matthew meant when he said Where your treasure is, there will be your heart, I think we're getting to the crux of the matter... Does that make sense?

John looks to me, then Grace, then me then Grace again, each windscreen-wiper movement of his eyeballs from her to me and back again accompanied by a Hmm? Hmm?

Grace says Yes, yes it does make sense, and reaches for my hand again.

I nod, looking at the space where the digestive biscuit was.

The grandfather clock ticks. It sounds like a zombie in clogs walking slow down a wooden staircase.

John speaks again. Okay. Let's get to the practical stuff. What music do you want at the service?

Grace sits forward. We want to walk down the

aisle to Stairway To Heaven, she says, smiling at me then John.

Hmmm, says John, slow-drumming the arm of his chair with hairy fingers. I don't think I know that one.

—

That night, I dream. And when I wake up I remember watching a film with Nannan about a ventriloquist who went mad, his dummy coming to life and speaking for itself. My dream is like the end of the film where the ventriloquist and the dummy are in the madhouse, all these mad devil-faces pressed against the iron bars of the cell door, laughing as the dummy gets up off his chair and walks towards the ventriloquist who screams. The dummy strangles him. I can't remember in the dream if I was the ventriloquist or the dummy.

I'm in a funny mood all day. I don't say much. I don't feel like it.

CHAPTER 34

Drink a bottle of cheap champagne

Mix with orange juice. A large Glenmorangie. Milk and blackish toast. Half a bottle of Blue Nun. Budweiser. Budweiser. Go to church. Say I do, etc. Budweiser. Murphy's. Jameson. Budweiser. Stella. Stella. Cake. Stella. Jameson. Stella. Vodka and orange. Vodka and black. Speech, speech. Vodka. Vodka. Double Jameson. Double vodka. Double vodka. Get carry-outs of barley wine. Say goodbye to aunties. Uncles. Mothers, etc. Stop car on M18. Vomit. Sleep. Dream of dim-lit hallways and a black door. Wake up between Scarborough and Robin Hood's Bay. Her not saying much. Driving.

CHAPTER 35

You love her because

She feeds your dog ice-cream, hers, bought from the van on the sands, his paw crooked in her hand, like her and the dog are shaking on it, against this white picket fence, this warm breath coming in from the sea, lifting the white line of his fur as he takes the last of it saving her nothing, in the shade of this harbour pub yard, these white walls behind, in front only grey-green sea, and that lifeboat slope, a cobbled slipway down into the sand, the pincers of this cove holding the scroll of this ocean by the throat, and that red-brown sailboat, a wife of one day, and the thin radio of a child's voice, tuning in and out like something half-remembered, or half-forgotten, and now you have done this thing, happiness, a bolt draws back, a heavy door opens, ten minutes late by the high-tide clock.

CHAPTER 36

We look at a dinner table laid carefully for four

On the windowsill behind the table sits half a dozen birthday cards. Through the window we see a sun-blushed garden where Chris and Grace are stood looking at row of peas dripping with pale-green pods. We watch as Chris and Grace take a few steps further down the vegetable patch then stop, Chris pointing to something behind a bean row. He smiles, then him and Grace laugh. We cannot hear what is said between them, nor can we hear the birds that sing all around them, the lowing of the cattle behind the garden wall, or the screech of an impatient sow at an overpopulated trough across the farmyard. What we can hear is the sound of Billy's voice to our left.

BILLY: I didn't mean it, Mum.

Through the archway that leads from this dining room we see a kitchen. With their backs to us, stood at the kitchen sink are Billy and his mother.

We see that Jean is peeling potatoes and shaking her head in silent dismay. She puts a glistening skinless potato onto the breadboard to the right of her, takes an unpeeled wet potato from out of the sink, and then begins to scrape the skin away, stroke by stroke. Billy is looking out of the window. He turns to face his mother.

BILLY: C'mon, Mum. Don't spoil your birthday. I'm sorry. I didn't mean it.

A pause. The sound of scraping.

JEAN (*still peeling the potato*): Have you any idea how awful I felt? In front of my whole family? Not to mention Grace's family? At my own son's wedding being told that I'd spoilt everything?

Jean places the peeled potato onto the breadboard, sniffs, then takes another potato from the sink. Billy leans an elbow on the worktop, and turns to face his mother.

BILLY (*slightly exasperated*): But Mum! I was drunk! I only said it because you kept turning the music down.

JEAN (*raising her voice*): Once! Aunty Glenda said it was hurting her ears! It didn't need to be that...

BILLY (*cutting in*): Bollocks to Aunty Glenda! She's a miserable old cow any...

JEAN (*cutting in*): Listen! It's my birthday! And I'm not having it ruined by my own son swearing at me!

Jean peels the potato in quick short strokes. Billy, with both elbows on the worktop, hands holding his head, looks out the window. He sighs. Pause. The sound of scraping.

BILLY (*softly*): Look, I'm sorry. C'mon. Please. Let's not fight.

He puts his hands to the worktop and looks again to his mother. Jean takes another potato from the sink, starts peeling then starts to cry a little. Billy puts his hand on her shoulder.

JEAN (*still peeling the potato*): You scare me Billy. It scares me to death that you're going to end up like my dad.

Billy takes his hand from his mother's shoulder and sighs.

BILLY: I wish you wouldn't. I'm not like him. At all. I wish you'd stop saying that.

He looks out the window again. Jean puts the peeled potato on the breadboard, takes another unskinned potato from the sink. She begins peeling it.

JEAN: There was something on Radio Four last week. It said it can be passed on. It said…

BILLY (*cutting in*): Rubbish! I'm nothing like him. He was an alky, Mum, and me? I like a beer. Big difference.

Jean puts the peeler and the potato down. She wipes her hands on a tea towel then turns to her son. We now see them both in dark profile against the window.

JEAN (*quietly*): You have his mouth.

The kitchen door opens and in walks Grace and Chris. Grace is carrying a yellow bucket crammed with runner beans, and a smile that lights the room.

GRACE: Billy! I want a veg garden!

CHAPTER 37

To do

Saturday.
Move furniture out of front room. Take old carpet up. Sand skirting boards, window and doors. Have ham sandwiches for dinner. Nip into town. Choose magnolia because it's cheap and looks okay. Get a roller and brushes. Go home with a sense of purpose. Wipe all surfaces down. Talk about tomorrow. Eat chips and curry sauce from Chinky across the road. Drink a bottle of Blue Nun. Talk more about tomorrow.

Sunday.
Put first coat on walls. Put first coat on skirting boards, window and doors. Have spread cheese on crumpets for dinner. Make love on bare floorboards. Put second coat on walls. Put second coat on skirting boards, window and doors. Stand back and say Looks okay, doesn't it. Talk about tomorrow. Feel happy and accomplished.

Monday.

Move stepladders, paint pots etc, out of front room. Measure floor. Nip into town. Buy cheap brown carpet. Laugh at effort of loading carpet into car. Tie boot down with Billy's belt. Have cheese sandwiches for dinner. Lay carpet. Feel happy. Smells nice, doesn't it. Make love on carpet. Laugh whilst wiping little wet patch up with tea-towel. Bring furniture back in. Hang curtains. Feel happy and accomplished. Drink four cans of Stella. Talk about being happy and staying happy. Go to bed and sleep with spines touching all night.

Tuesday.

Open envelope addressed to Billy. Shout **GET IN!** Talk about new job at builder's merchant as a new start towards everything being right and good. Talk about being happy and staying happy. Talk about no more fuck-ups. Sit in newly painted front room that smells of carpet. Drink coffee with morning sunlight stretched in golden oblong across both your bare feet.

Sunlight

2 a.m. Upturned pyramid glints in tilted half-Bell's.

You fuck off because you fuckin want to

And why the fuck shouldn't you? One thing's for sure, if you stay you fuckin suffocate, suffocate in fucking normality, and normality is her fuckin chipping away at you night and fuckin day and all that other **FUCKING SHITE** so pocket that bottle fill your bag with that cider that lager them barleys grab your fucking bank-card fags cash stick your guitar on your back and get the **FUCKIN FUCK OUT** and yeh the birds are singing and yeh the sun is up and yeh this is the fucking start of it so **C'MON** get down that **FUCKIN** road.

(A lorry. Give it some thumb and what do you know.)

Yeh mate, yeh, Sheff's good. Goin fuckin walkabout, know what I mean? When you've had a fuckinough you've had a fuckinough, yeh?

And fair enough he looks at you like you're a fuckin headcase but what the fuck, you don't give a flyin fuck what he thinks and you tell him, tell him what the **FUCK** were I thinking about? Gettin fuckin married for fuck's sake! Fuckin hell! What a **CUNT!** Might as well just nail my fuckin arse to a wall, yeh?

And yeh he looks sideways at you half-iffy/half-like-he-knows-what-the-fuck-you're-talking-about growling his gear-stick telling you he's been married twenty-three years less for murder blah blah blah but he's still fucking married inhe but you're gonna humour the sad cunt cos he's taking you to Sheff for the start of it all and all is freedom from fuckin **FUCKERS** who want to tie you to a fucking chair do this do that do the fuckin other, **FUCKING FUCK OFF!**

Wanna drinka this? Nah, course you don't, driving yeh? What? Ahhh right, yeh I'll get the fuckin fuck out, fucking stupid old twat, yeh go on **FUCK OFF** stupid **FUCKER!**

(Slam the fucking door. **BANG!**)

CUNT!

Ahhh so fuckin what go lie back on this grass drink this fucking wine not worried not worried at all cos this is the fuckin start of it get that fuckin guitar out and fucking **FUCK YOU** nosey bitch seen enough or **WHAT? FUCK OFF TO YOUR SAD FUCKING FUCKING** wherever it is you're fucking goin to in your sad fucking little car **WELLLLLL JIMMY PLAYED HARMONICA IN THE PUB WHERE I WAS BORN...**

Fucking **WHAT? YEH? SEEN ENOUGH? FUCK**

THE FUCK OFF! WELLLLLL, JIMMY PLAYED...
YEH GO ON, FUCKIN FUCK YOURSELF! ...
PLAYED HARMONICA IN THE PUB WHERE I
WAS BORN ... PLAYED IT FROM...

Well well well, what do you fucking know.
Here come the fucking busies. Hello you fucking
wankers, yeh yeh slow down take a good fucking
look you fucking titty-headed fuckbags, **LOOK!
THIS IS WHAT THE FREE FUCKIN PEOPLE OF
THE FREE FUCKIN STATE OF FUCKIN BILLY
DO!**

Yeh, that's it, get out of your fucking fucking...
HEY! WHAT'S DIFFERENCE BETWEEN A
COP-CAR AND A FUCKIN HEDGEHOG,
EH? HEDGEHOG HAS PRICKS ON FUCKIN
OUTSIDE YEH?

What the fuck's it got to do with you? So I'm
just drinking this nice fucking bottle of fucking
Leibfraufuckingmilch on a fucking Friday morning
in the fucking sun, so what's the fuckin problem,
eh? So what if it is a fucking Thursday, excuse me
Mr fucking Ploddyplodplod.

HEY! WATCH THE FUCKING GUITAR
CUNTIE! HEY! NO NEED NO FUCKING NEED!
C'MON THEN YER FUCKING PIG FUCKERS
LET'S FUCKIN HAVE IT THEN, YEH HOW DO
YER FUCKIN LIKE THAT YER FUCKIN...

—

In this cell you are small. They've taken your belt and your shoelaces. You break a little. You put your hands over your face so they don't see. They don't listen when you shout for water, Please. Your tongue is so dry it feels too big for your mouth. You don't sleep. Someone behind the door shouts **BASTARDS BASTARDS**. You think you can see an old man crouched and watching you in that dark corner over there. You try and make spit to drink but you can't. In the morning they give you half a plastic cup of warm water. Across your tongue they drag a cotton bud which they drop into a plastic bag with your name on it. They take your fingerprints, your photograph, and then when you get home, she tells you she's pregnant.

CHAPTER 40

Scarlett, look!

Those are your stars, your moon. Can you see? See how big the universe is? And this earth is just a big ball spinning through the everything, never stopping, always turning, for ever and ever, and I'm your daddy, Scarlett, and I'll love you for all time, with everything I have, and you'll have nothing to be scared of, ever, because I'll protect you, and care for you, and love you, and you'll grow ever beautiful like those stars, that moon, everything, my Scarlett, my sweet baby girl, and this everything starts with you, and I'll leave all that shit behind, like this is the start of everything, all over again, all those bad stupid fuck-ups, never ever again, because now I have you, and you have me, and I won't let you down, ever, and I promise on the stars, the moon, the everything, because I love you Scarlett, your daddy loves you.

CHAPTER 41

And then they are looking at

*An empty red-yellow Punch and Judy booth.
Scarlett is eating an ice-cream, kicking her heels
back against the pushchair in anticipation of the
show, mint choc-chip dripping off her chin onto
her denim dungarees, her father now laughing as
he leans over on the grass to wipe his daughter's
chin with a tissue, his daughter pulling her face
away in this game they play, C'mere rascally rascal,
and the orange eye of the sun hangs succulent
and full, blessing the lush deep greens of the park
and the gathered mums that sit islanded on tartan
blankets, amid Tupperware and pushchairs and
cool-boxes, the static crackle of their excited
offspring fizzing the humid noon like a midge
cloud in a wooded-lane hollow, and Scarlett now
holding out her ice-cream for her father to taste
in this other game they play, and now the devilish
cackle as she pushes the ice-cream against her
father's closed mouth, smearing mint choc-chip
across his gurning stubbled face,* **MMMMM,** *now*

closer, **MMMMM,** *now,* **GIZZAKISS!** *And now the squealing daughter tries to wriggle away from the mint choc-chip monster, her escape foiled by the pushchair straps, the monster's kiss now smearing green across the pale cheek of the child,* **STOP IT DADDY! STOP!** *And now the two small hands flat-palmed turn the father-monster's face towards the red-yellow stage,* **LOOK DADDY! LOOK!** *as the red-cheeked red-nosed hunchback puppet appears and the show begins...*

PUNCH: Hello boys and girls!

CHILDREN/SCARLETT: HELLO!

PUNCH: Have you seen Judy?

CHILDREN/SCARLETT: NO!

PUNCH: I said, HAVE YOU SEEN JUDY?

CHILDREN/SCARLETT: NO!

PUNCH: Can you help me find her?

CHILDREN/SCARLETT: YES!

PUNCH: JUUUUUDY! JUUUUUDY!

CHILDREN/SCARLETT: JUUUUUDY! JUUUUUDY!

JUDY (*enters stage left*): What is it? Who's shouting me?

CHILDREN/SCARLETT (*pointing*): THERE!

176

THERE!

PUNCH (*looking left and right*): Where?

CHILDREN/SCARLETT: BEHIND YOU!

PUNCH: Where?

CHILDREN/SCARLETT (*pointing*): THERE! THERE!

Punch moves from one end of the stage to the other. Judy moves in opposites to him until they bump into each other centre stage and fall over.

(*Laughter*)

JUDY (*scolding*): What are you doing, silly Mr Punch?

PUNCH: Gizzakiss!

JUDY (*turning away*): No. I'm not in the mood.

(*Laughter*)

PUNCH (*firmly*): I said, Giz. A. KISS!

Punch grapples with Judy, giving her a forceful kiss.

(*Laughter*)

PUNCH: That's the way to do it!

JUDY (*flustered*): No it is not! That wasn't romantic at all, Mr Punch!

PUNCH: Let's dance!

JUDY (*turning away*): No. I'm not in the mood.

PUNCH (*firmly*): I said, let's **DANCE!**

Punch grapples with Judy in some kind of violent dance. Judy pushes him off.

(*Laughter*)

Punch slaps Judy across the face.

PUNCH (*dismayed*): You're a rubbish dancer.

JUDY (*flustered*): That wasn't very kind, Mr Punch!

Punch slaps her again.

(*Laughter*)

PUNCH (*firmly*): Go and make me my dinner.

JUDY (*meekly*): You'd better look after the baby then, Mr Punch.

Judy disappears, then returns with the baby, which she hands to Punch.

PUNCH (*confused*): What is it?

JUDY: It's the baby, Mr Punch. Look after her while I make your dinner.

Judy exits. Punch looks to the audience and shakes his head.

PUNCH (*to audience*): What is it?

CHILDREN/SCARLETT: IT'S A BABY!

PUNCH (*confused*): A what?

CHILDREN/SCARLETT (*louder*): A BABY!

Punch shakes his head. The baby starts crying. Punch drops it in surprise.

(*Laughter*)

PUNCH (*disgusted*): What a horrible thing!

(*Laughter*)

Punch picks up the crying baby. He shakes it violently.

PUNCH: Shut up!

(*Laughter*)

The baby cries louder.

PUNCH: I said **SHUT UP!**

(*Laughter*)

Punch shakes the baby even harder. The baby cries louder. Punch hits the baby's head against the side of the stage.

(*Laughter*)

The baby starts screaming. Punch hits the baby's head even more violently against the stage, then throws it out of the window, backstage.

(*Laughter*)

PUNCH (*joyfully*): That's the way to do it!

(*Laughter*)

Judy enters stage right. She is carrying a plate of food.

JUDY (*confused*): Where's the baby?

(*Laughter*)

Punch shakes his head. Judy turns to the audience.

JUDY (*anxious*): Has anyone seen the baby?

CHILDREN/SCARLETT: THE WINDOW!

JUDY (*starting to panic*): Where?

CHILDREN/SCARLETT: THE WINDOW!

Judy looks out the window.

JUDY (*horrified*): Oh my goodness! You threw the baby out the window!

(*Laughter*)

Judy hits Punch with the plate.

(*Laughter*)

JUDY (*distraught*): You wicked Mr Punch! How could you do such a thing!

(*Laughter*)

Punch exits stage left. Returns with a big stick. He beats Judy to death.

(*Laughter*)

PUNCH (*joyfully*): That's the way to do it!

(*Laughter*)

The policeman enters stage right carrying the baby. He glances at Judy who is laid motionless on the stage.

POLICEMAN (*sternly*): Mr Punch! Did you throw a baby out of your window?

PUNCH (*quietly*): No.

POLICEMAN: Are you sure?

PUNCH (*suppressing a giggle*): Yes.

POLICEMAN (*to audience*): Did any of you see Mr Punch throw a baby out of the window?

CHILDREN/SCARLETT: YES!

PUNCH: Oh no I didn't.

CHILDREN/SCARLETT: OH YES YOU DID!

PUNCH: Oh no I didn't.

CHILDREN/SCARLETT: OH YES YOU DID!

POLICEMAN (*firmly*): Mr Punch! I'm arresting you for throwing a baby out of a window! And (*glancing at Judy*) for beating your wife to death with a stick!

PUNCH: Oh no I didn't.

CHILDREN/SCARLETT: OH YES YOU DID!

POLICEMAN (*puts baby on stage*): Right, Mr Punch! You're coming with me!

PUNCH: Oh no I'm not!

Punch beats the policeman to death with his stick.

(*Laughter*)

The baby starts to cry again.

PUNCH (*holding his ears*): Oh no not again!

(*Laughter*)

Punch goes to hit baby with his stick. Enter Toby the dog, stage left. Toby starts barking at punch.

PUNCH (*to dog*): Shut up!

Punch goes to hit baby with stick. Toby tries to bite Punch.

PUNCH (*angrily*): Get off me you horrible hound!

Punch kicks the dog in the face.

(*Laughter*)

Punch beats Toby the dog and the baby to death with his stick.

(*Laughter*)

Punch drops his stick then looks around at the bodies scattered about on the stage.

PUNCH: Oh dear! What a mess!

Exit Punch. Returns pushing a sausage machine.

PUNCH (*to audience*): Does anyone fancy a bit of sausage?

CHILDREN/SCARLETT: YES!

Punch feeds the dead bodies one by one into the sausage machine. A long string of sausages come out the other end as he does.

(*Laughter*)

Punch surveys the empty stage.

PUNCH (*joyfully*): That's the way to do it! Now, let's have a lovely bit of sausage for dinner!

(*Laughter and groans*)

Unseen by Punch, enter the crocodile stage right.

CHILDREN/SCARLETT: BEHIND YOU!

PUNCH (*to audience*): What?

CHILDREN/SCARLETT: BEHIND YOU!

Punch turns around just as the crocodile gobbles the sausages up.

(*Laughter*)

PUNCH (*horrified*): My dinner!

(*Laughter*)

Punch fights with the crocodile, nearly getting eaten in the process.

(*Laughter and shrieks*)

Punch retrieves his stick. He beats the crocodile to death.

PUNCH: Take that you walking handbag!

(*Laughter*)

Punch then feeds the crocodile to the sausage machine. More sausages come out the other end.

(*Laughter*)

PUNCH: Now that's what I call recycling!

(*Laughter from adults*)

Enter The Devil, stage left.

PUNCH: Who the hell are you?

(*Laughter from adults*)

THE DEVIL: Exactly!

(*Laughter from adults*)

PUNCH: What?

THE DEVIL: I am The Devil! And I've come for your soul!

PUNCH: Well, you can't have it. I'm using it.

(*Laughter from adults*)

THE DEVIL: You have no choice, Mr Punch! According to my records, you have made sausage-meat out of your wife, your baby, your dog, a crocodile and a policeman! In short, Mr Punch, you have been a very, very, bad man!

PUNCH (*dismissively*): Oh no I haven't.

THE DEVIL: Oh yes you … **AAAARGH!** Enough of your silly games! I am The Devil! And I have come for what is mine! (*turns to the audience*) Has Mr Punch been very very bad, boys and girls?

CHILDREN: YES!

SCARLETT: NO!

The Devil prods Punch with his fork. Punch yelps, then beats The Devil with his stick, who runs off.

THE DEVIL (*crying*): I want my Mummy!

(*Laughter*)

PUNCH (*dancing to exit stage left*): That's the way to do it! Bye bye, boys and girls! Bye, bye! Bye, bye!

(*Applause*)

CHAPTER 42

Jack is my dad's dog

But Jack sits in the backseat with me. Then Mum pulls up, stops our car by the campsite toilet, asks me again if I need to go and I say I don't because I don't. So Mum gets out, says Just be a minute you two, but that doesn't count right because that leaves three of us left: me, Dad, and Jack, who puts his paws on the back of Dad's seat, sticks his nose out the half-open window, starts snorting and snuffling, his slavver dripping down the glass, and it makes me laugh, but Dad just rubs his face with his hands, makes a sound like a balloon going down, tells Jack to **SIT!** and that he's **NOT IN THE MOOD THIS MORNING!** and **QUIET!** And then Dad spins round in his seat, shouts **JACK!** who's still snotting the window, now barking at that poodle and that fat lady in pink. **GET DOWN!** says Dad, **GET EFFING DOWN!** and he grabs Jack by the throat and pushes, and I don't like it, and Jack don't like it, and he growls and snaps angry at Dad's arm, and Dad shouts that F word again, slaps Jack in the face, and Jack falls back onto his belly, makes that whiney sound his eye blinks twitchy, and he shivers like he's cold, but he's not cold cos we're on holiday, and Dad lights a fag, and Mum gets in the car, and when we get there I look at the sea.

CHAPTER 43

Nil-nil last-minute direct free-kick

And up you step, **BANG!** Toe-poke the fucker Ronald fucking Koeman roof of the fucking net straight past that gobshite cunt of a keeper, **GET FUCKIN IN!** And yeh they get mards on and yeh there's argyfuckinbargy net still billowing lads yelling in your face grabbing your head **YES BILLY-BOY!** Stevie yelling **KEEP IT TIGHT KEEP IT FUCKIN TIGHT!** as you run back into position but it don't matter anyway ref blowing up two seconds after they kick off, **GET FUCKING IN! COME ON YOU CROOKED SPIREITES!**

And back in the bar, it's big fuckarsed grins all round, first pint necked in one Phil spilling half his down his shirt like a fuckin girl, Pongo slapping Phil on the back as he jips up lager down his trackies, Stevie already getting the next ones in and Eyup, notice them fuckers ant come in for one? Laughs all round, Tubby saying Nah not for me gottabeup in morning, and you grabbing his sack saying Don't be a **FUCKING PUFF GET IT DOWN YER YOU**

BIG GIRL'S FRONT-BUM, now feeling the phone vibrate in your front pocket.

Billy. Have started. Mum taking me to hospital. Get there quick. :) XXX

And of course the lads all cheer and get you a couple in before you get gone, taxi twenty-two fuckin quid but what the fuck you're going to be a dad again, telling the taxi gadge all about the last-minute winner as you neck a barley, smoke a fag or two.

The nurse at reception is as fit as fuck. She puts her pencil down by her clipboard, says a tight-lipped Can I help you?

You say you have a pain, Here, as you open your tracky-top, flat-palming the crooked spire badge on your footy shirt. I think it's a broken heart, you say. Grin.

She just stares at you, so you hold your hands up in surrender, tell her your wife's having a baby. She stares at you for a second longer, sighs, looks down to her clipboard and picks her pencil up.

Name? she says.

Billy, you say. Grin.

The nurse tuts. No. Your wife's name. Her full name, she says. Miserable cow.

Hospitals make you feel sick. The corridor is hot and there's no air. The floor squeaks as you walk through bad smells. Somewhere a woman is making a low groaning sound. You look at the nurse as she walks at your side and you start to say something funny about the noise, but you don't finish it. The nurse stops at a door, knocks, then turns the handle. She turns and walks off leaving you looking through the open door at Grace who is sat-up in bed, right hand on her swollen belly, a big white clip on her forefinger that has a cable attached to it, the cable connected to a machine on wheels. She half smiles at you.

Behind her, sat in a high-backed chair, is her fat mother, Joy, who looks at you like you just took a shit in her handbag, her flabby jowls turning little half-circles as she pulls another grape from the half-eaten bunch stood on the little cupboard by the bed.

Well, look who it isn't, says Joy all sarky, spitting a grape seed from her dog-bum gob into a scrunched-up tissue.

And yes you spike back, and yes she takes another pop, and yes your wife tells you both to pack it in, and yes you say that you will if she does and Anyway what the fuck is SHE doing here, and yes the fat cow sticks another grape in her fat gob and sputters Well somebody had to, and yes your wife will start crying saying For God's sake I'm having a baby, please stop it, and yes you're about to say you will if SHE does when the door opens to that frosty-titted nurse telling you to **KEEP IT DOWN THIS IS A MATERNITY WARD NOT A MINER'S BLOODY WELFARE,** and yes your fat cow mother-

in-law pulls a smuggy-fuck grin as the door closes
with a clunk patting your wife's hand saying It's
alright darlin' it's alright he's just had a few again,
and yes you look to your wife who gives you the
daggers then starts puffing and blowing saying Here
comes another one, and yes you reach over to hold
her hand as her mother makes a grab for the other,
and yes your wife makes a funny groaning noise and
closes her eyes then opens them with a snap pushing
your hand away still holding on to her fat mother's
paw, who's glaring spite at you as your wife calls you
A SELFISH BLOODY BASTARD through clenched
teeth, and yes that's about all you can take so you
fuck off slamming the door behind you walking
quick-foot down the corridor, giving the frosty-
titted nurse a **CATCHYALATERBAYYYBEEE** as
you exit stage left, light a fag, find a pub just down
the road, and yes you might have a couple.

Easy.

Stroll back down the squeaky-floored corridor
humming Rainy Night In Soho, not giving a fuck
and why should you? You feel good. You feel the
power of comfort knowing as you do that this
baby is yours, not that spiteful bitch-eyed sow of a
mother-in-law's.

And sure Grace is pissed off at you but so what?
It'll not be the last time. What does today matter
when tomorrow comes around? The past is past is
past and fuck all else matters.

You open the door. The room is dim, quiet. No Grace, no fat bitch of a mother-in-law. Quiet. Where the fuck are they?

You think about turning back, back up the corridor to find frosty-tits when you realise something is swaddled amongst the blue sheets at the bottom of the bed. You step closer. The baby has a white woolly hat on its head, and is dressed in a pink something that you can't quite register because you can't take your eyes from the face, a face with thin little purple lips, a face with blue-root veins running a thousand tiny rivers through thin onion skin, the eyes that have sunk below blue-black eyelids and nothing moves.

Quiet.

You feel a jag in your gut as you look to the bare arms resting on the little chest, at the thousand little blue rivers under red-blotched grey, the tiny red-blue fingers with their tiny purple nails.

Closer, you move your hand towards the baby, this baby that sleeps breathlessly and is so cold to the touch, and the blue-black sunken eyelids are still, and the thousand tiny blue rivers are still, and you take a tiny cold hand in yours as the floor moves and you vomit, and you keep vomiting, down on your knees by the bed, the brown-yellow sick splattering the shiny grey floor as a thin voice behind you says What are you doing?

You turn to see a woman who is not your wife

or your mother-in-law or a nurse, and the woman stares at you with red dead eyes and the saddest face you have ever seen as you climb out of your puddle of spew, **WHAT** are you **DOING?**

And you push past her out of the door, Sorry, you say, Sorry, all the time knowing that this is not your baby, that your baby isn't dead like this baby, that your baby isn't.

CHAPTER 44

We take turns to stand up in Miss Walker's class

And we read out what we've written. Miss Walker asked us to write the title first which is called What I Did at Easter. We go in alphabetical order so I go after Zoe Parker even though my name's Scarlett. This is because it goes on last names not first. I wrote about going to horse racing with Mum and Dad and Joe, and everyone laughed when I said the bit about Joe being sick in the car, and that baby sick smells like horrible yoghurt that smells for as long as dog poo does. Miss laughed as well when I said the bit when Dad asked a jockey for a tip and the jockey told him his horse Red Hand, so Dad put twenty pounds on it but it was rubbish and came last.

The jockeys were funny too, they're only a bit bigger than me but it's not funny when they smack their horses with whips. Mum said they don't really smack them, it just looks like they do, but to me it looks like they really do do.

Natasha Godly said that when horses break their legs the jockeys kill them.

I don't like Natasha Godly, she tells fibs behind your back and says her mum and dad don't like my dad.

When I read out the best bit everyone cheered. It's the bit about Merry-Go-Round which is the horse I picked which won at ten to one which meant I got eleven pounds back. Its colours were green and red which are my favourite colours, and when Dad got back with the money I waved it in the air but didn't throw it like I was in a film or something because it might have blown away.

I didn't write about the bit where Joe is crying so Mum has to take him back to the car, and I want to buy a double 99 ice cream with my winnings but because Dad needs to pick his next horse I can't, so I kick his beer over like a little river down the steps and Dad shouts **IDIOT!** smacks my bottom so my feet jump up.

CHAPTER 45

The Tuesday night gallon of ale fact and fable quiz

Question one. What happened to the fly when he flew into the honey jar?

Question two. Who just stumbled into the bar and is being served Guinness with a treble Jameson chaser and can't quite read the exchange of looks between the barmaid and at least three tables of regulars?

Question three. Why is the wolf confused by the ideology of who is allowed to eat the lamb?

Question four. What the fuck are you looking at?

Question five. When the donkey ingested nothing but dew because he thought it would make him sing like a grasshopper, did he a) sing a beautiful song that made the buttercups cry, or b) die a slow and painful death with the whole meadow laughing at him?

Question six. Brian and Des of the local pub-quiz team The Pit Props deem the puff at the bar to be unable to handle his ale. Is this view of masculine measure endemic to working-class patriarchal hegemony, or is it just in here?

Question seven. What happened to the hungry mouse when he slipped through a small hole in the grain basket to eat his fill?

Question eight. Don't you think you've had enough?

Question nine. When the crazy old maid kept her nose pressed to the empty wine bottle exclaiming Sweet creature! Was she extolling the delicious scent left by the wine, or did she have a certain mutation of the DRD2 gene? Or a lack of the HTR1B gene? Or a defective PER2 gene? Or an inherent low-level of the brain-emitted chemical Neuropeptide Y?

Question ten. Can you just leave, please?

Tie breaker. Who saw beauty in a cloud slicing the moon, then poked a number into his phone from the half-lit doorway, gleaned from the pub before this, a half-doubt of acting now fired by another slammed door, a Sure I'll sort yer, the night now moving like a slow riverboat to a branch-draped midnight bend, and then the other number poked, the Yeh ten minutes mate, the fag smoked under an orange arc of streetlamp, watching the headlights hum up the hill like wild-eyed dogs, not this one, not this one, then the tapering engine below a boxed bump bump bump, a window rolled down to the treble of music exotic, Taxi for a Mr Billy?

Yeh.

CHAPTER 46

Because

The house loomed black beyond the last lamppost.

Because it stood three floors high on its own bricked-off hillock.

Because the taxi bhangra fades when someone says my name.

Because he steps out from the shadow of a brick-built bus stop wearing studs that glint on his face.

Because he tells me to come inside he'll sort me.

Because inside is a long dim hallway, doors with numbers and a flight of orange-lit stairs.

Because his flat has two other blokes on a dirty sofa.

Because the fat one is familiar and the sleeping one not.

Because the man I rang from the pub says How much? I say An ounce.

Because the fat bloke smirks I say What? he says Nothing.

Because the man goes into a dirty kitchen, puts half a soap bar into a dirty microwave, ping.

Because he says Fifty, gives me a warm brown block that fits in my palm, then my pocket.

Because he grins and glints says Want to put some in a mix?

Because I take my gear out, give it back to him with the money.

Because he passes it to smirking fatso.

Because fatso unwraps it, flicks a lighter to it, flame licking a corner.

Because I want to watch how much he crumbs off but can't.

Because the bloke I rang from the pub waves a freezer-bag half-full of pills in my face says **FIVE HUNDRED OF THE FUCKERS!**

Because he grins and glints says Want one?

Because I say Yeh.

Because I've not done them before I say I have.

Because I swallow it, take another.

Because fatso passes a bottomless plastic bottle curling with white smoke like spunk in a bath.

Because I nearly cough my ring up.

Because I tell them to put some different music on.

Because This is SHIT.

Because fatso laughs I say What? he says Nothing.

Because I need water.

Because I think I'm going to chuck up.

Because back from the bathroom my face is drip-wet with sweat.

Because the bloke I rang from the pub says Ten more for the pills.

Because I've only got five he says Slate.

Because I have to go now.

Because the door won't open.

Because when it does I fall through it.

Because the man picks me up says That way don't forget.

Because there are too many hallways and too many doors.

Because I fall down the last half of the stairs.

Because outside I find the road.

Because outside I find the moon.

Because outside I find home somehow, remembering trees and bus stops and pubs, that I didn't get my gear back, that fatso's kids go to school with my kids, that next-door's koi-carp pond brings a river to my sleep, that eddies slow hush through a fern-filled gully, first light breaks white, through pine to a sway of open hand.

CHAPTER 47

You are six

Today is your birthday. You wear a badge on your blue school sweatshirt that says so. You look at it as you stand by the school gates waiting for your mum to fetch you.

I

am

6.

Your badge was on a birthday card that you opened this morning. You woke up earlier than usual because it was your birthday. It was still dark outside. Your mum and your dad were still asleep when you went into their room. Your tummy had a tickle in it. Their bedroom smelt funny, like pears or old apples.

You put your hand on your mum's shoulder and said, Mum.

She woke up quickly, sucking her breath in fast, her eyes looking at you funny like she couldn't see.

You told her it was your birthday and she smiled.

You and your mum and your sister Scarlett waited

downstairs for your dad. Mum said your dad was tired. Your presents and cards were in a pile on the table like a little pyramid. You did about pyramids at school. They were built in Egypt for the pharaohs to be buried in. You liked that they were buried with their treasure. Your teacher Miss Honeyman said it was because the pharaohs believed they could have their treasure in the life after death. She also said that sometimes the pharaoh's slaves were buried alive in the pyramids with the dead pharaoh. Everyone in your class went URRR and Jodie Turner said That's horrible. You said that you thought Jodie was right. Miss Honeyman gave you a silver star for good debating. Your teacher said that good debating is when you talk about things and you see someone else's point of view.

By the time your dad came downstairs you'd eaten all your Cocopops and you were trying to guess what was in your presents. He put his hand on your hair, rubbed your head so the bristles crackled and he said Happy birthday Joe. Then he sat down and breathed out long. You smelt that smell of pears or old apples again.

A car horn pips and you look up from your badge. It's your grandma in her little yellow car and not your mum. When you get in the car your grandma gives you a wet kiss and says Happy birthday Jojo. She smells like the sweet shop in the Market Hall. She says your mum is still making your birthday tea so she came to fetch you instead. Then she says something about your hair but you don't say anything.

Your grandma says she's taking you to Toys'R'Us so you can choose a present. She says it's better this way because then she can see you get your present. She tells you that's why she only sent you a birthday card and a Pokémon deck to open this morning. You get that tickle in your tummy again and tell her Okay. She says that when your mum was six, her and your granddad bought your mum a little bike with a basket on the front. Then your grandma goes quiet and starts to cry a little. You know she's crying because she says in a croaky voice Let's have some music, then she turns the radio on.

You look out the window at the houses going by.

Red door blue door brown door red door white door.

Your grandma does that croaky voice thing every time she talks about your granddad. He died a few years ago, and your grandma often says If only he were here to see you. Sometimes though, she says that your granddad watches over you and Scarlett and your mum from Heaven.

Once you asked her if he was watching Dad too, and your grandma said Ohhh yes.

At Toys'R'Us your grandma says you can spend twenty pounds. You choose a skateboard with Pikachu on the bottom of it. That leaves you with five pounds left so you choose another deck of Pokémon cards. You choose a deck that has a shiny Charizard in it. You like Charizard because he's a bit naughty and doesn't always do what his trainer Ash tells him to do.

When your dad is happy and having fun with you he says that Pokémon is a form of slavery. He says this is because the Pokémon trainers keep their Pokémon trapped inside the Pokéballs until they need them to fight a battle. You tell him it's not slavery because the Pokémon want to do it and anyway the trainers are kind to their Pokémon. Dad says Pants when you tell him this. It makes you laugh when Dad says Pants.

On the way home your grandma says So who cut your hair then? The council?

You look at your shiny Charizard. When you wobble it, it changes colour.

You tell your grandma that your dad cut your hair.

She says Good God did he have to cut it so short? and then she rubs your hair with her hand.

Charizard goes red then orange, red then orange.

It's a blinkin skinhead, your grandma says.

Your dad said he was sick of the nits and sick of using the nit-comb on you. You didn't like having nits. They made your head itchy and you didn't like insects living in your hair. Your mum washed your hair in special shampoos but they didn't work. They smelt horrible. Your dad said last week that he'd had enough. Your sister Scarlett was crying because she said her head was itchy too. She said she'd die if she had nits. You didn't want your hair shaved off but your dad told you to stop being a girl, his hand on the back of your neck as you sat on a stool in the kitchen, your hair falling onto the lino in little brown clumps, the shaver buzzing against your head making everything wobble, *bzzzz bzzzz bzzzz*.

Today you are six.

Mum and Dad and Scarlett and Grandma and Nanna and Granddad sing happy birthday to you. You blow your candles out and make a wish. You can't tell anyone what it is because if you do it won't come true.

After tea, Grandma and Nanna and Granddad go home and Dad plays Pokémon with you. Then you and Mum and Dad and Scarlett watch Pokémon The Movie.

Scarlett likes water Pokémon like Ash's friend Misty does. Mum likes Pikachu because she says he's cute. Dad likes Meowth. He says it's because Meowth has attitude.

Dad tells you to drink from his beer because it's your birthday. You tell him you don't like it. Mum tells Dad not to give you beer. Dad calls her a mard-arse.

When you go to bed you think about how Mewtwo

felt sad in the film and then he gets all angry. You felt sad with him, and it made you feel a bit like crying. Mewtwo said he was sad because he was made as a grown-up by scientists so he couldn't remember things from when he was little because he was never little. This made him want to fight and beat all the other trainers with his army of Pokémon clones that he made just like he was made. Mewtwo said at the end of the film that he was just looking for meaning, and he didn't want to be told what to do by the scientists that made him. You asked your dad what Mewtwo meant by meaning, and your dad said it meant something worth living for. Then he trumped really loud and squeezed his beer-can flat.

Dad is funny sometimes. You listen to his voice coming from downstairs. He's singing again. The light from the landing means you can still see some things in your room. Your school clothes are hung on the back of your door and it looks like another you without your head or your feet. Your birthday badge glitters a little.

You are six.

Your badge says so.

CHAPTER 48

0898 696969

Hello! And welcome to Cum Calls! Stay on the line to talk to one of our hot girls who are just aching to meet you. Press one for Michelle, who loves to talk dirty while she plays with her toys. Press two for Shantelle, who would love to share her sexy secret fantasies with you. Or why not press three for Tracey, who just adores threesomes and is dying to...

Hello? Yes, this is Tracey. Well, hello Billy, are you feeling horny tonight? Good. Well, I'm 22, slim, blue eyes, auburn hair and...Yes, I do like threesomes as it happens, do you? Good, because just last night I was being fucked from behind while I licked my girlfriend's pussy. Shall I tell you all about it? Oh good, I'm glad you're hard already, why don't you put that big cock in your hand while I tell you all about it? You don't mind if I play with myself, do you? Good, because it's such a hot story, and...

Er, yes Billy, I am from the south. London actually. Oh, right. That's in the north, isn't it? I thought so. I could tell from your accent. Northern boys make me feel so horny… Anyway, last night there was me, my boyfriend and my girlfriend and… Oh, right. Yes, I can hang on a minute while you get your cigarettes.

(…)

Right, now where were we? Ah yes, so me, my boyfriend and my girlfriend were having a drink at mine, and my girlfriend, who's never met my boyfriend before, says…

Jameson? Ha! Yes, you can pour me one, Billy. So anyway, she says to my boyfriend…

Sorry? Oh. Well that's what I'm here for. To cheer you up. So you take that big stiff cock in your hand and…

Oh? I'm sorry to hear that. Perhaps my wet pussy is just what you…What?

No, I can't meet you. It's against the…

Do I what? Look, I'm sorry. Listen, I'm going to have to ring off. Yes, I know you're paying a pound a minute, but this isn't the Samaritans, darlin'… Yes, I'm sorry you're feeling that way, but I don't see what I can…

You're going to what? Listen. I have to go now. Please don't call again. Goodbye.

From the house across the back gardens, Scott and Mandy watch from the dark of their bedroom window as the undrawn curtains of number thirteen provide a free screening of tonight's seedy cinematic presentation. The star of the show is that dirty little

Herbert called Billy, who, for the last ten minutes
has been sat half-wanking on the sofa, telephone
held between shoulder and ear, glass and fag in one
hand, his cock sporadically held in the other.

Both Scott and Mandy agree that Billy is a pervert,
a sad drunken dirty little pervert. And yet, despite
their low opinions of the pervert Billy, neither Scott
nor Mandy can admit to their shared disappointment
when the perv at number thirteen puts the phone
down and pulls his trousers up, whereupon Mandy
then closes the thin gap in their curtains and both
her and Scott return to bed, where they will fuck
eagerly, almost desperately, Scott coming well before
Mandy, and having to listen to her pleasuring herself
to climax in the dark, the bed trembling to a rising
judder, while Scott, token leg laid across the shaking
ankle of Mandy, ponders upon the pervert Billy,
while the drunken lost-child of a man at number
thirteen across the back gardens thumbs through
the telephone directory, pretend suicide breadknife
northward still on the settee beside him, until he
finds the page of listed Rileys, and begins ringing
them all one by one, starting with the obvious M's
for Mick then spreading outward amongst all the
other sleepy-eyed Rileys within a forty mile radius,
raising them from their beds as the slow violet dawn
approaches, asking each Riley in turn who picks up
their telephone, man, woman, or child, Are you?
Are you married to? Is your father my father?

CHAPTER 49

Dear Billy

I'm not very good at writing letters, as you're about to find out. I think it was the right thing to do to write to each other after our chat on the phone the other night. Like you said, we should take it slow and get to know each other if that's what we both want. Thanks for your letter and photographs. I'm pleased you have a family. You all look very happy. I enjoyed reading about your life so far, and feel I have caught up a little. As for your first question, back in 1966 I was not unlike yourself, always fooling around, daft about music, especially the Rolling Stones who I still like. I saw them recently at Wembley with my wife Maureen. I met Maureen in a town near Glasgow, and she's my second wife. We've been together for 10 years and we're very happy.

Anyway, after me and your mum split up (a few months before you were born) I married a girl in 1968 called Janice, and although we had two kids (Claire and Stephen) I will never know why we married. I don't know whether it was because I was looking for a way in life, or whether I was just mixed up about things. At the time I was working at Trebor, and I got offered a contracting job in Scotland through a mate of a mate. Me and Janice had only been married for a year or so but it was more money so I took it. From then on I travelled with work and didn't really see Janice or the kids much.

Not much to tell after that, other than I was working hard and got into a couple of bits of trouble. It was stupid stuff, scrapping and the like. And then in 1983 I met Maureen. I left Janice soon after, and me and Maureen lived in a caravan near Kilmarnock for a while, and a few times the kids would come and stay. They got on with Maureen and everything was fine. When the contract work stopped I decided it was time to settle down back here, and an old mate offered me some work at his timber yard in town. He even put me and Maureen up for a bit while we sorted a place to live. We got a mobile home (a caravan on bricks) near Whitt Moor. After that I started my own building business and things got much better. I have 12 men working for me now, and the funny thing is, my ex-wife and Maureen are really good friends. As for the kids, Claire is married to Dave and has two boys, Kyle (6) and Jordan (2). Stephen is living with his girlfriend Jade, and they have a girl called Aymee who is nearly 1.

In your letter you say it hurts that I never contacted you. I can't explain this fully in a letter. There are many reasons why I didn't, and maybe I can tell you when we meet, if (as you say in your letter) that's what you want to do. I think it would be better at a neutral place rather than at your house or mine. If you want I could pick you up from the Nelson car park one Friday or Saturday night (it's just across from you isn't it?). I might still be barred from there (long story, ha ha!) but we could go to a quiet pub I know and have a drink. My home phone number is on the business card attached.

All the best,
Mick

PS. Call me at home if you want to talk again or meet up.

CHAPTER 50

Hello Mum

No, nothing's up. Just thought I'd ring and see how you are.

Yeh, they're fine. Scarlett's on a school trip to White Post Farm, and Joe's got his sports day on Friday.

Yeh, Friday. Fancy coming?

Sure. Well, it starts about one. Come round about twelve for a cuppa?

Yeh, egg and spoon race, relay, and, something with beanbags, I think.

Yeh, should be fun.

Don't know. Not seen the forecast.

No, not today. Had flu all weekend so I thought I'd put a day in.

Yeh, probably. Feeling better anyhow.

Yeh, got the day off on Friday.

Oh, she's fine. How's Dad?

Great stuff. And how you doing?

Good, good. Yeh, er, listen Mum, I've, there's something I wanted to talk to you about.

No, no, nothing's wrong. It's just, well, I, er, I had a letter last week from Mick Riley.

Mum?

Mum don't. Listen, it's, Mum, it's nothing to get upset about.

It's fine. Really. It's just, look, I haven't said anything because, well, I didn't want to upset you.

No, it was, well, I knew his name didn't I, and I, well, I...

Yeh, I did want to know.

No, I'd looked in the phone book but he...

No. Derbyshire Times. An advert. A complete fluke really. Just flipping through it a couple of weeks ago and there it was.

Yeh. A building firm.

Yeh, he was fine about it. A bit surprised, I guess.

Mum, you don't have to get upset. It makes no difference to...

Yeh, I did. I had to find out.

Yeh, I've got the letter here. Want me to read it out?

Mum?

Mum, that's fine, I totally...

No, I couldn't go my whole life and not...

Yeh. Next weekend, I think.

Mum?

Mum, it doesn't make any difference to...

No, I'm not going to rush into anything. Promise. And Mum? Please listen. I'm not doing this because...

No, no I'm not.

Yeh, I promise. I just had to know. I'm not looking for another dad.

CHAPTER 51

A swift couple for the nerves

Then at five to seven I wander out into the Nelson car park and wait. All these years of not knowing and here I am, waiting on the bloke that fathered me. I sit on the wall and smoke a fag. Through the pub window I can see the big railway clock hung over the bar.

Five past.

Ten past.

Quarter past.

I light another fag and make a decision. Five more minutes then fuck it. It's strange, but I almost start to feel relieved.

As the big hand reaches the four I tell myself it's for the best, throw my dog-end down and slide my arse off the wall. I start to walk when a silver Jag pulls into the car park. A burst of starlings spiral up from the tarmac, and through the windscreen, grinning, the driver holds a flat palm up as he swings the car across my path.

Fuck.

I walk slow around the back-end of the Jag towards the driver's side. The electric window whirrs down and there he is. Big grin, gold chain, suntan.

Billy?

Mick?

He leans back and pushes the passenger door open, and with grin still fixed he nods towards the seat. As I get into his car the smile on my face feels like it's made of brick. We look at each other for what could be a few seconds or half an hour. Apart from his blue eyes he looks just like me, but fatter. We shake hands and he doesn't let go.

Well? he says, and I hear myself laugh, a laugh that doesn't sound like me. I loosen my grip. He doesn't let go until I make a slight tug.

I knew it was you, he says, I've seen you before.

Yeh? I say. My voice sounds thin so I sit up straight-backed and tighten the muscles in my stomach.

It was in Halfords, he says. A few years ago. I saw your name badge.

Yeh?

Yeh. I was going to say hello I but didn't. Thought you might not want to talk to me. He shrugs, pats the steering wheel then turns the ignition key. He grins again. His top lip glistens a little as the engine purrs. Shall we go for a drink somewhere? Don't think they'll serve me here, he says, nodding towards the Nelson, laughing.

We drive through the orange-red sunlight and make small talk. I take quick glances at him while he drives. It occurs to me that I should feel something for this man but I don't. Or do I? It's strange but I picture myself hugging him, crying and shit, but the thought of it makes me want to punch myself in the face. He talks about his building firm and I picture myself punching him, that same punch I've given him every time I've thought about meeting him.

I look out the passenger-side window.

He pushes a CD into the player, and the intro to Sympathy For The Devil flickers like a midge-cloud between us. He smiles at me. I smile back.

—

In the pub he tells me that he's thought about me lots. I look at him as he talks. Is this what I'll look like when I'm older? I watch his fingers as he raises his pint to his lips. He has fingers like mine. Or am I just thinking he does? He asks me how I've been. I'm sick of small talk now. There are things I need to know.

Why didn't you ever contact me? I ask.

He looks down into his glass. Because I didn't want to stir things up, he says. He looks up from his pint, looks me straight in the eye. I don't look away, and for sure there's something there, something bruised.

Didn't your mother talk to you about me? he says.

I drink to the bottom of my glass in one tilt. Bits, I say.

Like what?

Like, how you were a burglar, I say.

My words seem to hang like fag smoke between us.

He laughs, long and hard, then finishes his pint in one.

I'll get us another, he says, patting me on the shoulder as he heads to the bar.

In the next pub he knows the landlord. It's a shitty dive in a scrubby little village near town. I watch how the landlord looks at Mick, listen to how he talks to him. The landlord likes Mick. You can see it, hear it. Mick asks me what I fancy and the landlord looks at me.

This is my son, Billy, Mick says.

I nod and smile. The landlord grins, shakes my hand.

He's a grand man, your dad, he says.

We sit in a blush of sunlight by the pool table. I watch dust float in the air for a moment.

So what do you want to know? Mick says.

Why you didn't want me, I say.

Mick's eyes twitch, then narrow. He sighs.

I did want you. Your mother didn't want me. Your grandma hated me. I tried. Really. I wrote to your mum when she was pregnant with you, when she was in that home in Sheff. Told her how much I loved her. She wrote back saying she didn't want me. Believe me Billy, I really loved your mum.

I say nothing because I don't know what to say.

Mick drinks. Still do, he says.

Something jags inside me, like the drop of a weighted rope. I imagine my mum hearing this, my stepdad.

I saw you at the Town Hall steps, he says. When you were a baby. I thought you were being adopted. That was the plan. But your mother kept you. She didn't want me though. And that was that.

Mick seems to harden. We both drink, and I feel myself softening. My mum has told me nothing good about this man, and however I imagined this moment, however I saw this conversation past the point of me punching him in the face, it was nothing like this.

I'm beginning to realise, probably for the first time in my life, that even those closest to you can tell you half-truths, lies. This man, in the fragments I've been given, was painted a complete bastard. Maybe he was back then. But he doesn't seem a bastard to me here, now. He just seems hurt.

Tell me about your mum and dad, I ask Mick as he puts his empty glass on the table, wiping his sleeve across his mouth.

He sighs.

My dad was from Ireland, he says. Buggered off when I was five. My mother died when I was seven. I were brought up by my aunty. He shrugs, picks his pint pot up, wobbling the glass a little as the froth begins to settle in the bottom.

There's a moment's silence between us. I become aware that I'm copying him. I put my glass down.

Where in Ireland was your dad from? I ask.

Dunno, he says, smiling.

We have Guinness and a double Jameson each to celebrate our Irishness. I'm happy to have Irish in me and I tell Mick as much. I tell him about Nannan's dad being Irish too, and a strange look comes over Mick's face. I remember what he said about Nannan earlier. I decide not to mention her again.

We have another Guinness and double Jameson. Mick puts his hand on mine. He tells me he's sorry for not getting in touch.

Tell me about my brother and sister, I say.

He looks at his watch and smiles.

You're meeting them in half an hour, he says, It's your sister's birthday.

—

We listen to more Rolling Stones in the car. Loud. We drink cans of Holsten. We joke about fuck-ups. We swap stories of brawls and scrapes, almost shouting over the music and the rush of warm air coming through the open windows. I like Mick. A lot. And as we get out the car at the Saltergate Social, I realise that all my life I've been missing this, that all my life I've been trying to be good and failing, that all my life there was no need to try and be something I wasn't.

We walk across the car park shoulder to shoulder and everything starts to occur to me at once. This is my father. This is the part of me that I've been denied my whole life. My dad, who's as far from a fucking angel as you're ever going to meet, and look at him: happy, smiling, laughing at life's fuck-ups, half-drunk from behind the wheel of a silver Jag.

CHAPTER 52

My half-brother stole a car

Drove it drunk to Whitt Moor, missed a bend and bent a lamppost, ran to my half-sister's bleeding and never got pinched.

My father calls him Little bugger, puts a triangle of pints down on the table, goes back to the bar. My half-sister shakes her head. Smiles. Says, Tell him the rest of it, Ste, Tell him why you stole it.

My half-brother drinks. Grins. Says, It belonged to that twat. Moved in a week after she'd chucked me out. So I wrote his Mondeo off. Ha.

My half-sister tuts. That's not all of it, she says, Tell him. Tell him what you did before that, Ste.

My father puts two bottles of Grolsch in front of me, says Got you two cos we're on pints, yeh?

Go on, my half-sister says. Tell him the rest of it. Tell him what you did to the house.

My half-brother grins. Lights a fag. Says, She deserved it, the slag.

Then he tells me this.

I went round to see her, to sort things out with

her and the kid. But they weren't in so I went for a beer. Waited. And later when I tried again still no one answered. So I went round the back. Got in by the dicky kitchen window to leave a note. And when I got in some twat's work-boots were by the backdoor. Car keys on the key hook. Trousers on the fuckin clotheshorse. So I took a shit on her bed. Used it to write bitch on the wall. Pissed in her knicker drawer. Took a breadknife to her dresses. Went into the kid's room and turned the cot upside down. Pulled the arms off a teddy. Stamped on a doll's house. All of which I'd paid for in the first fuckin place.

And my father laughs. Says Little bugger. Drinks. My half-sister shaking her head saying Oh Ste, you and your temper.

CHAPTER 53

Got any Irish in you?

And she says not, so I ask her if she'd like some. Karen laughs, as does my half-sister Claire. Claire's husband Dave laughs too. Ste laughs so much he spits lager back into his glass. Karen's husband John doesn't laugh. He just stares at me over his pint pot. John has a neck as thick as his head and one continuous eyebrow. I look away. Ste gets up and goes over to his new fiancée's family who are sat at the other side of the social club. A small group of kids are throwing each other about on the balloon-strewn dancefloor to Agafuckindoo. I go over and ask the DJ if he's got any Stone Roses. He shakes his head, looks at me like I've just asked for the 18fuckin12 Overture. He puts The Birdie Song on, for fuck's sake, and I say what about The Pogues then? He slides his headphones to one side, says Later. I say Ta cunt, and he says What? as I walk away.

At the bar my father is gabbing to three blokes.

This is my son Billy, my father says, then buys

me a treble Jameson. He tells the blokes our story, and they pat me on the shoulder and soft punch me in the chest as he tells it. I buy another treble and a bottle of Pils, head off to where Claire is dancing to Adam and the Ants.

Claire is my height, same colour hair, same nose, same mouth. She does this little wiggle when she dances. She smiles when she sees me coming over. She wiggles again as she smiles. I like Claire. She sometimes has a look on her face like she's just done something naughty. It's well cute. I give her the Holsten, start dancing with her.

LIKE A SCHOOL FUCKIN DISCO, I shout in her ear.

She smiles, puts a hand on my shoulder, pulls my head to her mouth. **WHAT?** she says.

IT'S LIKE A SCHOOL FUCKIN DISCO, I shout. **THIS SONG WAS SHIT THEN AND IT'S STILL SHIT NOW**.

She laughs, pulls me to her mouth again. I like the smell of her breath.

DON'T WORRY ABOUT IT, she says. **JUST DANCE**.

So I do. Of sorts. I notice monobrow John is staring at me from our table in the corner. Muppet.

It's hot so me and Claire go outside for a fag. She says it's ace I got in touch. She says she likes having a half-brother. She's said these things before but I like hearing her say them again.

We put our hands together, flat-palmed and look at how the shapes are the same.

We do this sometimes.

I kiss her on the cheek and I tell her I love her.

She says I love you too, Billy, then she asks where Grace and the kids are. I tell her they've got something on with Grace's mum. It's a lie of course, and I don't like to lie, but it's better than saying Grace didn't want to come because she thinks there's something not right with you lot.

Behind us, the door opens to a dull puff of Culture Club. I fucking hate Boy George.

Dave says I ought to come inside because thicko John says he wants to do me for what I said to his missis. It's probably taken the dumb cunt this long to get the joke. I need another drink anyway.

My father stands alone at the bar. He buys me another treble Jameson then tells me he wants to sponsor my five-a-side team with a new kit. We chink glasses on it.

I ask him where Maureen is tonight and he just shrugs, says something about her not feeling well. I've only met her once before. She didn't really talk much.

Ste comes over and my father offers to buy him a pint and a vodka. He looks at me and Ste and says, My boys. Ste says he's come over to get a round in for his new fiancée's family so my father buys the round for him. He fucks off with two full trays of drinks and my father says how he still loves my mum. He's said it before, but I still don't know whether he means it or whether it's just the ale talking. Roll With It by Oasis comes on and Ste comes back over, grabs my arm, drags me onto the dancefloor. We jump about, arms around each other's shoulders, punching the air amongst a litter of kids doing likewise. Ste gives me a sloppy kiss on the cheek as Oasis dissolves into that shit No Limit song. He tries to make me dance to it but he's got no fuckin chance.

I love my new family. They make me feel like the jigsaw is finished. I start walking back to our table but fat-neck John is still giving me the deadeye.

I turn and head back to the bar.

I didn't mean anything by it, I tell John, putting a pint of Stella in front of him. Here, I say. Peace offering.

He just looks up at me, starts drinking the pint that my father bought him.

Me and Claire mooch off to dance to Funkytown.

HE REALLY IS A BIT OF A CUNT THAT JOHN, I say in Claire's ear.

DON'T WORRY ABOUT IT, she says, her hand on the small of my back, **JUST DANCE**.

———

In the toilet cubicle, our tongues wrestle like little

snakes in each other's mouths. We needed to talk after the last time. I don't know what it is but I can't help it. We can't help it. Since the last time I tried to forget about it. I did forget about it. But here we are again, and realising that you want to fuck your half-sister is a strange place to be in.

Claire says she wants me, wants me and wants to run away with me. I pull her tight into me, my cock pressing against her cunt-bone, both hands up her skirt, fingers soft-digging into her arse-cheeks, and we half-fall, stumbling against the toilet door, my right-hand travelling, and Claire saying Don't, what if... My ring-finger slipping inside her, the thought flashing across my mind that I could be fingering myself here, and I want her, want to fuck her, my sister, my half-sister, my whatever she is, who unzips me, unbuttons me, pulls me out, starts slow-wanking me, now sliding down me, tits pressed into my chest, my belly, now kissing my cock, my hand still wet finger-tipped and now down her bra, slow-tracing the O of her stiff little nipple as I watch her lips part, her dark eyes looking up at me as she slow-takes my tip into her mouth, her warm-wet lips sending a judder from my cock-end to my spine, and I push, gently, slow-urging her onto me, feeling her warm-wet tongue flicker around me, and it's like I'm watching this, myself above myself, my cock in my half-sister's mouth, and I will come into her, come **AND YOU KNOW ME SHARON, DON'T TAKE NO SHIT FROM NO**

FUCKER SO I SAID FUCK YOU BITCH! YOU'RE THE ONE WI A CUNT LIKE A WIZARD'S SLEEVE, AAAHHHAHAHAHAHAHA!

And my heart thumps, Don't move, Shush, and Claire looks up at me, trying not to giggle, my cock softening by the second, drooping like an unwatered rose in her hand, and when the bints have finally gone, me and Claire agree that this isn't the time or the place, but we want each other, want each other badly, but if we get found out all hell will break loose, so we have to be clever, and we kiss, long, then off she goes, back down that dark hallway into the social club, and after a minute or two I do the same, heading straight for the bar, grinning to myself, Christ-all-fucking-mighty I just nearly spunked in my half-sister's gob.

—

I'm glad your grandma died, my father says, bozz-eyed and shifting weight from one foot to the other. I wanted her dead then, and I'm glad she's fuckin dead now, the interfering old bitch.

I tell my father he's a cunt, and if he doesn't shut his gob I'm going to twat him one.

People standing around the bar are looking at us, and I'm telling my father that if he ever says anything bad about my nannan again I'll glass him in the fucking face.

I leave without saying goodbye to anyone. I never want to see these fuckers again. Full stop. I light a fag under a streetlamp, look up to a white moon as the club doors bang bang a damp echo across the car park. I turn to look, and brick-shithouse John is steaming across the tarmac towards me, fists clenched. I chuck my fag and run, run like fuck down the road, the stupid fat-necked bastard dragging his knuckles further and further behind me, and of course he doesn't catch me, no one ever has.

CHAPTER 54

Empty

Is what you feel. If feel is even the right word. You go to sleep hating yourself, and wake up feeling the same way. Feel. An absence of. And yet you feel it. This weight that snakes itself around your gut, yet seems to be outside of you. It's like you're a blur in-between. Like the shadow of a shadow of a hook, pulling at you somewhere both outside and in.

Yesterday you thought about hanging yourself from a certain beam in the outhouse. And then you thought about the kids, so you considered that tree in the woods instead.

You don't want to live in this skin anymore. There is no light.

You look into your sandwich box on the dirty table in front of you. You'll not eat. You've not eaten properly for three days now. Four days ago you left the scene of the worst fuck-up you've ever committed and there is no way back into the light. And there never will be. You want to tell Grace about it but you can't. You want to tell your kids that you are a bad bad man and you don't want to be, but you can't.

You should kill yourself. Have done with it.

Through the canteen window you watch as a fork-truck rumbles by. How did you even get here? Your boss has told you twice this morning to pay attention. You've messed up three orders already today. You cannot count. You cannot think. You are considering getting up from this table and walking out. And then you'll keep on walking. You don't care where you go. There is nothing left. You are empty.

The canteen door opens and your arsehole winks. There are only two tables in here and there is no escape from conversation. You just want to be left alone.

Hey.

You look up from your sandwich box. It's the new bloke, Curtis. He smiles at you and you can't return it. He sits bang opposite you. You press the lid back onto your sandwich box.

Not hungry? he says.

You shake your head. He pulls a yellow Tupperware box out of a carrier bag and pulls the lid off it. Inside is pasta and salad. He pulls a silver fork from his inside jacket pocket and jiggles it in the air.

TA-DAA! he sings, plunging his fork into the pasta, and then, You're Billy, aren't you?

You don't even have the energy to stand up and leave.

Yeh, you say, feeling your hands cup your head.

Not feeling too good? he asks through a mouthful of pasta.

Just tired, you say, each word feeling like a concrete boot on your tongue.

Ah, he says.

Curtis soft-chomps another mouthful of food. You look up and his twinkly blue eyes blink at you. You look down to his mouth and watch his little moustache wriggle over his thin lips. He swallows.

Wilt thou then, O mortal, cling to the husk which falsely seems to you the self? he says.

You feel your face pinch together.

What? you say, your voice a heavy pebble dropped into the well of your head.

Wu Ming Fu, Curtis smiles, forking half a tomato into his mouth.

What?

An old Chinese poet, Curtis muffles, his Adam's apple rising with the swallow.

Oh, you say, feeling your thumbs press hard into your temples, your palms forming a visor across your eyebrows.

You feel Curtis looking at you and you feel vulnerable, sliced open. Eyes closed, the sound of fork against Tupperware feels like little tin birds pecking at your skull.

Ever read Kafka? Curtis chirps, soft-chomping again as the fork-truck rumbles by.

You have no energy to fight this. The little tin birds peck-peck and a hot worm wriggles somewhere deep in your brain. You move your head slow right then left.

No.

Ooh you should! Try The Trial! It's fabulous! There's this guy who gets arrested but he can't find out what he's guilty of. It's amazing!

You hear the rustle of a carrier bag, followed by the sound of a flask cup being unscrewed, followed by a flask lid being unscrewed, followed by the trickle of liquid.

You don't look up.

Slurp.

We're all on trial at some time or other though, aren't we Billy?

The words Please, Fuck and Off tread soundlessly through your head.

Slurp.

You shuffle in the hard plastic chair that holds you.

Dunno, you say.

Ah, Billy, sings Curtis with a chuckle, I myself have stood many trials. Many, many trials.

You hear his fork scrape against the Tupperware box. You feel Curtis waiting for a response. You have none. You want to get out of here. Now. You will your legs the strength to stand. Your chair legs scrape back.

Do you read at all, Billy?

You get to your feet. You look into Curtis's twinkly blue eyes. He smiles. You shrug.

You should, he says, his grin showing a sliver of tomato skin across his teeth.

You turn your back and move towards the door.

Don't forget your sandwich box, Curtis coos.

You turn and pick it up, surprised at how much your hand shakes.

Try Oscar Wilde! he blurts as you pull the canteen door open.

You turn and look at him.

What?

To deny one's own experience, is to put a lie into the lips of one's own life!

Curtis smiles. You hear the ticking of the clock on the wall. You hear the needles of birdsong outside. You feel open and known to this annoying cock sat looking at you.

Everyone knows everything.

The shadow of the shadow of a hook tugs from deep.

The boss sighs when you tell him you're sick, and you have to go home.

CHAPTER 55

You speak it into the pillow

Eyes closed tight, you're sorry, you're so very fucking sorry, and in this curtain-closed afternoon you hear only the breathe and sniffle of those you call wife and daughter and son, who sit around your blackened matter as it hides under duvet and eyelid, this bedroomed hot-fug promise of never going back, answered by those pattering tones of We love you Dad, and We'll help you get better, and from that deepest underground a guttural sob again finds echo through that rancid hole, and It's not your fault Dad, It's not, and the wife now stifling that tide, that grave-silent soliloquy of What have you done to us? That glass half-empty in her hand, that white pill in her open-palmed other, Sit up, Sit up and take this, the words aired downstairs to her children still swimming her head like a blind fish in a mile-deep cavern, It's not your dad's fault, It's not, We can help him.

CHAPTER 56

You will never know the name of these birds

But as they settle across the pond, you begin to wish the motorway, and its constant hum, were not so close, so you could hear these dusk feeders, as they circle, then land, on this mirror-skin of water.

You watch closely, trying to imagine what sound the shadow of feather on water makes, when something spooks these birds, and they take flight, in a clatter of soft glass, breaking, then falling back into place.

CHAPTER 57

And now we look at

The interior of a stifle-untidy family car, slow-crawling a north-easterly exit of the M1, the driving mother, the father, the daughter and son, the sad-eyed border collie all occupying this cramped space, where the dim crackle of radio and engine backdrop their humid worldview of litter-strewn verge and number plate, the dog soft-punctuating with a tongue-lolling pantpantpant, head hanging out the half-open left-side rear window, its shuffling rump now nudging the nine-year-old boy, who elbows back, says **GERROFF JACK,** *returns to his Gameboy Pokémon Yellow, sending Jigglypuff out to use sing against Jessie's Arbok, the boy's twelve-year-old sister gazing out the half-open right-side rear window, teen magazine on her lap, and God it's hot, and How long until we get there? To which the driving mother replies An hour? Maybe more? And by her side with cigarette hanging out the wound down passenger-side window, the sunglasses and stubbled husband, taking a swag from the* *squash bottle markerpenned with a smiley face and the name Billy, one-quarter of the night-before's prepared supplies happily assembled by this wife and mother, each with their own name-scrawled drink and Tupperware box of food, each containing that lovingly put together quartet of sandwiches, bag of crisps, and by now half-melted Mars Bar, for this, their first holiday in two years, that week-rented three-storey fisherman's cottage overlooking Whitby harbour, last night's talk of tomorrow's sound of seagulls and sea, the feel of sand between toes, of evening strolls along the shoreline, all subtexted by the unspoken hope of things sorted, of Billy now leaning forward and turning the radio up, of CONFIDENCE IS A PREFERENCE FOR THE HABITUAL VOYEUR OF WHAT IS KNOWN AS...*

BILLY (*turns to face his kids in backseat*): **PARK-LIFE!**

Scarlett and Joe look at each other and roll their eyes.

BILLY: Come on, babies! **HOL-I-DAY!** (*wags his index fingers like a conductor*) **AND MORNING SOUP CAN BE AVOIDED IF YOU TAKE A ROUTE STRAIGHT-THROUGH WHAT IS KNOWN AS** (*cups his right ear towards kids*).

SCARLETT/JOE (*half-heartedly*): Park-life.

Billy pulls a mock sad face at them both. Grace turns the radio down. Billy turns in his seat to look at her. He tuts.

BILLY: **BORR-RING!**

GRACE: I can't hear the engine, Billy.

BILLY (*drinks from squash bottle*): And what's the engine saying to you, Grace? (*imitates an engine*) Brrrrummm-brrrrummm, Graaaace, Graaaace, you're borr-ring.

GRACE (*smiling, play-slaps Billy on the knee*): Shut up.

Billy drinks from the squash bottle again, screws the lid back on, places the bottle into the well between the front seats. Billy then twists in his seat, reaching back to squeeze Joe's right knee. Joe looks up from his game and frowns.

JOE: What?

BILLY: So Joe, how's the Pokémon slave trade going?

Joe rolls his eyes then smiles sarcastically at his father. Billy turns his attention to Scarlett, who is absorbed in her magazine. He flicks the face of the young boy on the cover. Scarlett twitches then looks over her magazine at her father. Billy holds a packet of Polo mints out to her.

BILLY: Polo-lo-lo?

SCARLETT (*returning her gaze to the magazine*): No ta, Dad.

BILLY: So who's the hottie on the front?

SCARLETT (*from behind the magazine*): Dunno. Just some boy.

Joe looks over his Gameboy at his dad.

JOE (*deadpan*): Dad, you're weird.

BILLY (*smiling at his son*): Polo-jo-jo?

Joe leans forward to take a mint. Billy pulls the packet away from the boy's reach.

BILLY (*imitates gills with his hands*): Sucker-**BLOWFISH!**

JOE (*returning to his game*): Fair enough.

Billy starts prodding the boy's knee with the packet of Polos.

BILLY (*robotically*): Am I buggin you am I buggin you am I buggin you am I...

JOE (*looking up with a snap*): **YES!**

BILLY (*holding mints out again*): Polo-lo-lo-jo-jo-jo-jo?

JOE: **NO!**

GRACE: For goodness sake you two, cut it out! It's too bloody hot for this!

Billy turns back to face the windscreen. He puts a

hand on Grace's knee.

BILLY: Soz. Just seaside excited.

A moment's peace is broken by the dog whimpering.

SCARLETT: Jack needs a wee.

JOE: Me too.

GRACE: Service station coming up.

BILLY: Can't wait to get on that beach at Robin Hood's Bay.

JOE: Why is it called Robin Hood's Bay?

BILLY (*sucking on a Polo*): Dunno. Maybe Robin Hood lived there for a bit?

SCARLETT: I thought Robin Hood lived in Sherwood Forest?

GRACE: Isn't he fictional?

JOE: We did him at school. Miss said he was real but a lot of the stories were made up about him. In songs and stuff.

BILLY: One day they'll sing songs about me.

JOE (*sings*): I'm a creep, I'm a weirdo…

They all laugh. Billy turns and points a finger at Joe in mock threat. Joe grins at his father.

GRACE: Here we go.

They pull off the main road into a service station. Billy

takes his drink from the well and unscrews the cap.

BILLY (*drinks*): You lot nip to the bogs then, and I'll take Jack for a slash.

And now we look at Billy slipping the lead over his panting dog's head through the open backdoor, the mother and her children crossing the tarmac to the toilets, Billy now walking the dog to the grass verge, fag lit as the dog sniffs the waste bin, cocks a leg and pisses long, Billy watching as his family disappear behind the brick-built garage, him now dragging Jack back to the car, that sunrise in his belly as he bends to pour water from a plastic bottle into a red plastic bowl, all is good, all is sorted, and the dog bows down to drink, Billy now rummaging his rucksack in the boot, bottle of squash stood waiting by the cool-box, a glance to the garage, now topping the bottle up, now screwing the top back on, now skipping across to the waste bin dropping that empty Vladivar in amongst the trash, the smiley-faced squash bottle placed back into the well, now dragging Jack back into the car, now sitting back down in the passenger-seat to take a drink, sucking on a Polo to tell himself he's bossing this, that none at all ever was never going to work, that a self-set limit was agreed on as the only way forward, that what they don't know won't hurt them, that this is a holiday for fuck's sake.

CHAPTER 58

Christ allfuckingmighty

What twat stands on a windowsill puts his hands on top of a stuck sash-window then yanks it up to try and shut it? Like, no chance of getting your fucking fingers trapped in it is there? What. A fucking. Mong.

Look at you. Crucified in your fucking Spiderman pants three floors up inside a fisherman's cottage smack-bang in the middle of Whitby fucking harbour like some fuckarsed Jesus. You're gonna die, Billy boy, this window's gonna fall through and you're gonna die in a great fuckarsed smash of blood and glass all over that fuckin alley.

Maybe I should shout for help? Yeh, great. Can see it now. Coppers, fire brigade, ambulance, every fucker in Whitby looking up at some daft spazz bluebottled inside a window wearing nothing but his fucking underpants.

Fuck.

How long are Grace and the kids gonna be?

Yes, telefuckingvision, thanks. I'm glad they're

going to fucking post. Great. Just help me down from this fucking windowsill will you, and I'll crack one of those Stella's open, light a fag and watch the fucking race. Nice.

FUUUCK. My fingers are fucking hammering. What if they go all black and drop off like when you get frostbite? Great. Fucking stumps for fingers. Lovely.

Well, Billy boy, you've really gone and done it this time haven't you? Why didn't you just go to the beach like they asked you to? You could have been sipping a cold one listening to the sea watching the kids build sandcastles glegging a bit of passing gash but no, you had to stop in and watch the fucking horses didn't you.

Ah. Here we go. Seven furlongs. Come on Merry-Go-Round. **COME ON THEN MERRY-GO-ROUND! GO ON!**

Oh woopdifuckingdoo. How appropriate to this afternoon's entertainment to be beaten on the fucking line. Red fucking Hand? How can a 25-1 pit pony beat that field? Utter shite.

Fuck I need a piss.

At least it'll be a good one to tell the lads if I don't fucking die pancaked all over them cobbles down there taking three fat Geordie kids out with me.

Fuck, will you look at that seagull's eyes.

Current betting. Evens: Grace and the kids return within the hour, releasing Billy to much laughter and cold wet tea-towels wrapped lovingly around bruised fingers followed by the drinking of six cans of Stella followed by another trip to the offy followed by a wild drunken fuck when the kids are asleep.

3-1: Grace and the kids return within the hour, releasing Billy to initial laughter followed by spits of gnarl over the length of time they were out followed by cold wet tea-towels wrapped carefully around bruised fingers followed by the drinking of six cans of Stella followed by another trip to the offy followed by inexplicable 2am rantings.

10-1: Grace and the kids return within the hour, releasing Billy to minimal laughter followed by spikes of gnarl over the length of time they were out followed by cold wet tea-towels wrapped half-arsed around bruised fingers followed by the drinking of six cans of Stella followed by another trip to the offy followed by inexplicable 2am rantings followed by a cold loveless fuck followed by a half-sleep riddled with bad dreams about a dark wood followed by Joe waking at 9am to find his dad sat on the doorstep drinking from a near-empty bottle of Thunderbird asking passers-by what the fuck they're looking at.

50-1: The window falls through, Billy dies horribly, end of story.

CHAPTER 59

If after the fall

You rise from undergrowth as sapling, hide as tree in trees, arms outstretched as branch and branch, finger-leaves tremble, blood-sun bleeds through pillared dusk, now hide behind see-through eyelids, hearing bent old song from gramophone unwound, slack-slow belly-voice treacles lowing moan, stump-finger piano drunks a darkling birdsong, Billy, Billy, look at me, and there she stands, erotic creak of limbs, bark-lids lift to blink white blind eyes, bent breasted trunk bending slow to show moss-haired slit, Fuck me Billy, fuck me, and uproot you will, dry twig-fingers she wraps around, tug-wanking pull into mossy hole, and warm, and sleek, and velvet-lush the mossy-mouthed slit, your knees now tight around the fuck-trunk-she, dull-husk rub of bark against your belly, Fuck me Billy, fuck me, deep as deep into dark dank hollow, tickle-sting pinpricks of unseen ants seething at the bell, fuck-trunk-she moaning cattle-call low, snake-shapes entwined with gramophone unwound, push-fuck, push-fuck,

fuck-sudden gush of cum-blood you, ragdolled back onto forest-soft floor, geyser rush of crimson arcing the dark-leaf canopy, a fountain smear of you that wilts, lolling bluebell-limp as rook-scraw warning makes you flinch in thin skin, and it's coming, and you know it, that legless demon pounding over dead-leaf carpet on flat-palmed sprint, arms as legs, rotting stump of cock dragging the dry earth, and it's coming, you hear its sand-rasp pant, now see its hollowed-out eyes and pin-tooth grin, this soundless scream of you and it's here, there in the clearing, gnash and pound close and closer, **WAKE UP, WAKE UP AND RUN,** but these legs will not carry so you fall, and you keep falling, this fast-passing of rain-pregnant cloud you grasp at nothing, bracing for the pain that never comes because now you are here in this half-mooned bay where you run, feet finding loose-lever over hollow drag-clank of cobble, chasing the shoreline to that far cove-claw, that hatchet-jag of whitewall cliff, this ever-inward creep of sea darkening the black-brown pebbles, a thousand gull-wing clatter of wave breaking on rock-fist, impassable, so see it, see it and understand, know that you were dropped like a dead stone into this, so listen, listen to the voice, Behind you grew a tree, its husk is your ferry, its fruit will be your sustenance, trust all serpents, and when you get there, pray to nothing.

CHAPTER 60

The first thing is the smell of dog shit

Second is the wine tastes of piss. Maybe the wine is piss? Either way, I'm not opening my eyes yet, and the bottle goes back to the floor.

The clock ticks. The birds sing.

The smell is too much and I sit up in bed. The dresser-chair is lying down on its side and I'm wearing yesterday's clothes.

There's a trail of brown mush from the rug to the door. The dog has shit in the night.

I let him out the front door and he wanders down the drive, pausing at the open gate to look back, once. I can't be arsed to take him a walk anyway.

In the living room is a broken glass. It sits under the table, jagged teeth skyward like a little crystal bear-trap.

In the fridge sits two cans of Stella. I take them both upstairs and run a bath. Then I ring for a taxi. Twelve-thirty. That gives me forty minutes.

The house is too quiet so I put some sounds on. Rum, Sodomy, and the Lash. Loud. The bath water is too hot so I toss off while the water cools. I think of the new neighbour bent over, me fucking her from behind. Her arse is small and firm, but wobbles ever so slightly. My hands grip her hipbones as I push into her. She looks over her shoulder at me as I come.

I drink Grace's Blue Nun while I watch through the kitchen window for the taxi.

There's a woman in some kind of uniform looking up the drive. She has something in her hand that looks like a dog lead. She takes a couple of steps up the drive and my dog appears around the gatepost. This is not something that makes sense so I open the door to sort it.

I ask her, What you doing with my dog? My voice sounds strange and I realise I haven't spoken today.

I found him wandering the street, she says.

So?

I'm the dog warden. A neighbour said the dog lived here.

So?

Your dog could have caused a road accident.

What?

If you allow it to happen again, I'll have to report it.

The taxi pulls up behind her. My dog looks at me with his big sad eyes and I suddenly become aware of the bottle of Blue Nun in my hand. I put it down on the drive and walk towards the woman.

The taxi-driver winds his window down and says my name with a question mark. I tell him Yeh, then grab the lead out of the woman's hand, unnoosing my dog who wanders toward the house wagging his tail.

I hand the lead back to the woman. I tell her to go away. The taxi-driver looks on.

She says, You can be fined, you know.

I tell her to get the fuck off my property, pushing her once, twice towards the street. She says something about assault, pulling a notebook from her pocket as she walks away.

On the taxi ride in, the driver says Some women want to be men but are just lesbo cunts. Then he tells me Some women are just slags who use their cunts to make men stupid. He lets me drink Blue Nun and smoke. He's alright is Brian, and we agree to go out for a jar sometime.

The cash machine says I can withdraw a maximum of seventy quid. My overdraft is seven hundred and stands at six-twenty-six. I walk across the square towards The Angel with a spring in my step.

I haven't been in here for years. As the barmaid pours my Guinness I add a Jameson to the order. I say Ta and smile at her. She doesn't smile back. I take a seat by the window and look out to the market square. Some udder-titted mother squats down in front of a pushchair wagging a fat finger at her kid. The kid wriggles and kicks out. The mother slaps the kid across the legs, picks a pink dummy up from the pavement and sticks it in the kid's gob.

I go get another Jameson. The miserable cow behind the bar still won't smile. I tell her to cheer up, that it might never happen. She just says One-eighty, putting the glass down on the bar with a clack.

Must be rag week.

I drink up and head next-door. The Anchor.

My tongue feels dry and fuzzy so I ask for a Heineken. I sit near a fuddy-duddy forty-something couple who are eating steak and chips. I drink, then ask them if they've heard of The Pogues. The woman ignores me, but the man looks up and frowns.

The Pogues, I say, Ever heard of them?

The woman still doesn't look up. The man looks back to his plate, starts sawing at his steak, mutters something about Fairytale of New York.

I tell him I played rhythm guitar on that, and he looks back up at me, his skinny lips parted, a sliver of steak hanging off his paused fork.

Really? he says.

Yeh, I say, Really.

I tell him how they're a really good band to work with. Easy. Don't give a fuck.

The woman coughs a little when I say fuck. I say fuck every other word now, watching her eyes half-blink on the kick of the K. Her husband says something about trying to have a quiet meal. I pretend not to hear and tell him about the time me and Shane had a gang-bang with four Thai birds on the last tour. I bet him he's never fucked a Thai girl up the arse while she's licking out a slanty fanny, and he stands up quick with a scrape of chair legs, walks over to the bar. The woman puts her knife and fork down and stares at her plate while I tell her about how me and Shane nearly got shot by gangsters in Holland over a crack deal.

Someone taps me on the shoulder.

I turn around and it's a pot-bellied dwarf who says he's the landlord and can I please leave now.

I drink up steadily in one, eyeballing him the whole time over the glass. I reach over to the woman's plate, grabbing a handful of chips as I leave.

In The Crown I talk to a couple of gadges I used to half-know. They don't seem to remember me too well. I tell them I used to hang around with Grady, Blue and Newt some years ago, and they both make noises like they remember me. I tell them that I'm a drug dealer now, that I can get them anything they want. They tell me they don't take drugs. One of the gadges gets up to go to the bar and I try and sell the other some Prozac the doctor gave me. He says he's not interested. I push three pills out of their little foil pockets and wash them down with barley wine.

I drag a fingernail under the bold lettering on the packet that says **DO NOT MIX WITH ALCOHOL**.

I laugh because it's funny.

The gadges are boring so I sup up and fuck off.

The Bull is quite la-dee-daa, all green velvet and wood panels. I watch traffic for a while, counting how many cars are red. It seems to me that more cars are red than any other colour. I go to the bar and get another three barleys. When I get back to my table a girl in horse-riding gear is sat at the table opposite. The boy next to her looks like he's just been on manoeuvres with the Territorial Army, all camouflage combat gear and big black boots. As he drinks his head twitches. It looks like he's winking, but he's not.

I pour two barleys into my pint pot. The girl smiles at me. I smile back. Under the table I can see the bump of her fanny in her jodhpurs. I drink, feeling my guts tighten as I watch her legs part slightly, close, then part again. I look up. The girl smiles again, and I realise she's watching me watching. He's looking at me too, but as I catch his eye he twitches then looks down to his drink.

The girl soft-coughs. Hello, she says, My name's Eve, and this is Andy.

I smile and nod, feeling strangely fucked and tongue-tied. My heart's beating too fast and there's a bumpbumpbump in my ears.

Billy, I say.

Hello Billy, says Eve, a curious grin creeping across her face. Andy nods. I nod back then realise he could be just twitching. I take another drink.

That's a good look, I say, nodding at Eve.

Eve looks herself up and down, as though surprised to find herself dressed this way.

Yeh, she says, still grinning that curious grin. Been riding. She reaches down to a carrier bag by her feet and pulls out a riding crop. She swishes it from side to side above the table.

Me and Eve laugh, a laugh that feels loaded. Andy laughs too, but a join the dots kind of laugh, like someone who doesn't quite get the joke. My mobile phone buzzes. I take it out of my pocket. It's Grace. I turn it off.

Eve puts her mouth near Andy's ear, says something quiet. His face does half a dozen quick little twitches as she whispers. I drink and look out the window as another red car goes past. I hear Andy clear his throat. I look back to them both. Eve is grinning. Andy twitches then says something so fucked I cough some barley wine back into my pint pot.

Say again?

Andy looks to his lap. Eve giggles. Andy takes another drink, puts his glass down, then glares at it. Twitch.

I said. Me and Eve. Are getting married next week. But Eve. Wants a last shag. With someone else. First.

I look from him to her and back again. I open my mouth to say something but I don't know what to say so I just laugh. Andy scowls and takes another drink. Twitch.

Eve leans over and kisses Andy's cheek. It occurs to me that he looks a bit mental.

She looks bladdered.

Oh Andy, don't be so miserable, she chirps, leaning into him. You can fuck someone else too, remember.

I laugh. She laughs. It's as though the whole fucking room laughs. All except for him.

Eve sways a little as she gets to her feet. She picks her stool up and puts it beside me. My heart bangbangs so loud in my ears it sounds like someone's playing a kick drum in the room upstairs.

Eve sits down next to me. Well? she says.

My cock stiffens in my jeans. Andy picks his stool up, plonks it down opposite me.

He sits, pulling a pack of fags from his combat jacket pocket. Twitch.

Well? says Eve again, her fingers tapping a horny Morse code on my leg.

My gut fills with mercury. I take a drink, then another. Eve's fingers tap higher up my thigh. My cock throbs in time to the kick drum. I glance at Eve. She's quite fit. She smiles, and her left eyeball goes a bit bozzy. I tell myself not to be such a coward.

I think it's a good idea, I say, putting my glass

down, feeling myself grin as I pour the last barley into it.

Andy offers me a fag, does another half dozen quick twitches as he lights it for me. I take this as a good sign. I take a drag, then put my hand on Eve's thigh as Andy flicks his ash, his eyebrows making a little V towards the bridge of his nose. He stares into the ashtray. Twitch.

Are you sure you want to do this? he says to Eve, his eyes now watching my hand move between her legs.

Oh Andy, she sings, curling her bottom lip down and pulling a sad pantomime face, You promised, remember?

He takes a drag on his fag, blowing the smoke out sharply towards his lap. Okay, he says, rubbing a hand across his forehead, As long as I'm there too. Twitch.

Eve answers for me. No. Just me and him. Here. In the bog.

He sits bolt upright, leans over the table grabbing her wrist.

No, he says. This is stupid. Come on. We're going. Twitch twitch.

OH-WAN-DEE, she moans, in a weird baby voice that makes her sound retarded, now pulling back against his grip. **WU PWOMISED!**

I DON'T CARE! he says, twitch twitch, yanking at her wrist again and standing up. **COME ON!**

WE'RE GOING! NOW!

This makes me angry. And I tell him so. I tell him he's not her fucking owner, and if she wants to fuck, then she wants to fuck, and he can go fuck himself.

HEY! she says, spinning around to face me, Andy still tugging at her wrist from across the table. **DON'T YOU TALK TO MY ANDY LIKE THAT!**

The next thirty-seconds are a little blurred. I know he shouts **BACK OFF!** and I chuck the rest of my drink at him. I also know she jumps on my back and starts scratching at my face like a psycho cat bitch as I land one on his nose. I also know the table turns over, and there's a sound of breaking glass. But the thing I know most is that punching a girl in the face when you have a hard-on is like nothing I know of.

They wouldn't serve me in The Bell because my face was bleeding. So I turned my phone on, rang Grace to come and fetch me, and on the way home I told her all about the idiots you meet when you're out for a pint, that I was sorry I buggered off, and that from now on we'd just have a quiet drink at home because I'm sick of it, sick to the back teeth of fucking idiots.

CHAPTER 61

And you will

Ask the neighbour round for a barbeque seeing as her husband is away on an oilrig again. And you will all sit in the sun eating pig and sweetcorn and chicken. And your kids are much older than her kids but they'll still play together. And you and Grace and the neighbour will drink a box of Liebfraumilch before five. And then you'll bomb down to the offy for another, and a twelve-pack to boot. And when you get back you and Grace will have a little set-to about the twelve-pack and the credit card bill. And you will say Oh c'mon, and Chill the fuck out will you? And the neighbour will say Back in a mo. And when she climbs back over the wall you'll see her pink knicker gusset as her leg swings over. And then you will feel a tightening in your cock. And she will say Look! I brought tarot cards! And then she will tell Grace's fortune. And you won't pay any attention and go paddling with the kids in an inflatable pool decorated with Simba and Pumbaa and Timon. And the neighbour will smile at you because you make her kids laugh. And by nine all three of you will be pretty pissed but only two of you will be smiling. And as the sun drops behind the rooftops the neighbour will take her kids for a bath and bed, and then Grace will usher Scarlett and Joe inside likewise saying No no no, it's school tomorrow. And you will carry on into the twelve-pack. And Grace will call Turn it down please from the bathroom window. And under your breath you will tell her to Go fuck herself as you turn Definitely Maybe down one-half of a notch. And when you sit back down on the still-warm plastic garden chair and put your bare feet on the table the neighbour will be smiling from her kids' bedroom window. And you will wave and blow her a kiss. And you will see her laugh through the glass but she won't blow you a kiss back. And by half-ten Grace and the neighbour will be back outside with you. And then you will throw wood onto the barbie. And then Grace will complain about the smoke. And you will ignore her, and continue to play accidental footsie under the table with the neighbour. And by eleven, Grace will say she's off to bed because she's up at six. And you will just say Bye and not persuade her otherwise. And when the backdoor closes the neighbour will say Your turn now and shuffle the tarot cards with slender fingers. And now she will say This is you, waving the Knight Of Wands in front of your face. And you will say Why? And she will say, A man below forty born under the sign of Aries. And now you will say How do you know I'm Aries the Ram? emphasising as you will, the Ram. And she will smile and say Oh, you'd be surprised what I know, and you will feel another tightening in your cock. And then she will say This is what covers you, placing down The Hierophant. And then she will say Weakness, and you will say Bollocks, and she will laugh and you will too, all the time still playing accidental footsie under the table. And now she will say This is what crosses you, placing the Nine Of Swords upside-down on your Knight Of Wands. And she will smile and you will say What? and then she will say Imprisonment, ha ha. And now you will both drink, and then refill your glasses with Liebfraumilch, putting Fleetwood Mac's Rumours on the CD player because she likes that one, and yes, you will both sing the hook-line to Second Hand News, then look at each other for longer than is usual for people who aren't shagging. And then she will say This is what crowns you, putting the Five Of Wands above your Knight Of Wands saying Struggle. And you will laugh at this saying Too fucking right. And now she will say This is beneath you as she places The Fool on the table causing you both to laugh long and loud until she pats your hand saying, A lack of understanding, Billy. And now you will light a fag, drink, hooking your ankles around her bare heels. And now there will be a silence bar Fleetwood Mac as you watch the colour rise soft in her cheeks before she sits upright moving her feet away. And then she will say This is behind you, dropping the Page Of Pentacles upside-down on the table saying Cursed by a bad omen. And you will place one leg by hers until your skin touches saying Well, this is going really well isn't it? which will make her laugh again as you top both your drinks up. And then she will drink and so will you. And now she will say This is in front of you, putting down the Six Of Swords saying, A voyage. And you will say Where are you taking me, Alice? And she will blush softly again but look into your eyes all the same saying, It's more where you're taking yourself, Billy. And you will say Oh. And then she will say This is you, and place Judgement onto the table, saying Consequences for past deeds, and you will say Great, I'm fucked then, and she will smile but not look at you. And now she will say This is your home, putting an upside-down Ten Of Cups onto the table, laughing, and you saying What? and her saying Quarrels, Funny, you will say. And then she will say This is your hope, placing the burning Sun in front of you both saying Well, happiness, and you saying But I am happy, stroking your toe down her bare leg. And now she will smile, saying And this is your future, and The Devil will have both a man and a woman naked and chained to his cloven-hoofed legs, his black eyes staring out at you from the tarot card, and you will say Oh, I was hoping for The Lovers, and then, Want to play something else?

CHAPTER 62

Truth or dare?

Truth, she says, and so I ask her.

I was having my hair washed, she says, and I came. Right in the shop. The girl asked me if the water was too hot. Or something.

She drinks. I drink. We both drink, then, Dare, I say.

Kiss my arse, she says. So I do. Right on the pocket button.

I drink. She drinks. I top us both up.

Truth, she says, and so I ask her.

I'd have to say my husband, she says. Though these days he prefers toys. I prefer real ones.

She drinks. I drink. We both drink, then, Dare, I say.

Kiss my face, she says. So I do. Her chin tilts, just.

I drink. She drinks. I pour us another.

Truth, she says, and so I ask her.

She says, You. Sometimes.

She drinks. I drink. We both drink then, Do you think he's faithful? Truth, she says.

So I tell her.

CHAPTER 63

She's a FUCKIN LIAR!

Listen, Grace… Last night as soon as you'd gone in it were truth or dare kiss my arse and that, the nights are getting cold and that barbie's gone out, so over the wall blue label next-door this duty-free litre we're talking and that, and dancing and that, and she's saying stuff and I'm saying stuff, then me like a twat goes to kiss her again and I'm sorry and I'm stupid but I'm totally hammered and now it's fuckoff, she's pushing me out and I'm like **WHAT?** Then all day been thinking thinking done nothing at work rough as fuck and I'm thinking I'll tell you tonight when it's right when both kids are in bed, then this afto back home, let the dog out when **BANG!** there she is all daggers and deadeye and face red as fuck, so I ask her What's up? and she's practically yelling **CAN'T Y'REMEMBER? CAN'T Y'REMEMBER?** and I know exactly what she's on about but I don't want a scene so I just say Look… **BASTARD** she says (What?) **BASTARD** she says. So I'm thinking wait on and I'm telling her so, saying

YOU TELLING STORIES OF FIRST COMES AND DILDOS HOW LONELY YOU GET AND WHY DON'T WE DANCE AND WHY DON'T WE DANCE and I'm stupid I know but KERPOW chucks me out turns out, she's only gone and rung him in DUFUCKINBAI telling him Billy did this and Billy said that and if I were you I'd stay behind that FUCKIN WALL cos he's flying back tomorrow and he's NOT FUCKIN HAPPY and I swear to you now as I did do to her, I never said SHIT he were shagging Dubai, I said, I. Don't. Know. I DON'T KNOW? she says, I KNOW ONE THING...

CHAPTER 64

This is the way

The house shuddered and wheeled, passing out before birdsong, to when the kids twitched and stir, eyes at the half-open, door-hesitant and sleep-slow, finding a path barefoot past this aluminium that glass, stopping only to look at the broken chair, each other, a dad curled up on the dog shelf, the fire that was, now grey ash and bottle tops, this is the way, again, Cocopops and too much milk, a balancing act up a narrow staircase, get into bed with Mum, don't spill.

CHAPTER 65

You suppose home is where the heart is

And now you've moved into this new house you suppose things can only get better, given time. You also suppose you've made your bed, and surely, every woman has to put up with her man being a dickhead every now and then. Like they say, you pays your money and takes your choice, but when he throws a sickie like he did last week, again, it worries you loads, because now you've taken on a bigger mortgage you've got more to lose, and as per, you seem to be shouldering all the weight. Again.

Worrying about things never did anyone any good though, did it. But then again, what if things always end up going bad, and he never gets any better? It's like you're both just going round in circles.

He stops. He starts. He fucks up.

But, you suppose, it's like your grandma used to say, what you lose on the swings, you gain on the roundabouts. What goes up, must come down.

Although sometimes you wish to good-God-all-friggin-mighty he'd just find normal for more than one blue moon a month, and actually stay there.

But, least said soonest mended etc, and anyway, God knows you know by now that if you say something when he's on one it'll only make him worse. So best let sleeping dogs lie and all that. Unless of course he's on a downer, and needs to talk, needs to say he's sorry, needs to make those all-important promises. Which, when you think about it, you know he'll always break.

Funny. Though it isn't. It'll never cease to amaze you the things he tells you. But then again, truth really is stranger than fiction. And at least he tells you the truth, hearing it straight from the horse's mouth, so to speak. Which is tons better than hearing it from someone else. Like your mother for instance.

What is it they say? Seeing is believing? Well, you'll never believe what your mum said Joyce Farmer's husband said he saw Billy doing to that pub letterbox back where you used to live. So there you go. Seeing is believing. Although you certainly don't believe your mum will ever see the good in Billy. Or that someone could actually shit into a letterbox.

All said, you suppose it's quite simple. You're stuck between The Devil and the deep blue sea, but Joe and Scarlett need a dad, so no way you're just going throw the baby out with the bathwater and leave him, are you.

No. You need to make the best of what you've got, and remember them that live in glass houses shouldn't come downstairs and tell him to get to bed because he has work in a few hours then try and grab the can from his hand. Because it's right, it is better the devil you know. Even if he does scare you when he's like that. Sticks and stones may break your bones, but when he calls you a cunt in front of your kids it still hurts.

You suppose he's getting worse again. There's no smoke without fire and yesterday you found three empty vodka bottles in his sock drawer, so you're going to have to take the rough with the smooth, even if sometimes when you make love, he just fucks.

Into every life a little rain must fall.

This'll be the third mattress you've had.

CHAPTER 66

On the fifth day of Xmas

What did my true love give to me? I ask Joy, seeing as it's my turn to ask.

Grace's mother sucks her flabby jowls in and wobbles her head from side to side. She looks like she's just eaten a whole lemon, sour-faced fucker she is, rind and all.

You shouldn't say Xmas, she says.

I take a drink.

Why?

She says, Because it takes the Christ out of Christmas.

Grace shuffles in her seat.

Grace's brother Victor nods in agreement as Scarlett and Joe busy themselves with a Chinese puzzle from a cracker.

Grace's younger sister Hope puts a Quality Street in her mouth. I watch her lips for a second, hearing myself sigh, the pissiness hissing out of me like a car tyre on Mischievous Night.

Joy glares at me across the table. I look away and

flip the card over to check the answer.

It's for a piece of pie, Mum! sings Grace, trying to stick the pin back into the hand grenade.

Fuck. I hate Christmas. Who's idea was it to play Trivial Pursuits? Couldn't we have just watched Goldfinger? I put the card on the table and drink. Yum. Tullamore Dew.

C'mon Mum, says Hope, her thin voice ever on tiptoes.

She's well fuckable, but Christ her voice. She sounds like one of those floaty-gobbed mediums, breathing questions into the air for the dead to answer. Must be all those years of living with her mother.

I look at Joy. She smiles, and her lips look like two earthworms fucking.

Five. Gold. Rings, she says triumphantly, like she's just discovered penicillin, the atom, and the absolute Biblical proof that her son-in-law is Satan.

I flip the card over and look at the answer again, fighting the tug of a smirk.

Sorry. The answer says Five *golden* rings.

I pass the die to Victor. Scarlett and Joe are giggling into their palms.

Victor passes the die back to his mother.

Close enough, he says, Grace rifling the bag for a pink piece of pie.

Poor Victor. Cadfael bald-patch at thirty. Still living with his mother. No girlfriend. Face like pig-farmer's bucket.

Here you go Mum, says Grace, slotting the pie into her mother's pie-holder.

Joy shakes the die again, smug-fuck look on her face, turbulence from her bingo-wings shivering her dress, udders shuddering somewhere below the table.

I drink, get up to change the CD. Hope starts telling Grace about her reflexology class.

Your foot has pressure points that are connected to the rest of your body, she breathes. Inside, and out.

Before reflexology it was aromatherapy. And before that acupuncture. She never sticks at anything for longer than a month or two. Grace says her sister is trying to find herself. I have no idea what that means.

I pull Screamadelica from the CD cupboard, smiling as I press play because I know it'll annoy the fuck out of Joy. I busy myself with drinks in the kitchen while Scarlett asks Joy her question.

Grandma, what are you if you're myopic?

Oh! I know this one! says Grace.

She's so cute when she gets excited about stuff. She sounds twelve.

In the kitchen, I drink from the bottle.

My-opic, myyy-opic, says Joy through the chomp of another Quality Street.

Joe appears by my side so I take the bottle from my mouth, fill my glass and grin at him. Is there anymore Tango? he says.

Joe helps me carry the drinks through into the front room. Scarlett says, No Grandma, it's near-sighted.

She shows Joy the card.

Well, short-sighted is the same thing, Joy says, Victor grunting his agreement.

I knew that, says Grace.

I put everyone's drinks in front of them. Joy shakes the die again, her flabby jowls working yet another Quality Street. In front of her stand ten wrappers twisted into ten little foil goblets. Five more wrappers wait by her elbow to be twisted in her fat fingers. She lands on the blue pie square, singing OOH! PIE AGAIN!

No kidding.

Victor slides a question card from the box.

Right Mum, says Victor in his stupid too-serious question master voice, What city's main thoroughfare is O'Connell Street?

Easy, I say.

Joy ignores me. Grace smiles. She looks quite cute in that Santa hat. I bought her some red crotchless knickers for Christmas. A dildo too.

OOH! EDINBURGH! yelps Joy, nodding her fat head and picking the die up.

WRRRONG! I sing. It's Dublin.

I raise my glass and toast to Erin go bragh. I knock it back in one.

Oh, I forgot you're Irish now aren't you, spikes

Joy, Victor snorting his fake laugh.

Pogue mahone, I grin. In my mind is a ripple of applause.

What does that mean? asks Hope.

She has nice eyes too. Big and brown like Grace's. But sad looking. I bet they look great when she comes.

Kiss my arse, I tell her.

Hope laughs. I watch her eyes narrow then close. That's how she'd come.

Victor shakes the die. The look on his face as he moves his counter is the same look he wears when he watches the horses. It's somewhere between stifled rage and desperation. His eyes narrow to the size of a blackbird's, his mouth to the shape of an Alsatian's bum-hole. He's the worst gambler I've ever known. It's a badly-kept secret that his mother took his credit cards off him. In a two-horse race he'd back the one called Glue.

Yellow, he says, sucking air through his Alsatian-hole. History.

He squints like he's doing a difficult shit as Joe slides a question card out of the box. Joe's eyes scan the words, his mouth moving slightly as he takes the words in. I drink. My son clears his throat.

Uncle Victor. In Genesis, who married his half-sister Sarah?

I'm about to say something about Phil Collins being a dirty fucker but I stop myself.

Joe says, What's a half-sister?

I get up, glass in hand.

Drinks? I say, looking at no one.

A mumble of no's send me off into the kitchen as Grace explains to Joe what a half-sister is. I see a flash of Claire on her knees. I shake my head as though shaking an Etch-A-Sketch.

Tullamore Dew is very easy to drink.

I hear Joe go **URRR THAT'S SICK TO MARRY YOUR HALF-SISTER!**

I take the bottle from my mouth and top my glass up. Joy tells Joe that we have to forgive Noah, because the Bible was written a long time ago, and things were different back then.

I put the bottle back to my lips.

R.E. at school. Lot's wife being told not to look back, but she does. God turning her into salt. Lot taking his daughters to a cave. They get him pissed. Then fuck him.

I screw the top back on the bottle and I hear Grace saying Sorry to Joe, that it was Abraham not Noah. Joy goes Ooh, sorry Jojo.

I go back into the front room, drink, put my glass on the table, sit down. Is a bad thing not a bad thing if you don't know you're doing it?

I look at Scarlett, her tongue poking out the corner of her mouth as she tugs at the Chinese puzzle.

Joe sits flicking Joy's goblets into a bowl of peanuts.

Billy.

Billy.

I look across to Grace.

Your go, she says, pointing to the die in front of me, question card poised in her hand.

I shake, and land on brown.

Right Billy. According to Bau-de-laire, whose loveliest trick is to convince us that he doesn't exist?

I drink.

The song has finished.

It's quiet, and everyone looks at me.

———

We leave the blinds open because the snow has started to fall, flickering specks caught in the orange glow of the streetlamp. Grace has the crotchless knickers on and I'm fucking her from behind, and with my right hand, I nudge the dildo between her arse-cheeks. I rock on my knees, Grace holding the rail at the bottom of the bed as I push the dildo in a little.

No! she whisper-shouts, Don't like it!

I take it out and carry on fucking her, my left hand on her hipbone, the now-wet sides of the slit-crotch knickers rubbing the length of my cock as I push in, pull out.

Outside, the snow falls faster in the orange glow, looking like shivering bacteria in the eye of a microscope as I push the dildo up my arse, the orange-lit bacteria shivering faster as I move the dildo in and out, a mechanism of Holy-fuck between the three of us: me, Grace and the dildo, a perfect symphony of rubber and flesh, each pushing against the other as the other pulls back, and as the streetlamp fades to black, I see Hope's sad brown eyes closing with the come, and Grace low-moans, and the picture changes to Scarlett, and I shake my fucking head till the Etch-A-Sketch changes to slate, but too fucking late, *And he knew not when she lay down, or when she arose*, and my arse-lips push-kiss the dildo back out, falling unseen and shitty onto the pillow in the half-light, and some things you don't even have to see but you know, you just fucking know.

Door locked

Key hidden.

Throw clotheshorse at her.

Leave by kitchen window.

Pub.

I get into town early

Have a couple. And when he gets there he's brought a girl. She's called Jane. She's a punk single mum with green eyes. Me and Jane talk while Curtis gets them in. Jane has a big smile. Curtis gets back from the bar laughs too much. I think there's something else.

We walk up to the next one in the rain. Jane walks in the middle with a brolly. We link like a chain. I fancy Guinness and a Jameson. I think Curtis is going to tell me something. Inside I look out. The fountain is lit. I run a joke through my head I don't say.

Jane talks of how she met Curtis ten years ago. That's nine more than me. Jane buys the next round insists she can afford it. We all have double vodkas the jukebox is loud. Jane and Curtis are dancing. Two old men are watching from the snug. Fuck em.

This pub is quieter. We sit near a pool table. Jane is funny. Curtis says he's queer. I laugh and say Whatever, mine's a barley wine (five in the last).

We watch Jane piss in the church doorway. She sidles like a crab. She leaves pissy footprints on God's flagstones. She sings Space Oddity at the moon. She puts her hand down the back of my jeans. I copy.

Jane lives in a rented room. A big old house on the edge of town. Her room is at the top near a dirty kitchen. A scruffy old blonde with too much rouge is smoking a cigarette by a dirty sink. She hugs Curtis by name.

And this is Jane's landlady Marjorie. And I am Curtis's friend from work. Marjorie's teeth are yellow. Jane says she'll only be a minute. She comes back in pyjamas. They're striped.

We drink tea from a dirty kettle. Curtis and Marjorie laugh lung-bleeders. Jane says she's tired, takes me to see her room.

Jane has lots of records. Crass. The Damned. Discharge. The Fall.

Jane gets into bed. Jane says turn the light off. The streetlamp looks red. She has a wide kiss. She has a soft lumpy tit. She has a kid. Where's the kid?

Jane says Be quick, pulls her pyjamas down yanking my belt pulling down my pants and jeans in one, Come on, her big tongue my fingers inside she's bending my cock down up inside she lets go of breath, says Don't let them hear, What about the? Come, she says, Injection, she says, What? It's okay, Come, Just, Come, Just be, Quick.

The light snaps on and the landlady squawks.

Curtis is gob-smacked, Jane is laughing, I'm trying to pull my trousers up, Going I'm going, and the landlady's yelling of men and bastards, over the banister, down the stairs, and the night is cold and the moon is red and Curtis says, What in the name of fuck were you thinking?

Death, I tell him, And the taxi costs more than I got, yeh?

CHAPTER 69

Now you are looking at

*A black and horny Devil scaling the church organ
pipes like a cloven-hoofed spider, who now sits
astride the big bass pipe, leering, knowing, and it's
in his eyes, black and blacker, looking into what
you are, into what you have become, a yellow-
toothed grin breaking its black scaly face like a rip
in a rain-pregnant cloud, and you know, and The
Devil knows, and the moon reaches white fingers
bruise-purpled through stained glass, the church
now Hell's hub spinning the night earth faster,
moon-eye through that window, now that window,
now that window, the Saviour picking up his cross,
carrying it up to the hilltop, nails now driven
through feet and hands, The Devil laughing like
shards of glass hitting a marble floor, and he will
show you the everything and all, a kaleidoscope of
jag-rope sins that cannot be unseen, and you are
falling, grabbing at nothing as that stone-slab floor
cracks open, and this is where you belong, down
down to the sound of iron and chain, of teeth-*

grinding cogs in flicker-lit shadow, of...

GRACE (*off screen*): Billy. Billy. Wake up.

And now we are looking at Billy and Grace's bedroom. A chair lies on its side. A broken pot dog lays headless under the curtained window. A can of Guinness toppled and black-spewed by the bed. Grace, dressed in black work clothes and frown, stands over the curled crumple of Billy, half-covered by the flowery duvet, still dressed in yesterday's scuffed jeans and booze-spattered Celtic shirt. A low groan.

GRACE (*soft-shaking Billy*): Get up. It's seven-thirty.

BILLY (*groans*): Can't.

GRACE (*shaking him a little harder*): **GET UP!**

BILLY (*pulling a pillow over his head*): Can't.

And now we see Grace kicking the bedpost, leaving the room by a swinging door that clatters its brass knob against the wall, Billy now turning over slow onto his belly, peeping out from under the pillow for a moment to glimpse the scene.

BILLY (*disappearing back under the pillow*): Fuck.

*We watch for one whole minute as the clock ticks.
From outside, we can hear the birds sing, the low
dull rumble of traffic. Billy twitches, as though
bitten by midges.*
*Heavy footsteps on the stairs. Then Grace enters
the room with a coffee cup in her hand.*

GRACE (*placing the cup on the bedside table*):
Drink this. Get up. Go to work.

BILLY (*from under the pillow*): Can't.

GRACE (*slapping the bed*): **GET UP! NOW!
YOU'LL GET THE FUCKING SACK IF YOU
DON'T GO IN AGAIN! GET UP!**

BILLY (*from under the pillow*): I think last night,
I...

GRACE (*making for the door*): **WHATEVER!
JUST GET UP! NOW!**

BILLY (*from under the pillow*): But...

GRACE (*exiting*): **GET UP!**

We hear Grace heavy-footing down the stairs. The

clock ticks. We hear a door slam.

BILLY (*from under the pillow*): Fuck.

We see the bedside clock tick: seven-forty, eight o'clock, a quarter past ten, the clock stops.

And now you are trying to leave the dark woods by a bramble-strewn path that scratches your naked body. Ahead you see the thinning of the trees, a clearing in the half-light, and beyond this, a hillside blessed in a golden blush of sunlight, this perfect treeless hill that rises up and up into the light. You run, stumbling, kicking against the thorny undergrowth, your skin ripped by a thousand tiny claws, the blood now wet-warm down your legs, the sound of your own breathing a thin desperate echo, and then, you stop. In the clearing stands the lion, the wolf, and the leopard. They begin their slow lope towards you, and you try to scream.

BILLY (*waking with start*): Christ.

And now we are looking at Billy sat up in bed, slow-lifting the duvet, a dark flower of piss blossoming across his jeans.

CHAPTER 70

It's the Garden of Eden

It's from a Flemish tapestry called The Original Sin, says Curtis.

The three of us are standing halfway up his stairs looking at the picture.

I look at Curtis's face for a moment with its little moustache and twinkly blue eyes. The sound of a violin meows softly from somewhere above and I sense Grace fidgeting on the step below. I turn back to the picture.

There's two Eves, I say.

Curtis explains that the first Eve in the background, watched by the serpent, takes the apple from the tree, and then in the foreground, the other Eve gives it Adam to try.

It's the Tree Of Knowledge, Curtis says, pointing to the apple tree.

I ask Curtis why it's called that. He says it's because it grew the fruit of all knowledge, both good and evil, and anyone that ate from it had the knowledge of God. Hence, it's the Forbidden Fruit, he says, spreading his arms wide as though to say ta-daa.

I'm tempted to crack a joke about forbidden fruit in his direction but I don't. It makes him act even gayer when I say stuff like that.

What's the bird for? I ask, pointing to a red-yellow parrot in the picture.

Dunno, he says.

And the lion?

Dante, I think, he says, smiling.

I don't know what the fuck he's on about but I say Oh anyway.

This is the way of things between me and Curtis, him talking arty-farty bollocks and me saying Oh. It gets a bit annoying at times. Sometimes at work he calls me Eliza, like that thick cockney bint in that film, says he has to show me the way. It bugs me when he acts all queer with me in front of people at work.

Funny. He thought he was telling me something I didn't know last week when he said he was bent.

We carry on up the stairs towards the violin and I wonder if all bummers are like this, all classical music and arty shit. Then for a second I travel back and see cousin Raymond's hand turning the pages of a Batman comic, and then on the bus ride home with Nannan, a Spiderman sticker in my hand. A prize for not telling. Kerpow.

Curtis takes us into the front room of his flat,

where the violin snakes around the picture-covered walls like a sugared worm.

Nice, says Grace, looking around the room.

Why, thank a-you, says Curtis bowing theatrically, his little moustache thinning across the top of his thin grin. Grace asks him how long he's lived here and he starts to tell her a little life story. Grace and Curtis have got to know each other quite well over the last few weeks since he started giving me lifts home from work, inviting himself in for a cup of tea, getting matey with my kids, Grace insisting he stops for something to eat, and Ooh let's have a game of Scrabble. It's become a regular thing. Not that I've had any say in it. Grace said she likes having Curtis around. She says he's good for me.

Funny. If Curtis hadn't asked me out last week I wouldn't be in this shit now.

He disappears into his little blue kitchen, tells me and Grace to make ourselves at home. We sit on a brown leather settee and Grace looks around the room again. I put my hand on Grace's. She smiles.

Everything feels backwards. I didn't want to do this. I told Grace as much. Left to me I'd have just said fuck it, but Grace told me we should let Curtis help sort it out, then we could forget about it and get back to normal. Funny how I always feel closer to Grace when I've fucked up.

From the kitchen is the sound of a spoon clinking a cup, a kettle boiling then clicking off. Grace squeezes my hand as we lean back into the sofa. The violin is replaced by a flute. It sounds like something from a fairy tale. I close my eyes for a second and I imagine I'm in a wood, the moon full between bare branches above. Everywhere, red eyes peek at me from behind trees. I'm running.

Here we go, sings Curtis, placing a tray of four blue mugs on the carpet. Sorry it's instant, he says, The coffee-maker's buggered.

A door bangs shut below.

My heart beats faster.

Ah, just in time, says Curtis with a smile.

The door swings open and there she is. Jane glances at me then hugs Curtis. She looks a little different to what I remember. She lets go of Curtis then looks to Grace. Jane looks nervous. I stand up, and for some reason I shake her hand. She looks a little surprised. We both say Hello then she turns to Grace and says, Nice to meet you. I get a sudden flashback of Jane pissing in the Crooked Spire doorway. Grace says Nice to meet you too.

Curtis claps his hands together as me and Jane sit down.

Sonata Number Eight in C Minor, methinks, he says, and busies himself by the stereo.

Me, Grace and Jane sip our coffee, no one making eye-contact, the air between us no less the heavier for the pathetic tinkly piano now pitter-pattering the room.

What the fuck am I doing here?

Curtis puts himself in an old chair with embroidered patterns swirling all over it, sighs, then says smiling, Beethoven. Beautiful, beautiful, Beethoven.

Jane creaks in her leather chair as she bends to put her coffee on the floor. Curtis clears his throat.

Right then, he says, Let's get this daft little mess sorted, shall we? He smiles and nods at each of us in turn. Okay. Jane and I have spoken about this, and we both feel it's for the best if we get it all out into the open so we can all move on and be friends again, without any awkward atmosphere spoiling things. Sound good to everyone?

Jane smiles weakly.

The word friends makes my jaw tighten.

The piano tinkles. Curtis looks to Jane.

Jane?

Jane clears her throat then glances at Grace.

Grace. I want to say I'm sorry about what happened. I didn't mean to hurt you. I was really drunk. I'm Sorry.

Grace smiles tightly, then nods.

Thank you, Jane.

I look at the carpet for a moment, my toes curling in my trainers.

Jane says my name. I look up at her. She looks down at her lap.

Billy. I know you were drunk too. And that you

didn't know what you were doing. So I want you to know that I won't be putting any blame on you. And like Curtis said, I'd just like to move on and forget about it.

My head swims a little. I feel a heat in my gut. When I speak, the words feel like they come from outside of me.

What do you mean, blame?

Jane looks up, her big green witch-eyes saying something I don't understand. I'm struck with how odd-looking she is, how big her mouth is, how her head seems too big for her body. She looks back to her lap. Curtis coughs.

Look, he says. We were all drunk. Shit happens. And Jane is being good enough to let things go, so let's take it from there Billy, and get onto fixing things.

I glance at Grace. She's frowning. Curtis raises his eyebrows to me in some gesture of encouragement. I feel the heat rise like a midge-cloud in my belly.

I hear Grace say, Well, we'd like to put it behind us too.

I put my coffee mug on a little table by the settee and Curtis jumps up, collecting a blue coaster from a little pile on the mantelpiece. He puts one on the table then puts my cup on it.

Antique, he says.

My gut is still burning.

What do you mean, blame? What are you saying?

Jane blinks but doesn't look up. Curtis says my name. He pats the air in front of him.

Billy, listen. Let's be calm about this. Okay, granted, Jane admits she was drunk, and can't remember that much about it, but... He pauses, looking up to the ceiling as though trying to catch sight of the right words.

Curtis shrugs.

I stare at Jane. I feel Grace squeeze my hand. Jane won't look at me. I say her name. It feels hot in my mouth.

I don't get it. Blame?

Jane doesn't look up.

Billy, says Curtis softly, Jane's being good enough to let it go, so if I were you...

I've stopped listening. On my way downstairs I pull the picture of Eden off the wall and throw it at the door. I tell Grace to watch her step as we leave, her hand tightening in mine as I pull her over the threshold, up the garden path to the roadside, where the low sun strikes white off the car bonnet, Oh Billy, she says.

CHAPTER 71

Myself am Hell?

John the vicar waits for me to answer, raising a thick curly eyebrow, a soft smile spreading thin across his mottled face. I look down into my lap. I've no idea why I came here. I've no idea why I even knocked on his door, why I felt the need to come and tell him these things. All I know is that something black and heavy sits in my belly, making everything black, so black and so heavy that I can't carry it anymore.

What do you mean? I mumble, the effort of speech feeling like lifting a large rock above my head.

It's from Milton, he smiles, And it seems to me Billy, that what you're experiencing here, is guilt, which is a Hell that you make for yourself, a Hell that seems inescapable until you address the root of it, the cause of it, if you will.

I don't have a fucking clue who Milton is. But the words seem to make some kind of sense. I've felt like this before. I know I have. But this one won't go away. People at work are avoiding me. Curtis has been spreading shit. I know he has. I hate people. I want to be left alone, but I hate myself. Myself am Hell.

Have you been drinking today? John says.

Yeh.

Do you drink every day, Billy?

Sometimes.

Hmm, he says, raising a thick curly eyebrow. And do you find that your, erm, messing things up, as you put it, coincides with your drinking?

After a moment or two, I nod, because there's no getting away from it. Even so, and I can't explain it, but the sense that it's not just the drink is, and always has been, a dog chewing at my gut.

I look up from my lap and at the man who married me and Grace all that time ago. He's waiting for me to say something.

I've been with other women, I mumble, feeling the rock's weight again, And I feel bad about it.

I see, he says, rubbing his chin.

He waits for more, and for some reason I give it.

I got into a situation with a neighbour, and it went wrong. And then I got into something with a friend's friend. That went wrong too. And there's been others.

Something jags in my throat. I feel like a little boy. I feel pathetic and I hate myself.

John reaches over to his desk. I look up and he has a Bible in his lap. He frowns, licks his thumb, then flicks the pages over until he finds what he's looking for. He looks up from the page.

Can I read you something? he says.

I shrug. John looks to the Bible.

For God has done what the law, weakened by the flesh, could not do, sending his own Son in the likeness of sinful flesh and for sin. Thus he condemned sin in the flesh, in order that the law might be fulfilled in us, who walk not according to the flesh but to the Spirit. For those who live according to the flesh set their minds on the things of the flesh, but those who live according to the Spirit set their minds on the things of the Spirit. To set the mind on the flesh is death, but to set the mind on the Spirit is life and peace. For the mind that is set on the flesh is hostile to God, it does not submit to God's law, indeed it cannot, and those who are in the flesh cannot please God.

John looks up from the page and at me. His bushy eyebrows raise again. To set the mind on flesh is death, but to set the mind on the Spirit, is life, and peace. Do you see, Billy?

I look to my lap again, to my hands as my fingers join like church, like steeple. I say nothing.

Listen, he says softly, Human beings have an innate rebelliousness, in that we fight against the spiritual, the Godly. Saint Aquinas once said there can be sin in the will of every creature, considering the condition of its nature. Does that make sense, Billy?

I shrug again. I have no answer. John continues.

The poet Shelley called The Devil, Nature, and for me, this is the crux of the matter, that we all have this constant tension within us to do the wrong thing, to act on this Nature, this compulsion, which some would say is the very Devil himself speaking to us, tempting us.

John pauses, as though waiting for me to say something. I don't know what to say.

Can I ask you, Billy, do you accept God at all? He says this leaning forward and putting his prayer-ready hands between my face and lap.

No, I say, not even having to think about it.

I reach to my side where half a cup of cold tea sits on a three-legged table with a crucifix carved on it. I drink. I want a drink that isn't this drink. I want to get out of here. Soon.

You know, says John, If you accept God into your life, you'd be surprised how much of your burden he'd lift.

But I don't believe in God, I tell him, And I don't believe in Heaven, or…

Billy, he says, holding flat palms towards me, If you let yourself enter the Community of Faith, if you accepted the word of God, I can promise you that very quickly you would receive forgiveness through Jesus, who died then rose again, proving death is not the end, proving that whatever you've done, whatever bad deeds you've committed, God will forgive you, and lift your burden, because in the same way as Jesus showed us that death is not the end, God can show you that the Hell you're in right now is not the end for you, that you can rise again, in a new life, happy and peaceful, and all you have to do is to accept God. Do you see that, Billy?

John puts his hand on my knee. I twitch and he moves it.

I ask John what Jesus did wrong, and he blinks.

What do you mean? he says, his bushy eyebrows moving towards each other.

You said something about sin, and how God gave his son to show us about sin, or something.

John looks up to the ceiling. A grandfather clock in the corner ticks. Outside the window, sparrows flicker about on a bird table. A bus rattles by and the sparrows fly off.

Jesus died, says John, still looking at the ceiling, So God could show us that we were born into sin, and that through his redemption, we could be born again into Heaven, which is why he sent his only son to die for us. John closes his eyes a moment. When he opens them again he's looking at me.

So Jesus didn't do anything bad then? I say.

John sighs, frowns, then smiles. His smile is less soft than before. He picks at the seam of his trouser leg with one hand, his other rolling a soft drum-roll on the fat arm of his chair.

No, he says. It's a symbol of redemption. Of how

we are born within the grip of the Original Sin, of how Adam and Eve...

I stop listening for a moment. I see the picture on Curtis's staircase. The tree. The apple. The snake watching Eve.

...So when Jesus died and then rose again, God was showing us how to escape this sinful grip. Do you see?

Why didn't God want Adam and Eve to eat from the Tree Of Knowledge?

John coughs, then looks up to the ceiling again.

Because if they did, which they did do, they'd have the knowledge of God, of the everything, but more importantly, they'd have knowledge of all the evil man is capable of, which then gave them an awareness of sin.

I think about this a moment.

Why didn't God want them to know? I ask.

John shuffles in his chair. He looks a little annoyed.

You have children don't you, Billy? John says, smiling tightly.

I nod.

Well, as a parent you keep certain things from your children, don't you? Because they're simply not ready to know everything that you know, are they? It's like that with Adam and Eve. They just weren't ready to know, and they needed to put their trust in God. And they didn't, which is why we're all born into sin. Do you understand that, Billy?

I look out the window. Everything tumbles at me at once. We're fucked from the start. We arrive guilty without having done anything wrong. And according to John, we then have to live the dullest life imaginable. Just keep praying and keep clean. Keep dull dull fucking dull in the thin hope that some unseen God lets us off with the bad things we haven't even done so he can open his sparkly fucking gates for us. I don't buy it. At all. There is no God, just some fuckarsed rulebook invented by lying self-righteous bastards that wait around every street corner sharpening their tiny daggers of spite, itching to stab you in the face in some fuckarsed idea of truth, a truth that's so because a thousand and three backhand whispers down a thousand and three council estate jennels made it so: he did this, he did that, he did the fucking other. Fuck it. Life, is a fucking cesspit. Full of two-faced cowardly bastards who'll suck you off behind closed doors then run down the street screaming rape because they can't deal with the truth that every single fucking one of them is just as dirty a bastard as every fucker else.

I shake John's hand, leaving with little else said other than I'll think about joining his Community of Faith, which I won't, because now I know, know that I have to do something, and it has nothing to do with some stupid fuckarsed God. No. What I have to do is for my kids, because they need me, need me to protect them from a world full of lying cunts.

Outside John's gate, a stray mongrel pads up the street growling. I go to kick it in the face but it runs off. I'm beginning to understand. I need to get straight. Get sober. Get sharp.

CHAPTER 72

Hello, my name is Billy

And I think I'm an alcoholic. I glance around the circle of faces as I say it. At the slurry tramp with the fag-stained beard who ate nail-polish remover on bread, at the skull-headed sparrow-woman with pock-marked skin who's trying to get her kids back, at the forty-something salesman in a tie that says World's Greatest Dad who throws empties into the field behind his house then goes back in the dark hunting for dregs, at the redhead with the cleavage who says she's tired of giving herself away, at the twitchy bald bloke who never looks up and won't say what he's done, at the smiley old grey-haired black gadge with the gold front tooth who's been dry for thirteen years, at the pin-and-ink teardrop lesbo with no fingernails who beat her girlfriend unconscious with an ironing board, at the redhead with the cleavage, who smiles a smile that says Go on then, say it.

I feel myself take a breath.

I came here because I want to stop drinking.

I haven't had a drink for two days.

A burst of applause soft clatters around the room like starlings leaving one tree for another.

I take another breath.

I'm stopping drinking for my kids. They need me.

I glance around the circle again as I get another smattering of applause.

And for yourself Billy, says the black gadge, nodding sagely to a dull hum of agreement that bluebottles around the room.

Tell us your story, squeaks the sparrow-woman.

The dull hum bluebottles the room again. My palms are sweaty. I clear my throat.

Things turns to shit when I drink. My wife wanted me to stop ages ago. She says it makes me different. Like I'm a different person.

The bluebottle dull hums, and I'm surprised at how much I want to say these things.

I get sad. Like life has no sunlight. Then I drink even more. Get angry. Sadder. I end up hurting people.

The bluebottle dull hums again. I look at the shoelace on my left shoe. It's undone.

Go on Billy, says the redhead softly, Tell us.

My hands are twitching in my lap. And for some reason I see Nannan's hands, knitting needles tap-tapping, a quick tug to loosen more wool from the ball by her feet, tap-tap, tap-tap.

I clear my throat again. I can feel everyone watching. I want to say more things so I pretend no one is there.

A couple of years ago, I went to see Nannan in hospital. She was really ill. I'd fell out with my mum and dad. Still have. I said some things to them when I was drunk. I've done it loads of times. I guess they've had enough. Anyway, my dad rang me to tell me Nannan was sick. That it didn't look good. That I should go and visit her. But to be out of there before my mum and him went. He said my mum couldn't cope with seeing me. That she was too upset. So I caught the bus into town. Had a few before I went to the hospital. And when I got there I was pissed. And late. I only had twenty minutes before my mum and dad were due. I fell over a waste-bin in the hospital corridor. Got into a row with a nurse. And when I finally got to Nannan she was asleep. Inside this big plastic tent thing. She had a plastic mask on too. The noise of it was fucking awful. I sat down by her bed and just looked at her. She looked so old. And I couldn't make my mind up whether it was because she was so sick or ... or because I hadn't seen her in such a long time. And then, she just woke up and stared at me. And I think she tried to smile but I couldn't really tell. I held her hand. She just kept looking at me. And all I could think about was wanting a piss. So I let go of her hand. Told her I'd come straight back. But I didn't.

I went to the pub instead. She died that night. I didn't even say goodbye. And now … now every time I think about her I just hope to fuck she were too fucking sick to even know I was there, because, because the thought of her laid there waiting for me to come back is…

I can't say anymore to these people. I'm crying, and I feel like a twat. I look at no one as I stand up and leave. And from the top-deck of the bus I watch the houses go by as I drink the half-Bell's. I feel little tickles all over me like I'm rising up into the air, but inside it feels like I'm falling.

CHAPTER 73

The fat bitch tells me I'm barred

Tells me last time I came in here I caused so much trouble that the manageress decided that was that, says I walked out singing something about the I.R.A, waving a barstool above my head, which I smashed up in the car-park, apparently.

Fuck knows.

I want to tell her to stick her pub up her fat fucking arse, but the thought that this is the only pub in the village limps across my head like a leper ringing a bell.

I tell her that I'm sorry, that I was drunk, but she just shakes her fat head again, her chins wobbling like that red thing under a cockerel's beak.

I ask her, Can I speak to the gaffer please?

She says, Not here today, and her fingers tap a little drum-roll on the Heineken pump.

There's a silence between us. Then the door bangs behind me and this pissy old gadge shuffles in. He gives me a quick sneery look as he hangs his walking stick on the brass rail in front of the bar.

Over his shoulder a middle-aged couple are sat in the corner gawping.

Pint, Bert? sings fatso.

Please Barbara says Bert, rubbing a snuff-stained hanky under his big blotchy nose.

Fatso starts tugging at the hand-pull, her little pink sausage fingers whitening with the effort. She glances up at me, her lips quick-curving into a ghost of a smile.

She says, I think you'd better go.

Bert tuts, shakes his saggy head, looks at me out the corner of his eye like I'm not even fit to look at.

My lion sits up. **WHAT'S YOUR FUCKIN PROBLEM, SANTA-NOSE?**

I slap the rail, grabbing a bar-towel which I lob at fatso as I turn and leave.

As I cross the car-park my phone buzzes. It's Grace. I stamp on it till it cracks and it occurs to me that I still have the social down the road.

I fucking hate the place, but.

A slight diversion past the offy for a quarter-Bell's takes me on the road behind our house. It makes sense not to go the front way. Grace'll be home. I neck the Bell's in three then throw up in the jitty that cuts across to the club. When I stop retching there's a wet itchy-heat behind my ball-sack.

Shit.

I swing the club doors open to the grumble of bingo balls, taking a left to the bogs. I get myself into a cubicle. If I take my jeans and trainers off and someone looks under the door it's going to look a bit fucking weird I reckon, so I just pull my jeans and pants down and sit on the bog. I look down. In my red pants the shit looks like brown egg-white.

I take my lighter out my jacket-pocket, and holding the side of my pants off my leg I start to burn at the seam. This makes sense. If I just ripped them off shit'd splash everywhere. The smoke stinks plasticy, and I feel sick. I lurch my head to the side and throw up. The sick is watery-yellow. I watch as it runs down the scrawled cubicle wall.

U.D.M scab wankers.

MTFC.

Pakis out.

I cup the muddy gusset as I hold the lighter to the other seam. I can't hold them off my leg very well and some of the material melts onto me. When the seam finally gives I drop my pants into the toilet and turn to grab some bog-roll...

Fuck.

I decide the best course of action is to rip the lining out of my jeans pocket and use that. My arse itches and my ears crackle as I yank at the material. It takes a few tugs but the lining finally gives. Even with both pockets there isn't enough so I spit on my right hand then reach between my legs.

It's messy.

I pull my jeans up and do the zip and button with my left hand. It's tricky but I manage. My ears are still crackling as I flush the chain. My red pants bob back up, the shitty gusset forming a bubble in the bowl. A pocket-lining smeared with shit curls around my pants. It looks like a red sunrise over a valley of dirty snow.

I wait for a minute then flush again. The picture just changes to a featureless Santa wearing a shitty hat. I leave it, go wash my hands.

There's no soap so I rub my hands under the tap until the shit's gone. I notice there's still some under my fingernails as I pull open the door to the grumble of bingo balls.

Unlucky for some, thirteen…

A pissy old fuck in a flat-cap mutters past me to get to the bogs as I hold the door open.

I shake my head and tut. Some dirty bastard's left a right mess in there, I tell him.

RIGHT! LET'S GET THIS PARTY STARTED! cries the sad 1980s bleach-blonde twat sat behind a Bontempi on the little stage. A plastic *bum-tish bum-tish* is followed by the chords to something I really don't want to be hearing.

Agafuckingdoo makes me want to punch myself in the face.

Assorted scrubbers clutter around the bar trying to get served. Grey-faced dead-fucks asking for mild, fat slappers with bad perms for lager and black, home-tattooed hardmen in Mansfield Town shirts for Mansfield Bitter.

Guinness and two double Jameson's please, I ask the cleavage behind the bar. I pretend to scratch my top lip with my right hand. There's a faint whiff but it's not too bad.

I sit by the doors at the back of the club. If I wriggle on the seat it eases my itch. As I drink, my ears crackle with the sound of corn-stubble burning.

By the time I'm back at the bar the sad keyboard gimp has fucked off thank fuck, and the bingo balls start rumbling. I order the same again and the cleavage narrows her eyes at me. As she pours the Jameson's the big-chinned club-steward puts his prison-tattooed hand on her shoulder and says something in her ear. They both glance over at me.

Tenner in hand, I dip into my pocketless pocket and cup my nuts with the money.

When I take my seat again I notice a girl I used to work with has come in. She looks a bit like a boy in her tracksuit. Her boyfriend looks like a hobbit. I gulp my Guinness as I watch them study their bingo cards. They're just like the rest of them in here. Twitching with fuckarsed excitement every time they get a number, a quick slash of the pen then back to hovering over their bingo cards like their sad fucking lives depended on two fat ladies.

I'd still fuck her though. Even though she does look like a boy.

I neck a Jameson and light a roll-up. Some bozz-eyed heifer shouts **HOUSE!** and a disappointed sigh goes around the room. Hobbit boy and tracksuit girl point to each other's cards and discuss their failure.

What was her name? Sharon? Shannon? Shantelle? Ah, yeh. Shernice. Shernice O'Toole.

Back at the bar I manage to be standing behind Shernice when she gets served. She turns around with her pint of lager and black and I say Hello as the keyboard gimp hammers out Telstar.

Bum-tish bum-tish.

Shernice smiles, says Eyup Billy, fancy seeing you here.

Yeah, fancy. Council do it?

I point to her near-skinhead.

Oh, she says, blushing slightly, rubbing her many-ringed free-hand over the top of her head, Fancied something a bit different.

Something moves in my trousers.

Sexy, I say.

Shernice laughs, her cheeks still flushed as a staggering gadge carrying a froth-flecked pint-pot pushes past her to get to the bar.

Alan's off to the horse, she says, nodding in the direction of hobbit boy, who sits chewing a bingo card at their table, his eyebrows joined in a pubic V as he squints in our direction. I'll come and have a drink with you if you like? Catch up and that.

She smiles, and the ring through her eyebrow lifts slightly.

The Final Countdown dadada-daa's through the club wall as me and Shernice talk shit by the extractor fan. We mooch round the side of the building away from the doors because Shernice says Alan's mum is a nosy old cow. I run my palm over her near-skinhead and she giggles, and for the first time I notice she has the ghost of a little 'tache.

She tells me about getting signed for Town Ladies footy team and I tell her Well done.

I go to kiss her cheek on the N of done and her face moves so our lips meet. She kisses like a hungry miner eating a sausage roll. With her hands on my arse, she pulls me into her and I slip my hand up her Man U shirt. I kiss her neck, and watch the bump of my hand moving under the devil crest. Her tits are small and firm, her nipples tiny and stiff. I switch hands, running my left hand under her footy shirt, my right hand sliding down her tracky bottoms as she unbuttons my jeans. I stop kissing her neck as my palm cups a stubbly fanny.

Wow. Matches your head, I say into her ear as I push my middle finger up her. She makes a little sound in her throat that makes me want to throw her down on the tarmac, fuck her hips off right here and now.

I run a wet finger up to her clit as she pulls my cock out and I catch a shitty whiff of my earlier incident.

I hope to fuck it doesn't put her off.

We kiss hard as we wank each other, her lips twitching against mine as I soft-rub little circles at the top of her cunt. Her clit feels like one of her nipples, this tiny stiffening button that has her biting my bottom lip as she **OI! WHAT THE FUCK YOU FUCKIN DO-IN!**

We both freeze and look towards the sound.

Alan, backlit by a yellow streetlamp stands fists-clenched, and for the first time I realise that hobbit boy is also a stocky little fucker. Less hobbit, more troll.

BASTARDS! he yells, disappearing round the corner towards the club doors.

ALAAAAN! screams Shernice, chasing after him, **ALAAAAN!**

I look down to my cock and notice a streak of dried shit smeared down the shaft. I consider my fortune at not getting her to suck me off and I put it away, pointing northward still as I make a decision.

Opening the doors to Two little ducks, **QUACK! QUACK!** I understand that I have no fear of anything anymore. I'm better than all these fuckers put together, and not one of them can hurt me. I walk in there a lion, scanning the flat-capped, flabby-jowled masses for Alan, because I have to tell the little fucker, tell him how it is, how it will be, and of who, exactly, I am.

All the sixes...

YOU BLEEDIN DIRTY ROTTEN DEVIL! squawks a voice to my left, and there stands Bilbo-mum, fleshy bingo-wings draped around her sobbing stump of a son.

THEY'RE ENGAGED YOU DIRTY ROTTEN DEVIL! THEY'RE ENGAGED!

I take in the scene for a moment. Bilbo-mum consoling her dwarf offspring, Shernice kneeling by said dwarf, palms upturned in her pleading forgiveness, other assorted goblins gathered around them throwing me the daggers and tut-tutting their slob-lipped mottled faces in disgust.

YOU'RE A DIRTY DRUNKEN DIRTY DEVIL! yells Bilbo-mum, shaking a fat little fist my way.

I glance around the club, conscious of the quiet, of the sudden absence of grumbling bingo balls and Agafuckingdoo. The entire shit-hole watches on. Every man, woman and child, every inbred six-fingered sad-fuck peasant, every big-nosed red-eyed baggy-faced shit-shoveller, all of them, watching, waiting.

WHAT? WHAT THE FUCK Y'LOOKIN AT?

The whole room seems to tut and shake its head. The only noise is the extractor fan, and then a single sniggering cackle. A rook coughing its liver up.

Get out till you can handle your pop, someone half-shouts.

The room becomes a rookery, and in my head, the sound of a distant violin being struck with a hammer.

WHO THE FUCK ARE YOU LOT TO FUCKIN JUDGE ME?

The big-chinned club-steward grabs me by the shoulder. I push him over a chair and climb onto a table.

LOOK AT YER! SAT TICKIN YOUR FUCKIN LEGS-ELEVEN OFF WAITING TO FUCKIN DIE IN THE SHIT YOU WERE BORN IN PLUCKIN FUCKIN CHICKENS EVERY FUCKARSED DAY FOR THE MAN! BAAAA! BAAAA! YES SIR NO SIR, THREE FUCKING BAGS...

The table disappears from underneath me. There's bumping and lights flashing. The next thing I know my face hurts and the air is cold around me. A yellow streetlamp backlights dark faces above. Someone is shouting something about killing me if they ever see me again. Something wet hits my face and I guess at spit. Another light flashes as a sharp pain explodes in my ribs. Something crunchy is in my mouth. I feel it between my teeth like sand and gravel. There's a whining sound in my head but it sounds far away.

Everything becomes still.

I open my eyes and I'm alone on the pavement.

It hurts when I try and stand up, and after a couple of tries I get to my feet but I fall over again. I decide to try and find home this way, on my hands and knees.

As I slow-cross the road a car-horn pips. I don't

look up. Behind me is the sound of muffled music as I shuffle up onto the kerb.

I drag my knee through a pile of dog shit. I lay under a hedge to gather my strength. Above me the stars brighten then blur.

It's the Birdie Song.

It's the fucking Birdie Song.

CHAPTER 74

The gaffer's glass-eye stays open when he blinks

He calls it his all-seeing eye when he's ragging the lads. It might be funny if he weren't such a cunt. It's hard not to stare at it. I can't help but smirk when he gets narky. His glass-eye seems to get bigger and he looks like Popeye. He's well pissed at me today. I make myself look at the calendar on his desk.

August 22. Monday. Without contraries is no progression. William Blake.

And frankly, he says lifting his coffee cup to his lips, I was bloody appalled to hear of your behaviour, Billy.

He drinks, his good eye closing, his bad eye eyeing me over the rim of his cup. I say nothing, picking at a loose thread in my work-trousers. He puts his cup down, picks his pen up, looks to the notepad on his desk.

The clock on his wall ticks 8:45. 6. Behind me I can hear the muffled rumble of a pallet-truck. Behind him on the wall is a poster showing different sizes of breeze-blocks and lintels. He taps the pen on his notepad, clears his throat.

The manager of the hotel, whom, might I add, was absolutely bloody fuming, spoke to me on Saturday morning as me and Valerie arrived downstairs for breakfast. It wasn't something I wanted to hear.

He looks at me across his desk. I don't know which eye to look at.

What do you think he told me, Billy?

I shrug.

Pardon? he says.

Twat.

I don't know, Mr Grindley.

Though I think I do.

Right, he says, looking down to his notepad again, It seems that after my wife and I left the function room to retire...

He looks up at me again, his good eye half-closed in a scowl, his bad eye wide-open.

...A function room paid for by the new company owners. As was the four-course meal. As were the twenty-four rooms in said hotel so that we could all enjoy a good night. So the new company owners could get to know the people that work for them. Us. A builders merchant on the verge of collapse until they stepped in, whom, might I add, have been on the telephone to me already this morning regarding this very matter, and I'm telling you here

and now laddy, they ain't bloody pleased Billy-boy,
THEY AIN'T BLOODY PLEASED.

August 22. Monday. Without contraries is no
progression. William Blake.

ARE YOU LISTENING TO ME, BILLY-BOY?

Yes, Mr Grindley.

Twat.

He clears his throat again, looks down to the
notepad, tap-taps his pen on the page.

At around 2am, a guest approached the night-
clerk in the entrance lobby asking to be served
alcohol. When the guest was told that the bar was
closed, he pestered the night-clerk for a further
twenty minutes, which resulted in a desk-bell being
thrown across the lobby.

Grindley looks up at me.

Well? he says.

I think about this a moment.

I just asked if there were any more wine, Mr
Grindley. And I didn't throw a bell across the lobby.
I knocked it off the desk. Accidentally.

Grindley raps his pen on the notepad again, once,
with a loud PUK.

ACCIDENTALLY! ACCI-BLOODY-DENTALLY!
THEN HOW THE BLOODY HELL DID IT END
UP DINTING A BLOODY DOOR THEN?

I shake my head, shrug.

AND AS FOR MORE WINE! HADN'T YOU
HAD A-BLOODY-CHUFFIN-NOUGH? IT WERE

FREE DRINKS ALL CHUFFIN DAY!

Enough for some.

Grindley shakes his head, blows air out through kissy-lips, looks back to his notepad. PUK.

At some point in the early hours of Sunday morning, an unidentified guest wrote, all the way across the bar in tomato ketchup, FIGHT…Grindley looks up at me again… FOR YOUR RIGHT. TO PARTY.

A grin starts tugging at my face. My fingers dig into my thighs but the bubble in my belly is hard to keep down.

Grindley throws his pen onto his desk with a clatter.

I FAIL TO SEE THE BLOODY HUMOUR IN THIS, LAD! PARTICULARLY AS WHOEVER DID THAT ALSO STOLE A BLOODY BOTTLE OF PORT FROM THE SAME CHUFFING BAR, THE EMPTY BOTTLE OF WHICH WAS FOUND LATER IN THE LADIES TOILET, STUFFED INTO THE SANITARY TOWEL DISPOSAL, WHICH WAS ALSO COVERED IN TOMATO BLOODY KETCHUP FOR GOD'S SAKE!

Grindley leans back in his chair and folds his arms across his chest. He screws his face up, his good eye scrunched, his bad eye staring blankly. I'm still wondering what the fuck I was doing in the women's toilet.

AND! Grindley pops, leaning forward and

unflexing his face, **THAT ISN'T ALL OF IT. IS IT, BILLY?**

I start to say that it wasn't me with the ketchup, or the port, but Grindley leans into his desk and glares at me, his breath smelling like a damp carpet.

Apparently, at the after-dinner disco, you greatly offended the new MD's wife, didn't you, lad. He picks his pen up, looks down to the notepad again. PUK.

August 22. Monday. Without contraries is no progression. William Blake.

I don't know what you mean, Mr Grindley.

And I don't.

He sits back quick and slaps his hands on the desk.

SO SHE'S A BLOODY LIAR THEN IS SHE BILLY-BOY? SO YOU DIDN'T GROPE HER BACKSIDE? EY? THEN TELL THE MANAGING DIRECTOR TO EFF BLOODY OFF WHEN HE CAME OVER TO RESCUE HIS POOR WIFE FROM YOUR DRUNKEN BLOODY LECHERY?

Oh yeah. Now I remember.

Well? Grindley says, his lips all tight like a ventriloquist's dummy.

I think about this for a moment, and I remember she was pissed too, grabbing hold of me when that shit Whitney Houston song came on, and oh yeh, saying she liked my shirt.

I was only messing about, Mr Grindley. I wasn't…

MESSING ABOUT? MESSING A-BLOODY-BOUT?

Grindley leans forward again, his eyebrows arcing into the bridge of his nose, his good eye narrowing, his bad eye massive, a clay-pipe short of an Ah'll saves ya Olive, that damp carpet smell still fugging from his gob.

Yes Billy, he speak-whispers, I've heard all about what you call messing a-bout.

He glares at me. There is something like disgust or hatred on his face.

My guts fill with mercury. Since that thing with Curtis and Jane a few weeks ago some people at work have been weird with me. I didn't know whether I was imagining it or whether it was real. Me and Curtis haven't spoken since that night at his. Since then he's stayed over on his counter and I've stayed on mine. I've even avoided the canteen if he's in there. I've been getting a strong sense that Curtis has been telling people things. Some of the office girls don't speak to me anymore. Some of the lads are different with me. Some-times when I walk into the canteen people just stop talking.

Grindley picks his pen up, quick tap-taps it on his knuckles. I'm giving you a final warning, Billy. One more lapse and you're out. Get it?

My lion sits up. How? That stuff at the hotel was out of work. How is...

YOU'RE A DISGRACE TO THIS COMPANY!
he barks.

My belly starts to burn. I prod the desk with my
forefinger as I speak. So let me get this right. You
give us shit-loads of free booze then punish us for
being drunk? How does that...

NOT US, BILLY! YOU! YOU ACTED LIKE
A BLOODY ANIMAL! HOW THE HELL
DOES YOUR MISSUS PUT UP WITH IT? NO
WONDER SHE DRAGGED YOU OUT THE
CHUFFIN HOTEL BEFORE WE ALL GOT
UP! I BET THE POOR LASS WAS ASHAMED!
AND AS FOR BEING OUT OF WORK-
HOURS, YOU WERE STILL REPRESENTING
THIS COMPANY, YOU, YOU, BLOODY
IDIOT!

The word idiot hangs in the air a second.

Fuck this.

REPRESENTING? WHAT THE FUCK ARE
YOU ON ABOUT? YOU PAY ME SHIT-QUID
TO FLOG FUCKARSED BRICKS EIGHT HOURS
A DAY TO FUCKING BUILDERS IS ALL ... YOU
DON'T FUCKING OWN ME!

Grindley slaps the desk with both hands and sits
bolt upright, starts wagging a finger at me.

I'M WARNING YOU, BILLY! ONE MORE
OUTBURST AND THAT'S IT! YOU'RE BY FAR
THE WEAKEST LINK IN OUR CHAIN! YOU'RE
CONSISTENTLY BLOODY TARDY! YOU'RE

NOTHING BUT A WORK-SHY NAIL IN OUR BOOT!

Red-faced, he leans over his desk, finger still wagging, and I realise that we're both stood up. I smell damp carpet again as he leans even closer, so close I can see myself reflected in his glass eye. That look of disgust settles on his face again as his good eye looks me up and down, his bad eye staring dead-fish ahead. A fleck of spit hangs off his bottom lip.

And, I can tell you this much, he hisses, his good eye narrowing to a slit. I don't like what I've been hearing about you Billy-boy, I don't like it one little bit.

There's a moment's silence between us, bar the drone of Phil Oakey from the shop-floor radio.

I reach over and tap Grindley's name-badge with my forefinger, once, twice, then I tell him.

You know nothing, you fuck-eyed ignoramus.

He goes to slap my hand away but I'm already turning. Through his office-window I see a small crowd has gathered pretending to stock-check U-bends. Behind them are others, craning their necks from various counters across the shop-floor. I swing the door open, slamming it shut in my wake.

I spot Curtis half-hiding by a rack of security lights. I rip my name-badge off, spinning on my heel, throwing the stupid fucking thing towards Grindley's window as I turn and climb onto a pallet of floor tiles.

I point to Curtis over the rows of metal shelves. He blinks, then adjusts the angle of a Par38 lampholder like everything is normal.

THAT BENT-BASTARD OVER THERE IS A FUCKIN LIAR!

I start to get down from the pallet but I stop and point at Curtis again. His hand is over his mouth.

OH YEH. HE'S GOT AIDS.

Curtis disappears behind the cable shelves as something like a dozen bicycle pumps are drawn out, pushed in. From the shop-floor speakers Peak-FM says Rain, but as I leave the building the white sun glares off the black tarmac making me blink. I keep my eyes half-closed all the way home, and when I get inside I lock the door and close the curtains, curling-up in bed, my head under the covers, breathing the same air over and over again, a feather of sleep spinning downward like a sycamore seed, until I look down into that deep well through darklight, that moon-mirror glinting up from the pit, myself staring back at myself, the well-walls now crack and groan, I didn't, I didn't... that sound downstairs of the dog scratching at the backdoor, this tin-taste of blood as my fist hits my mouth, again, again.

I get up, let the dog out, go get lager vodka Blue Nun.

CHAPTER 75

We are now listening to

A telephone ringing. The telephone sits on a mahogany desk that sits beneath an arched window veined with lead. By the window is a painting of Jesus crucified. On the next wall of this small oak-lined room is a large bookcase, and by this, a door. The telephone is still ringing as the door swings open, and we see a black-haired, middle-aged priest come into the room. Through the open doorway we see a church, an elderly lady arranging flowers by the altar. The priest approaches the desk and looks at the ringing telephone. He wipes his forehead and neck with a white handkerchief. It is a hot and humid day and there is no escape from it, not even within the cooled air of the limestone church. The priest picks up the receiver.

FATHER DIMMI (*sighing*): Hello, Church of the Annunciation, Father Dimmi speaking.

BILLY (*anxiously*): Is that the Catholic church?

FATHER DIMMI: Er, yes, that's correct. How can I help you?

BILLY: I need to talk to a priest.

FATHER DIMMI: Well, I'm Father Dimmi. What can I...

BILLY (*cutting in*): I'm lost, Father.

FATHER DIMMI: Lost?

BILLY: Yes Father. Lost. And I want to be alright again.

FATHER DIMMI: Who am I speaking to?

BILLY: Billy.

FATHER DIMMI (*thinking aloud*): Billy... Billy... Are you a member of our congregation?

BILLY (*agitated*): No, but I need to confess, or something. Because...

FATHER DIMMI (*cutting in*): Wouldn't it be better to come into church and talk to me? I'm a little pressed for...

BILLY (*cutting in*): **NO!** I need to talk **NOW!** I feel bad and, and I need to...

FATHER DIMMI (*cutting in*): Billy. Slow down. (*softly*) What's troubling you?

BILLY: EVERYTHING!

FATHER DIMMI (*hesitantly*): Okay, I see... Are you sure you can't come into church and talk to me? I'm free between five and six tonight if that...

BILLY (*cutting in*): **NO!** I need to confess **NOW! EVERYTHING IS WRONG! EVERYTHING!** And if I don't do something about it something fucking awful is going to...

FATHER DIMMI (*firmly*): **BILLY!** Now take a deep breath! And please! I don't want to hear that kind of language!

BILLY (*quietly*): Sorry.

FATHER DIMMI (*collecting himself*): Okay. Now, I have to ask, are you actually a Catholic?

A pause.

BILLY (*quietly*): No... but I'll be one if it helps?

We see Father Dimmi move the receiver from his ear, then look at it with raised eyebrows. He sighs, then puts the receiver back to his ear, opening his mouth as though to say something but Billy is already speaking.

BILLY (*tearfully*): Father, please! I don't know what to do! I need to confess or something! Please!

FATHER DIMMI (*frowning*): How old are you Billy?

Down the line, we hear the sound of a beer-can

being opened. Father Dimmi narrows his eyes.

BILLY (*drinks, sniffs*): Er, thir-ty-two, no, thirty-three?

FATHER DIMMI (*flatly*): Are you drunk?

A pause.

BILLY: No! It's Tango. Honest. (*starts crying*) There's no way out...

FATHER DIMMI (*softening*): Now Billy, c'mon. Listen to me. I'll hear your confession. It's not the usual way but I will listen to you. Now take a deep breath and just speak truthfully. Tell me what's...

BILLY (*cutting in*): I'm drunk, and I tell lies! To **EVERYONE!** I'm unfaithful to my wife. Loads! People hate me. My mum and dad won't speak to me. I fucking hate **EVERYONE!** Except for my kids, who have a useless spineless pisshead for a dad. And I want (*tearfully*) I want to be left alone, but, I get so fucking lonely (*crying*) and I get angry, at everything, and I'm trapped, and I should just kill my fucking self...

FATHER DIMMI (*softly*): Billy, Billy, you're obviously in a great deal of pain, and very confused about life, but killing yourself is not the...

BILLY (*cutting in*): **WHAT ELSE CAN I DO?**

FATHER DIMMI (*softly*): Live, Billy! But you have to live in God. Look, in Psalms there's a passage where David speaks of how guilt lays heavy upon the soul. It might help... Just a moment... (*the dry sound of pages turning*) Here we go. (*clears his throat*) And when I declared not my sin, my body wasted away through my groaning all day long. For day and night Thy hand was heavy upon me, and my strength was dried up as by the heat of summer... (*clears his throat*) Now Billy, clearly you show a great deal of contrition for your sins, so...

BILLY (*cutting in*): Con-what?

FATHER DIMMI (softly): Contrition. You're sorry for what you've done, yes?

BILLY (*sniffs*): Yeh.

We hear the sound of drinking.

FATHER DIMMI: And because of this, because of your regret for your actions, your sins lay a heavy hand upon you, which is that feeling of guilt that you are clearly experiencing, yes? And because of this, through God, I can offer you absolution. But you Billy, you have to...

BILLY (*cutting in*): Abso-what?

FATHER DIMMI (*sighs*): Absolution, Billy. It means you'll be forgiven. And the guilt of your sins will be lifted.

BILLY (*perkier*): What? As easy as that?

FATHER DIMMI (*clearing his throat*): Well, it still requires a great deal of work on your part to...

BILLY (*cutting in*): But what if The Devil comes again?

A pause. We hear the sound of drinking.

FATHER DIMMI (*hesitantly*): Well... The Devil tempts us all, Billy. Daily. But through God we can learn to say no to sin. And God will give you this strength if you open yourself up to him. Listen. We all have three enemies, all of us, and they are The Devil, the World, and the body. And all three will ask of you to sin. But through the Holy Trinity you can fight these enemies. With the God-given strength of The Father, The Son, and The Holy Spirit. These three are your weapons in the war against The Devil. And you must arm yourself. You do you understand that don't you, Billy?

We hear the sound of drinking.

BILLY (*quietly*): I think so.

FATHER DIMMI: Now Billy, for ab... for you to receive God's forgiveness, you will need to do some work to show him that you're correcting your ways. And this is called penance.

BILLY: What's that?

FATHER DIMMI (*sighing*): It means you make amends. By righting the wrongs that you've done to others. And by doing the right thing you'll begin to walk the path of righteousness. Out of the dark woods, and away from The Devil by doing the right thing. Yes?

BILLY (*quietly*): Yeh.

FATHER DIMMI: And can I suggest you begin with your parents?

BILLY (*quietly*): Yeh.

FATHER DIMMI: And if you begin to redeem yourself with those closest to you, then I promise you, with the help of God, you will begin to see life in a completely different...

BILLY (*cutting in*): Do I have to say three Hail Mary's or something?

A pause.

FATHER DIMMI: No Billy, not really. But I do want you to do something for me. I want you to stop drinking for today, and I also want you to read Psalm Fifty-One. Think about what the words are saying to you. Okay?

BILLY (*quietly*): Okay. Thanks.

FATHER DIMMI (*cheerily*): No problem. And if you want to talk further on this matter then please come into church and see me. Goodbye, Billy. May God go with you.

BILLY (*quietly*): Bye.

With a sigh, Father Dimmi places the receiver down, then looks to the painting of the crucified Jesus by the rectory window. He wipes his forehead and neck with the white handkerchief again, then wafts it in the air as if shaking the sweat from the cotton. If you were watching this act as a fly on the wall then you would see a thousand priests waving something like a thousand surrenders, as the seeming object of their defeat looks down from a thousand crosses, a thousand crowns of thorn bleeding into two-thousand pained eyes of forgiveness.

And now we are listening to the sound of Billy pulling a cork from a bottle of Blue Nun, followed by the glug of the pour. We watch him drink, then turn pages of Joe's Good News school Bible that sits on the table next to the half-empty glass.

BILLY: Have mercy upon me, O God, according to Thy steadfast love, according to Thy abundant mercy, blot out my transgressions, wash me thoroughly from my iniquity, and cleanse me from my sin, for I know my transgressions and my sin is ever before me, against Thee only have I sinned, and done that which is evil in Thy sight, and Thou art justified in Thy sentence, and blameless in Thy judgement. Behold, I was brought forth in iniquity, and in sin... did my mother conceive me.

In the following few minutes, the front door will open and in will walk Grace, Scarlett and Joe. They will find Billy with his head resting on his arms, his arms resting on the table, and they will see the opened bottle, the empty cans, and they will understand. His children will say nothing of their father's eyes as his head raises up, of the blank nothingness of which only nothing comes, the dull murmurings of things to be done, the sweep of empty cans to the floor, the staggering exit and slammed door of this man called Dad, the mother now closing the book, now quietly opening kitchen cupboard doors as though what has just gone was nothing but nothing, the on-button of the television set giving the girl and the boy another place to be in, where nothing is really real, where they watch in silence as the Goosebumps story unfolds: this is what happened to the haunted puppet, and then this, and then this...

CHAPTER 76

And then this

Slow blue darkness has fallen soft, shade by shade
and star by star as he reaches the wooded lane
hollow, and he remembers these trees, the dens he
made alone, the long hours spent poking a stick
into the fly-tip river, searching for the treasure of
a marble-neck pop bottle, only to be smashed to
salvage the clear pearl, only to be catapulted against
the barn wall, the long-spent search full-stopped
by the dull pop of shard, the chalky star of impact
left on breeze-block, washed away always with
the first fall of rain, and behind him now, the dry
crackle of corn stirs in the wind as he aims his piss
at the barbed-wire, pleased at the hit, of the dew-
drops hanging from the grey steel, these teardrop
glints under white-eye of hunter's moon, and now
zipping-up he pulls the half-Bell's from his coat-
pocket, draining the last of the amber, the bottle
now flighted, swallowed by the deepening dusked
wood, now pleased at the crack-smash down below,
now lighting a fag and looking into the blue-black

pillared woodland below as an owl calls, as another gust of late summer wind shivers the drying canopy of leaf, as he spits onto the sign that says NO FLY-TIPPING, beyond which lies a soiled mattress, a split binbag spewing porn, a bicycle with no wheels, a broken doll's house, and there are things to be done, and as he turns to walk the lane to the home of his parents, a rook scraws, and the blue night darkens.

CHAPTER 77

Knock knock

Who's there? Billy, who now steps over the threshold, the stepfather saying We want no trouble, to which the stepson replies But you're my dad, and you're supposed to give a shit, now half-stumbling into the pine-dresser, this homemade crayoned birthday card saying WE LOVE YOU NANNA falling flat onto its smiley face, the stepfather now placing an oil-stained hand firmly on the stepson's shoulder, saying I mean it Billy, we want no trouble.

And now into the kitchen walks the mother, the tax of her son's condition to be read on her face as she props herself on the back of the chair, saying You haven't come to shout have you? Because if you have, you can leave now, to which the son replies Typical, how when I need you all you do is tell me off, and now the stepfather half-raises his voice, saying Sit, pulling a chair out from under the kitchen table, now flicking that switch on the kettle saying Jesus Billy you're a bloody mess, the mother saying Why do you do this? Can't you see what you're doing to yourself, to Grace, to Scarlett, to Joe?

And now Billy puts his face to the table, his hands over his head, mumbling something about Lost, to which no one says anything for half a turn of the thin hand that jerks its tick around the kitchen clock as the kettle rumbles to boiling point, the mother moving like a slow ghost across the room to pull three cups from a cupboard, the chink of a spoon against the porcelain of a cup, and Here Billy, drink this, and now the mother and stepfather watch as the red-eyed Billy sips once, twice at the black hot coffee, the mother now seeing her father's drunken eyes through the mist, that jag of a weighted rope, that knowingness that she is the bridge between that bastard and this, as down goes the coffee cup, shedding black tears onto the pine, the son fixing the mother with a bloodshot stare, You never wanted me, you should've fuckin dumped me like you wanted to, to which the mother covers her face with her hands, drawing her breath through her fingers, Oh Billy, please don't, and now the stepfather slaps the table, saying I won't let you do this to your mother, can't you see what you're doing? Can't you hear yourself? The mother now weeping the spider-silk words, You're my son, don't you understand?

And now the husband gently cajoling his wife to sit, the cause of her pain once again face down on the table, hands over his head, mumbling You lost me, mumbling My father, and now the mother looks to the ceiling, her arm across her chest, and Is that what all this is about? Now listen to me, that man was bad, he was just like my dad, don't you see? I made a mistake... and now the son looks up at the mother, eyes redder than a devil's, **THERE! SEE! I'M A LIVING, BREATHING, FUCKING MISTAKE!**

And now the mother puts an arm across her chest, leaning into the table, tears welling her eyes, her husband wrapping an arm around her shoulders, her now saying No, no, that's not what I meant, that's not what I meant at all, and now the husband raising his voice to the stepson, **saying I WON'T HAVE YOU SPEAKING TO YOUR MOTHER LIKE THIS!** And now the stepson saying **WHO THE FUCK ARE YOU TO TELL ME?** as the mother stands, her chair falling to the floor, **THIS MAN! HAS GIVEN YOU EVERYTHING! YOU SELFISH! BLOODY! BASTARD!** And now the son stands, shouting **YES MOTHER, I KNOW I'M A BASTARD!** as the mother moves slow-arched to the stairs doorway, No, she says, I can't do this anymore, her arms holding herself within herself, now reaching out to open the door, I'm going, she says, and now the stepfather grabbing the stepson by the collar, **C'MON, YOU'RE LEAVING!** leading the stepson to the backdoor, pushing him back out into the blue night, telling him never to think about doing this again, **EVER!** Billy now turning, red eyes glinting in the half-light of a hunter's moon, Love, he grins, Fuck off.

CHAPTER 78

He lifts the barbed-wire

And into the dark woods he slips. Through the black shifting canopy of leaves, the moon, a white splintering eye, is watching. Down and deeper he treads, stride by stride by the side of the dry fly-tip river he moves, stumbling through the crack-snap of the dark undergrowth. An owl screeches. Another replies. The last scent of summer's wild garlic hangs sour in the air. He stops to piss by a tree.

Love, he spits to the splintering moon.

Deeper into dark he goes, until finally, he finds it. The twisted trunk of the old den tree, the old corrugated sheet still leaning against the heel of the crook, the ring of stones that served as a fireplace, the rotting log that was once a chair.

In the half-dark he gathers dry-dead branches, snapping them right-sized for the fire, and then the short half-blind stumble to the fly-tip where an old Derbyshire Times will serve as kindling.

A rat, or a fox, or a scuttling something scurries in his wake as he treads flat the dead bluebells on his way back to the den, where he will light the night-fire, then lay himself down to sleep under the corrugated sheet and dream of that boy again, holding out that corked-bottle in outstretched hand, hooves glinting like oyster shells in the dying wilt of wild garlic, Hello Billy, he grins.

CHAPTER 79

Rough as fuck and wet with dew

Waking in a wood is fucked. I take a shit by a blackberry bush, wipe my arse on a dock leaf, think about my mother as I tread through nettles. Mist hangs low in the hollow. I think it still must be early. I guess at sixish. I vomit in the hedge-bottom as the post-van goes by.

When I reach the village the only shop open is the paper-shop. I buy fags, a Mars Bar, a can of Fanta. I've just enough money to get into town. My overdraft is fucked but I've still got my credit card. I sit in the bus shelter and wait. I'm cold.

The 83 is half-full with people going to work. I get a stiffy on the backseat. I fall asleep.

I wake up just as the bus pulls into town. The Crooked Spire clock says ten to eight. I chuck-up on the pavement as soon as I get off the bus. Someone says Dirty bleeder. The sick is orangey-brown. Fanta and Mars Bar.

I slide my credit card into the cash machine. It takes me three goes to get my number right.

Birthdays. Mine and the kids. The screen says I have a hundred and eighty quid credit left on my card. I take the lot, then head towards Supersave.

A half-Bell's and six cans of Guinness should take me through till opening time. It's eight-thirty. I walk past the market. The fruit and veg bloke is setting his stall up, and as I try and get past his van a lad comes out the back of it carrying a bag of spuds. He doesn't stop and neither do I. There's only one winner. He shouts Twat to my back as he picks his spuds up that are now rolling about on the cobbles. I head up past the DHSS then over the Courthouse grass to the cenotaph.

I sit and drink, start reading the names. I get as far as Evans G then understand these people mean nothing to me. I throw up again. It's blackish now. Guinness.

The Post Office clock says ten-twenty. I turn and face the other way. The sun comes out, thank fuck. I look towards Clarence Road where I used to live. From where I'm sat I can just about see the attic window. I think about Nannan. Funny. It was like I had two mums when I lived there. When one wasn't there I had the other. Then Mum got married. A new home, and her telling me that I had a dad now, and that I should call him Dad. From two mums to one mum, and she gave herself to someone else. Is that how it was?

I drink and think as I watch a sparrow hopping

about on the Courthouse grass. It stops to peck at something. Another joins it. Then another. I drink. Light a fag. It seems such a long time ago. Me, Mum and Nannan. I can't remember what it was like to be me back then. At all.

A crow lands on the grass and the sparrows fly off.

I'm a bad father. A bad husband. I'm probably a bad person too. There's no way to fix these things. It's too late.

I finish the Guinness. It's the last one. What day is it? I think I've done throwing up. There's still some of the half-Bell's left. I pocket the bottle for later. Pub.

I sit on the steps of The Market pub and wait. The Post Office clock says eleven but they're still not open. I decide to give it a few minutes before trying somewhere else. I've got about a hundred and sixty quid left. I'm going to make some decisions today. Something has to change. I might go to Ireland. I might just hitchhike to save money. Stow away on a ferry. Go to Dublin. Or somewhere quiet where I can think. Maybe by the sea. Somewhere I can start again. I'm tired of being me. Somewhere, something went wrong. I need to find right. I need to find happy. The sound of a bolt being drawn back makes me stand up. Ten minutes late by the Post Office clock.

Today, things are going to change.

I have lager because I'm thirsty. I sit by the window watching the market people on their stalls. I'm starting to feel better about things. If I go away, some people will get mad at me. But I can't let that stop me. I have to kill the me that got fucked up. Start again. Go live in a place where I belong. Get a job in a bar or something. I have another lager then take a walk across town towards The Punch Bowl. It feels good to wander. This is the start of it. I can go anywhere I want now. On the Co-op corner is an old gadge playing a mouth organ. He's shit but I throw him a fiver anyway. He says something like Thank you sir, but he doesn't take his mouth organ from his lips. He sounds like a pissed dalek. Funny.

The Punch Bowl is grubby, and the windows are stained-glass like in a church, but they're dirty so no light comes in. I have three barleys in a pint-pot and a double Jameson. I don't fancy staying here long. The landlord looks like an alky. His nose is red and swollen. I buy him a drink. On the wall behind him are a load of framed pictures. Most of them are wonky. The pictures are orangey-brown and show Chesterfield a long time ago. All the men have hats and moustaches. The roads look muddy and the women wear fat-arsed dresses. I want to be in another place in another time. When I get to Ireland I'm going to find a place by the sea that hasn't changed in a hundred years. I'll go to the pub everyday and sit drinking Guinness and proper Irish whisky. No one will know me. The Punch Bowl is shit, so I go for a piss then leave.

On my way across Knifesmithgate I walk past a Big Issue seller. She looks Pakistani. I give her a tenner. She smiles, says Thanks, then I ask her if she fancies a beer. She says not but I keep asking. She keeps saying no so I offer her a twenty. She bends down, starts putting her Big Issues into a rucksack, says I'm not a fuckin prozzer, then walks off quick. I light a fag and head for the Welbeck.

The Welbeck is all yellow Formica tables and dirty wallpaper. It looks like a Miner's Welfare. Two fat slappers are playing pool and cackling like witches. The skinny barmaid pours me a pint of Stella. She has a mole on the end of her nose the size of a brown Smartie. One of the fat slappers leans over to take her shot and half her tits hang out. They look like veiny balloons filled with pink custard.

I sit by the open door and look out onto the street. I need the sea. I need a place where no one knows me. I'm sick of people. People are ugly and tell lies. When I get to Ireland I'm going to live a hundred miles from anyone. I'll grow vegetables and have chickens. Who needs a fuck when a wank is easy. Who needs to talk to people when people are stupid.

This pint is off so I go to the bar and tell the skinny barmaid. She sniffs at it, says, Smells fine to me, luv. I shrug and tell her it must be her nose cancer that stops her smelling properly. She just stares at me. I leave, taking an ashtray with me.

I walk up past the Market Hall on my way to the Fleece. Town's getting busy. I look at people as I walk. Some people look at me funny, and I realise I'm a bit grubby after sleeping in the woods. I don't really give a fuck but I decide I need some new clothes. I walk past the alley that leads up to the Fleece and head towards Burtons. I need some new clothes for my journey anyway.

Burtons have a sale on suits. I pick a brown one and a white shirt. I've never had a suit before. I go into the changing rooms, put my coat on the chair, then take my jeans off. They're still wet from the woods. I take a swig from the half-Bell's, and look at myself in the mirror. I put my hand to the glass, flat-palmed. I say my name and watch the mouth move in the mirror. It's like I'm in two. I press myself against the glass and stare into the eyes. I breathe onto the mirror. Gone.

My pants are damp so I take them off too. There's a dark skidmark in them. My arse itches so I wipe it with my pants, throw them in the corner on top of my jeans. I remember my wallet is in the back pocket so I take it out and put it on the seat next to the ashtray. I have a sudden urge to piss. I pull the brown suit trousers on but the urge to piss gets worse. I figure I'm never coming back here so I piss on my pants and jeans in the corner. The piss takes ages. There's loads of it. I have to keep moving my aim because it makes a loud splashy sound if I piss in the same spot too long. I end up pissing on the wall so it runs soundlessly down onto my pants and jeans.

I look at myself in the mirror. The new trousers are a bit too big but I figure by the time I'm living off the land, eating vegetables and chickens, I'll have put some weight on. I try the shirt and jacket then look at myself. The jacket's baggy but I look like I mean business. I slide my trainers on and decide to leave my pissy jeans and pants in the cubicle. I throw my t-shirt over the top of them, pocket my wallet, grab my coat, then go through to the shop. I leave the ashtray. It would be a mistake to hoard things now. I need to travel light.

At the counter a zitty kid with a name badge that says Jez asks me if I need any help. I tell Jez I'm taking the suit and shirt that I'm wearing. He takes the tags off and rings it all up. It comes to eighty-nine quid. I figure this leaves me just enough to get to Ireland if I hitchhike. Jez asks me if I want put my old clothes in a carrier bag. I tell him I only have a coat. This seems to confuse Jez. He frowns then puts my coat into a carrier bag. I turn to go just as someone makes a noise of disgust from the direction of the changing rooms. I leave swinging my carrier bag, feeling good, feeling today is the day.

The Fleece is packed with footy fans and it occurs to me that this must be a Saturday. I used to like football. I don't anymore. All that tribal shit, like you belong to something. How can you love something that doesn't love you back? I drink quick, as all around me blokes in blue and white start singing.

OH CHESTERFIELD! IS WONDERFUL! OH CHESTERFIELD IS WON-DER-FUL! IT'S FULL OF TITS, FANNY AND SPIREITES! OH CHESTERFIELD IS WON-DER-FUL!

On the bus home I drink a bottle of Blue Nun and think about the sea. In a few hours I'll be feeling the waves under the boat. In a few hours I'll be starting my new life. I feel my inside rise. Maybe the kids will visit when I'm settled. Maybe I have to do this thing to make everything right again. Yeh.

When I get home Grace tells Joe and Scarlett to go to their rooms. I close my eyes so I can't see them. I think they've been crying. Only when I hear the sound of their feet on the stairs do I open my eyes, and I tell Grace that I'm going to live in Ireland.

She rolls her eyes and says Yeh right, sure you are. She sounds upset. I decide not to say anything else so I make a sign by pulling a pretend zip across my lips. She shakes her head and asks me where I was last night, if I've got any idea what I'm doing to the kids, and where the fuck did I get the suit from?

I make the sign of the zip again, and she sits heavy at the table, puts her head in her hands.

She says, Do you know how skint we are?

I don't reply.

I go to the cupboard under the stairs and drag my old sports bag out. Grace keeps talking. She sounds angry.

She says, Joe needs shoes, the car needs an M.O.T, the gas bill needs paying, it's Scarlett's birthday next month. And you, you haven't even looked for a job in weeks have you?

She stares at me. She's waiting for an answer. I look at her and shake my head. It looks like she's been crying too.

Christ, Billy, she says, Look at you. What the hell are you doing to yourself?

I put the bag on the table. I make the sign of the zip again, and tell myself I have to be strong. Grace shakes her head.

She says, Where did the money come from?

I take my wallet out the inside pocket of my new suit-jacket. I drop my credit card onto the table and point to it. Grace closes her eyes. Her lips make a kissy shape and she blows out a long stream of air.

IDIOT! she shouts, slapping the table.

I shake my head. I have to be strong. I smile. Grace stands up quick.

IT'S NOT FUNNY! WE CAN BARELY PAY THE FUCKING MORTGAGE AND YOU

SOD OFF BUYING SUITS AND DRINKING YOURSELF STUPID! I CAN'T EVEN AFFORD A FUCKING HAIRCUT! YOU SELFISH... LOOK AT ME WILL YOU! JUST FUCKING LOOK AT ME!

I look at her.

WELL? she says.

I do the sign of the zip again. She puts her hands flat-palmed on the table, then she swings forward, hard, smacking her head against the tabletop. She starts crying loud, then she swings forward again, harder this time, shouts **CHRIST**.

This is the worst I've seen her. I have to be strong. I have to do this. No matter what.

I decide it's better if I don't go upstairs to get my things. I should just go. The kids'll get upset. They can't see me. I have to be strong.

I grab the bag, go to the bottom of the stairs and pull some of my clothes off the clotheshorse. I go back into the front room stuffing the clothes into the bag. This is it. I'm going. Now. Grace stands in front of me, tears running down her face, a red O on her forehead. She slaps the bag out of my hand, screams **LEAVE THEN! JUST FUCKING LEAVE!** then she pushes me in the chest and goes into the kitchen.

I bend down to pick the bag up. The phone starts ringing. I can hear drawers being opened then slammed shut in the kitchen. I walk over to the phone and pick the receiver up. I'm going to put it straight back down, but for some reason I put it to my ear. I don't recognise the voice at first but after the third hello I realise it's my stepdad. I allow myself one hello then I make the sign of the zip. Chris sounds different. Like he's winded. He says There's no way of saying this other than just saying it. Then he tells me that my mother is dead. That she had a heart attack this morning. That they tried, but they couldn't do anything for her. That she's dead.

I put the phone down and walk into the kitchen where Grace is sat on the floor, pulling tight a handful of long black hair from her head as she saws through it with the breadknife, long black sheaves scattered about her like a nest, a sound like laughter, my own.

CHAPTER 80

We brought nothing into the world

And we take nothing out. The Lord gave, and the Lord has taken away. Blessed be the name of the Lord. We have come here today, to remember before God, our sister Jean, to give thanks for her life, to commend her to God our merciful redeemer and judge, and to comfort one another in our grief.

Let us pray. Almighty God. You judge us with infinite mercy and justice, and love everything You have made. In Your mercy, turn the darkness of death into a new dawn of life, and the sorrow of parting into the joy of Heaven through our saviour, Jesus Christ. Amen.

We will now sing one of Jean's favourite hymns, Morning Has Broken.

But.

You won't sing, will you.

You'll just stand up, the back of your knees pressing against the hard wooden pew as you stare straight ahead at the coffin, imagining the carcass inside, that lifeless thing that was once your mother, now looking down to your hands as the voices sing Sweet the rain's new fall, and all you will see are the faces of your mother's two sisters when you got here in that long black car, their reddened eyes narrowed and accusing, their trembling mouths on the cusp of telling it, your uncles curbing their contempt as they drape arms around their crying wives, turning their backs as one in a stifled mutter of loathing, you, the son that killed the mother, inch by inch, the bile and spite of years wrapping barbed-wire tendrils around her heart until...

As children of a loving Heavenly Father, let us ask His forgiveness. For He is gentle, and full of compassion. God of mercy, we acknowledge that we are all sinners. We turn from the wrong that we have thought and said and done, and are mindful of what we have failed to do.

And in the flowers lay the faces of your cousins, turned heads blossoming with indifference as you followed the coffin down the aisle, the same indifference you drew from your stepfather's sister in that long black car journey here, that same journey where you avoided the eyes of your stepfather, the air between you musk-heavy as orchid scent.

For the sake of Jesus, who died for us all, forgive us what has past, and help us to live each day in peace. Amen. Today we remember the life of Jean. Wife to Chris, mother to Billy, and mother-in-law to Grace. Grandmother to Scarlett and Joe, sister to

Julie and Belinda, and aunty to Barry, Daniel, Jason and Lance. Lord, we pray for these left behind to mourn the passing of Jean, as we pray for all of Jean's family, a loving family that loved and cherished Jean in turn.

And now let us sing another of Jean's favourite hymns. Abide With Me.

But.

Once again. You won't sing, will you.

You'll just stare at the coffin with its gold-plated handles and darkened pine finish, a box carried in here by men you didn't know and never will, placed on these pedestals in front of you as the soft staccato barks of crying women punctuate, What but thy grace can foil the tempter's power? Your eyes following the cracks between the bone-grey slabs from the coffin to your black-shoed feet, and the lace of your left shoe has come undone, Through cloud and sunshine, Lord, now look to your daughter by your side, who cries for her Nanna stiff and sunken-eyed in that box, your son as pale as a lily, moving his lips to Death's dark sting, fixed to the hymn-sheet in awkward hands, limp fringe hiding his eyes, not seeing, not wanting to see, and by his side stands his mother, your wife of seventeen years, those long dark locks scissored, and do you feel it at all?

God of mercy, Lord of life. You have made us in Your image to reflect Your truth and light. We give thanks for Jean, for the grace and mercy she received from You. For all that was good in her life. For the memories we treasure today. Saviour in mercy, hear our prayer. Lord, Your mighty power brings joy out of grief. Life out of death. Look in mercy upon Jean's family who mourn. Give them patient faith in times of darkness. And strengthen them with the knowledge of Your love. Amen.

And now, Jean's son Billy will say a few words.

You walk slow. You think you hear the whispers. You finger the piece of paper in your pocket as you walk the narrow staircase up to the pulpit. You look up, once. Faces. You breathe in. Out. You look down to the coffin.

You speak.

Love. If it means belonging to someone, then I belonged to my mum. She had me in the Sixties. We lived with Nannan. She's gone too. My mum wasn't married when she got pregnant. She had to go away to have me. People treated my mum like she was bad because she got pregnant. People made her feel bad to be a mum. She was going to give me away. Nobody would know she'd had me. Then people wouldn't have called her bad. But she kept me. She told me once, that when I came out of her, and she held me, she knew she couldn't give me away. So she kept me. She took me home. People treated her like she should be ashamed. That's what people are like. Isn't it.

I was told I should read a poem out if I didn't know what to say. I don't know any poems. So I wrote some things down.

Mum.

I wish I could talk to you again. But I can't.

I wish we hadn't fallen out so many times. But we did.

I wish we could mend things. But we can't.

Everything always goes forward. Never back.

I should have been a better son. But I wasn't.

You should have given me away. Then I would've hurt someone else. Not you.

And you will not look up as you leave the pulpit. You will walk straight down the aisle and out the church, sitting down on the steps outside, and when they all come out they will cosset you, because now you are Jean's loving and penitent son that spoke the words, and then by that hole in the ground they will gather around you, a family tree wrapping its branches around your dull husk, Ashes to ashes, that dry earth falling through fingers onto dulcet patter of unhollow casket, that hollowed-out you helped into that long black car.

Pub.

CHAPTER 81

The wake is at the Blue Bell

I used to come here when I was younger. I used to go in the taproom though. The snug has a green carpet and red velvet curtains, horse-brasses on the wall. There are sandwiches and cakes on a table. There are people here that I don't really know. Everyone is talking quietly as they eat. Some people are standing up. Some people are sitting down. Me and Grace and Scarlett and Joe sit at a table near a window. The window is crisscrossed with lead like an old window. It's not old though, it's just pretend. On my paper plate is a salmon sandwich and two pickled onions. I'm not hungry. I drink some shandy then put the glass back down on the table. The sunlight shines through the drink, making a strange rainbow on the wood. I can hear Grace's mouth eating. Her hair looks okay short. She said so this morning. She said it makes her look younger. Scarlett said she likes it too. Joe said nothing about it. Joe's eating crisps. They crunch in his mouth. Scarlett says the sandwiches are nice and Grace agrees. I drink shandy again. My tongue feels itchy. Joe looks at me as I put the glass down on the table. We make eye contact for moment then he looks down to his plate. I ask him if he's okay. He says he is. Joy and Victor and Hope sit at the table next to us. Hope has a friend with her. Her name is Tina. I get the sense that Tina is fucking Hope because they look at each other in a funny way, and sometimes when they talk they touch each other on certain words. I think it's a code or something, a way of saying things to each other without actually saying them. Tina is pretty, like Hope. I chew my sandwich until it makes a little moshed ball in my mouth. The ball is hard to swallow. Victor eats with his head hung over his plate, scooping things up like a cat eats from a dish. I glance over at Joy's plate. She has a little castle of sandwiches moated by an orange circle of Wotsits. She talks with her mouth full.

It was a lovely service, she says.

Grace agrees.

Beautiful, Joy adds.

Hope and Tina swap sandwiches with each other. They sit side by side. Under the table I can see their legs are touching.

Joy says, Ooh, your mum would have loved the service, wouldn't she Billy.

I want to say No, she wouldn't, how could she, she's dead, but instead I glance over my shandy at her and make a noise like I agree.

Behind me, someone says my name.

Cousin Barry. He has a paper plate in his upturned hand. He looks like a waiter. His other hand is on my shoulder.

Alright Billy?

My smile feels stiff.

He pats the top of my arm, then thankfully he stops. I haven't seen Barry for a couple of years. He has a little moustache and a side-parting, which makes him look even more like a waiter. Behind him stands a woman with a wonky fringe. Barry looks around our table and smiles.

Lovely service, he says.

Beautiful, says Joy.

Barry ushers the wonky-fringed woman forward and says This is Jessica.

Jessica says Hello, then does a little wave at everyone.

Barry stands there grinning, his arm draped around Jessica. He looks like he's just won a teddy at the fair. From behind Jessica, Uncle Gerry and Aunty Julie appear. Uncle Gerry has two drinks. He puts a pint of what looks like lager in front of me, says Get that down yer, lad.

Aunty Julie bends down to my ear and whispers That was lovely what you said about your mum, Billy.

When she moves away from my ear she nods with her lips sucked in. Uncle Gerry pats me on the shoulder as I drink. It's definitely lager.

Aunty Julie tells us about Daniel. Apparently Daniel isn't here because he's somewhere in the Middle East with the army. The conversation flickers around me as I sit and drink. Grace catches my eye for a second as I put the half-drunk pint on the table next to the quarter-drunk shandy. There seems to be something in Grace's look. I get up and go to the toilet.

Pissing, I remember once in here when I pissed myself a little. Not too much, but enough. I stood here holding a lighter to the dark piss-flower on my jeans trying to dry it off. Someone came in and laughed at me. I think I must have laughed too.

On my way out the toilet some old gadge stops me to shake my hand. I don't recognise him.

Ernie, he says, Used to work on the farm. The pigs.

I pretend to be pleased to see him and I ask him how he is. He says he's sorry about my mum. Ernie says his wife passed away last year so he knows how I must feel. I nod, and for some reason I say Thanks.

Anyway, he says, pointing to the toilet door.

Back at the table, Chris is talking to Joe. It was strange talking to Chris after Mum died. Me and Grace went round because we had to sort the funeral stuff out. I was relieved in a way because it meant we had to talk. He cried when we talked about the coffin. I've never seen him cry before.

But that was good too, because it meant me and Grace had to comfort him, which meant it broke the awkwardness of it all. Before we went home I said I was sorry. He hugged me and said he was too. This meant everything was sorted, which was good.

I watch Chris and Joe talking to each other. Joe laughs and Chris play-thumps him in the arm. Grace and Victor are talking too. Victor says Yeh, had an interview there last week, bet I'll not get it though, and Grace says something about counting and chickens. Victor shakes his head then blows air out the side of his mouth. Joy and Hope are still talking to Aunty Julie and Uncle Gerry.

Definitely, says Uncle Gerry. Burn me up rather than worm fodder any day.

Joy laughs.

Hope says something about being put into the sea so her soul can travel the planet. Tina says me too. Hope seems louder now she's with Tina. Under the table I can see Tina's hand on Hope's thigh.

I drink. Scarlett is still eating. I watch her. She must feel me looking because she looks up from her plate and half-smiles at me. I feel myself half-smile back. People say she looks like me.

Billy!

I turn to see Aunty Belinda coming toward me, arms outstretched. She hugs me hard and says into my ear Your mum would have loved what you said.

She lets go of me, kneels by my side so our faces

are at the same level. She has a glass of wine in her hand. The other hand pats my leg.

She says, How you feeling, luv?

I drink the last of my lager, and putting the empty glass to the table, I say Okay ta.

Oh Billy, she says, her bottom lip tightening, How I wish you and your mother could've gotten on better.

I look to the carpet for a second, and I figure I'm going to say Me too as a full pint clacks on the table in front of me. I look up. It's my cousin Jason.

There's another one in at the bar for you Billy-O. He raises his thumb. Alright Mum? he says to Aunty Belinda.

She smiles, says Yes ta, luv.

I raise the glass to Jason as he turns and heads back to the bar. Aunty Belinda pats my leg again, her hand remaining on my leg as I drink.

Daft, she says, pat pat, That's how we are though.

I drink, she drinks, I ask her what she means.

Dunno, she says shaking her head, But it's like we never realise what we've got until it's gone.

I nod, drink, then say Suppose so.

A hand slaps the table. I look up to see Joy nodding her head quick with eyes wide.

You got that right! she says, wagging a finger. Me and my husband Willy were always at it. Hammer and bleedin tongs we were. Always bloody bickering at each other. And then, **POOF!**

She clicks her fingers in the air.

Gone! Just like that!

Aunty Belinda stands then sits down on the stool that was Victor's, starts talking to Joy about Grace's dad.

If I was in a cunt of a mood I'd be tempted to ask Joy if poof! meant buggering off with a barmaid then dying of throat cancer several years later. Instead, I drink up and head to the bar.

Jason's brother Lance buys me a double Bell's. I don't know Lance that well. He's Aunty Belinda's youngest, and even though he's in his twenties he still seems to be a little boy. We talk about football as we drink. He follows Chesterfield. I don't follow anyone, but I used to like Liverpool, and then tried to get interested in Celtic. I feel fake as I talk, like I'm pretending, so I listen to Lance mostly. He tells me about Chesterfield's new signings. I don't know either player but I still go Oh yeh, like I do.

Uncle George comes to the bar and buys us all a drink. Lance doesn't make eye contact with his dad, and Uncle George seems to be pretending that him and Lance are best mates.

There you go, Lancey, he says, handing his son a pint of Heineken.

Ah, footy isn't what it was, Uncle George says. Too much money in it now.

Neither Lance nor me say anything.

No more Georgie Bests no more, he says, shaking his head.

Lance drinks. So do I.

Better off with the horses, he says.

I finish my whisky. Uncle George gets me another.

What you got in the Gold Cup, Billy?

I shake my head. Nothing, I say.

He tells me and Lance to put our money on Red Hand.

You'll get a good price if you get it on now, he says.

I watch his Adam's apple rise then sink as he sups. His skin is dry-shiny like a lizard's.

I raise my glass, say Ta, then go back to our table where Chris is talking to Grace.

Yeh, he says, Try less grass clippings. And wee is great for breaking your compost down.

Grace laughs as Aunty Deirdre and her husband Tony sit down opposite them.

Tony says Yep, get yourself a little potty in your shed and get it chucked in, lass.

I watch them all laugh.

On the next table, Scarlett is talking to Joy and Victor. She glances up at me and smiles. I think we're better now. I light a fag and go stand by the window.

Scarlett called me a bastard when she came downstairs and saw her mum's hair. I think she thought I'd done it. I'd never heard her swear before.

I could hear her crying as she tried to tidy it up with the scissors. Then Joe came downstairs. He didn't call me anything. He just pretended I wasn't there. Grace told me to go away. I went to the shop and bought a half-Bell's, then I went for a walk to the ponds. I remember thinking about when we used to take Jack there. Sometimes we'd take a picnic. When we took Jack to the vet's a while ago, we all held hands and watched as the vet put Jack to sleep. Funny. They call it going to sleep, but it's not, it's dying. I remember his eye seeming to go cloudy as he died, but really it didn't. Why did I think it did? When I got to the ponds it was dark. The moon was out, and I was looking how it reflected in the big pond. It seemed to tremble in the water but there wasn't any wind. Some birds were singing. Odd chirps like the end of a conversation that made no sense to begin with. I could hear the motorway dull-humming too, and I remember wishing it wasn't there, so all I could hear was the birds. When I got back, Grace had told Joe and Scarlett about my mum. All three of them were crying. They all hugged me, and Grace said we'd have to pull together now. The next morning I was sick loads. I felt bad about everything but it was good that we all started being nice to each other. That seems to be what death does. Makes everyone nice.

I drink up and go to the bar. I order a treble Jameson and a Guinness. They don't have either so I have a pint of Murphy's and a treble Bushmills. I've not had Bushmills before. It tastes alright. I prefer Guinness to Murphy's though. An old couple come over and talk to me. They say my mum used to call in when she went for a walk down the lane. My mum used to take them tomato plants apparently. They say other things too but I'm not listening. Old people bore the fuck out of me. After a few minutes they seem to get the sense that I don't care and they go and talk to someone else. Good.

I order the same again as Uncle Gerry comes over to the bar. He pays for the drinks, talks about way back when, Them Sat'day afternoons round at Ena's. It's funny, because he talks about it like it was just Nannan's house and not mine. After a bit I stop listening to him, then Uncle George comes over in his lizard skin so I go back to standing by the window and light a fag. I don't want to talk to Uncle George. He's a cunt.

Through the window I can see the back of the old library. I remember nicking records from there when I was a kid. I still have some of them. Shame I threw my turntable at the wall.

You remember your cousin Raymond don't you, Billy?

I turn my gaze from the window. Aunty Julie has her arm around a tall bloke with a neat haircut.

Well, second cousin really isn't he, she says. Your granddad's, sister's, daughter's lad.

She looks up to the ceiling, and letting go of Raymond, she claps her hands together.

Phew! That took some working out!

Aunty Julie and Raymond laugh. Then Raymond offers me his hand. I pretend not to notice and put my pint to my lips. I notice a flicker of something in his eyes when I don't shake his hand, which goes slowly back to his side.

You remember don't you Billy? Your Nannan used to take you to see Raymond and your Aunty Della when you were little.

I nod.

Yeh. I remember.

Sorry to hear about your mum, Billy, Raymond says.

I nod again, drink.

Still like your Batman comics then, Raymond?

I watch his eyes. I see that flicker again. He looks to the carpet and laughs.

Well, I still have the collection, he says, But I don't read them anymore.

Ooh, is it any wonder? Aunty Julie says to Raymond. Bet you don't have the time, luv.

And then to me, He's got three kids to look after you know. On his own! And he's a policeman!

Raymond looks to the carpet again. His face is the face of someone being told that they're wonderful, when in fact they're not. And they know it.

Bringing three kids up on his own! says Aunty

Julie. Deserves a bloody medal, she says. Don't you, luv.

Raymond shrugs. He seems to be blushing. I feel a dagger in my hand.

What happened to the missus then?

He shrugs again. Better off without her, he says. Kids keep me happy enough.

I hear myself cough with a short pop of a laugh. I bet they do, Raymond.

The pissiness drips off my words like spit. He looks into my eyes for what feels like an age. Aunty Julie's hand strokes his arm.

I bet they do too, luv, she says.

Raymond is still staring at me. I grin. He looks to the carpet then turns to Aunty Julie.

Well, just thought I'd pop in and pay my respects. Got to get off. Got someone looking after the kids.

Aunty Julie makes an ahhh sound then hugs Raymond.

Well, it was lovely to see you, she says.

Raymond offers me his hand again.

Goodbye, Billy, he says.

I take his hand and he squeezes, too hard, his eyes fixed on mine. Take care now, he says.

I pull away from his grip, put both my hands to the side of my head like bat ears.

NANA-NANA-NANA-NANA RAY-MOND!

Aunty Julie laughs. Raymond pretends to, then

leaves. Aunty Julie pats my arm then heads off to talk to Barry and Jessica at the bar.

Through the window, I watch Raymond cross the road. He walks fast like he's angry, or like in a film when someone knows they're being followed, but doesn't want to let on.

I drink, and I feel like a coward.

Why didn't you tell Raymond any of the things you always said you'd say? I drink, thinking about what he used to make me do, like I'm watching it on telly, and then something occurs to me that I've never considered before, ever.

What if he didn't actually make you do it? What if you did it because you wanted to? Because you liked how it felt? Surely if you didn't like it you'd have shouted? Nannan was only in the next room, wasn't she. You, laid on the floor with your trousers round your knees, his fist moving up and down your cock while you, arm outstretched, hand wrapped round his cock doing the same, his other hand clasped tight over yours, pull and push as he straddles your legs on his knees, and then... And then that sense of wonder, his spunk on your belly, his face red as it untightens, the look in his eyes of being there but not. And then... you did it half a dozen more times after that, didn't you.

Wouldn't you have told someone if you didn't like it? Well? Wouldn't you?

I open my eyes. I look once at Joe, once at Scarlett,

then I leave by the backdoor. I call at the off-licence and buy three bottles of cheap vodka. I leave the village, start walking to the edge of here, to where the lane starts. As I near the woods I think about my mother. It makes me cry because I feel nothing. I drink from the bottle, understanding that I love no one. Not Grace, not Scarlett, not Joe. No one. As I see the dark lines of the trees, I know the day has gone to night, and nothing can bring it back. I climb over the barbed-wire. The only sound is that of myself, my feet that crick-crack the undergrowth, my breath as it leaves my body, my heart as it bumps in my chest.

The air is colder here.

I am alone, and it's getting darker.

CHAPTER 82

A rook scraws

It's morning, but through leaves I can see a star. A morning star is like an afternoon moon. Things mixed up. I poke my stick into the fly-tip again. A pigeon clapflaps. A cuckoo calls. Two hands make a cave, blow between thumbs but I don't.

I dig my stick deeper, lifting an old bike wheel and a bagful of broken plaster on top. Under the wheel is a doll with no clothes on, its head dinted so one of its eyes is sunken shut.

I drink, then try to spear the baby in its belly. It takes three goes, and when it goes it goes POK. I dance the dead baby over my head, turn in the air under leaves, blue eye winks at me so I swing the stick quick, send the dead baby flying through nettles till it hits a tree, stays stood up one blue eye staring, dinted eye still shut not looking but the other one is. Funny.

I drink, then pick up a piece of broken plaster, throw it at the dead baby like a bomb. I miss, so I bend down get another. This is a good game. I nearly hit it so I try again. The bomb hits the tree above the baby's head. It pops on the bark and leaves a pinky-white star. I try again. And again. The dead baby is smiling. It stares at me. I throw harder. I miss. I drink.

Hello Billy.

The voice makes me jump. I turn quick, and there stood between two trees is that boy again. He's smiling, and he puts his hands in the air like he surrenders. I'm holding the stick out in front of me like a gun. I put it pointing downwards by my side and I can hear my heart go bump bump. I put the bottle back to the ground.

What you playing? he says.

Bomb the dead baby, I tell him.

That's a good game, he says.

Yes, I tell him.

He comes to me through wild garlic and nettles, stopping halfway to look at the den letting out a long slow whistle. I pick the bottle up, drink, and when I put it back down he's by my side.

Let's finish the game, he says.

Yes, I tell him.

We take it in turns, him first then me. We both miss then miss again. We drink.

We need some luck, he says, and he bends down to pull up a dandelion clock that stands between dock leaves.

Blow, he says, so I do.

We watch the pale fairies float soft in the air, first going up towards treetops, then slow falling through spindly fingers of sun. We drink as the fairies fall. The cuckoo calls. I put the bottle down, and the boy says Riddle.

I want to tell him no, that I don't want to think about things, but before I can speak he tells it. He says Morning Glory chokes the corn so the angry farmer says Devil, but a happy girl makes a necklace blue, thanking God for the flowers.

I feel a bit sick. I want to tell the boy I've stopped playing with people.

He says, So who's right?

We drink, then as we bend down to get another bomb I tell him I don't know the answer, because I don't.

There is no answer, he says.

I tell him that's stupid, and he goes all quiet. I think he might go away, but he doesn't. We drink.

He says, Let's finish the game, and he points to the dead baby.

Look, he says, You're winning.

I look at my pinky-white star above the dead baby's head. He's right. I am winning.

He goes first again, and this time he hits the tree, bits of bomb a dry rain trembling the nettles below. He smiles. On the brown-green bark above the dead baby's head now are two pinky-white stars right next to each other.

We're the same, I tell him.

Yes, he says.

We drink. Then it's my go. I close my eyes and hope the dandelion fairies have brought me luck.

Go, he says, so I open my eyes and throw as hard as I can. My bomb explodes right next to the dead baby's head. The baby blinks as the nettles shudder.

You're winning again, he says.

I smile at him. We drink.

Let's have a rest now, he says. Are you hungry?

I tell him I don't know.

C'mon, he says, and I follow him to the blackberry bush. We kneel down in front of it. A rook scraws.

We should eat from it, he says.

We can't, I tell him.

Why? he says.

Because they're not ready for us. Look.

We look, and the blackberries are pale green with bits of red, not blacky-purple like they should be.

He tells me that I'm a scaredy-cat, that I'm a chicken, that I'm a cowardy-custard, so I eat. It's like a dare. The more he eats, the more I eat. Then I'm sick. A lot. I tell him I don't like being sick.

He says, So it's another riddle then.

Yes, I say.

So what's the answer?

I think about it, but not for too long because this one is easy. I wipe my mouth with my sleeve.

That I was right, I tell him.

Yes, he says, But you had to do it, to know it, didn't you.

We stay kneeling. We drink. I feel better now. He looks to the den.

C'mon, he says, Let's go inside.

We walk through nettles to get there. Some nettles poke up my trousers as I walk and my legs get stung. I go into the den and sit on the log settee. He has a dock leaf in his hand. He sits in front of me, rolls my trousers up to the knee and rubs where it stings. It feels nice. The dock leaf is cold on my skin. We look at the little white bumps on my legs. The little white bumps have red blotches around them. We drink. A pigeon clapflaps.

What's in there? he says.

I look to where the boy is pointing. It's my little cupboard in the corner where I keep things. It only has three legs. The fourth is a plant-pot. I'm not sure I want him to see inside, but it was nice what he did with the dock leaf so I tell him to look and see.

I watch him open the door. He smiles. Yes, he says. He puts the things on the ground and sits next to me on the log settee. We drink. We look at the things. He points to each and gives it a name.

Book. Cut. Fuck.

I like the boy. He makes me laugh. He picks up the thing he calls Fuck. We drink, and look at Tracey in red knickers. We drink, and look at Sapphire playing tennis. We drink, and look at Cherry laying on a settee with her eyes closed. We both like Cherry the best. I kneel down and pull at myself as he watches. When it comes out of me I look at him and not Cherry. We stay still for a while and listen to the wind play soft in the leaves. It sounds like water moving in a river. I close my eyes. I hear my heart bump in my ears like a flat-hand pat pat against a cushion, slow, then slower. When I open my eyes again a bluebottle trembles on the wetness below, feeding on what came out of me.

The boy laughs. I put myself away. We drink. I don't know what to say so I say nothing. I feel bad because he watched what I did when we looked at Cherry. I feel him watching me now. He says if I don't know what to say I should say a poem. He picks up Book and puts it in my hands. I look at it. It's blue and it's dirty and the edge of the pages are yellowy-brown.

Go on, he says, Say one.

I still feel bad so I just sit there looking at the book in my hands.

This one, he says, and he opens it in the middle, pointing, Here, he says, Say the words out.

I tell him I don't want to. Not on my own.

He says, Together then. So we do.

We say, A furious angel swoops like an eagle from the sky, grips the sinner's hair in his fist then shakes him, shouting **YOU WILL LEARN THE RULE! FOR I AM YOUR GOOD ANGEL!**

DO YOU HEAR? KNOW THAT WITHOUT QUESTION YOU MUST LOVE THE NEEDY, THE SPITEFUL, THE DEFORMED, THE DUMB, SO THAT YOU MAY MAKE FOR JESUS WHEN HE COMES, A CARPET OF TRIUMPH WITH YOUR CHARITY! THIS IS LOVE! YOU MUST ACT BEFORE YOUR HEART EXPIRES! LET THE GLORY OF GOD SET IT AFIRE! RAPTURE! THIS IS THE TRUE DESIRE THAT CANNOT ROT! And the angel never ceasing chastises with love, beats the blasphemer with giant fists, and yet still, the damned man forever insists, NO! I WILL NOT!

We look at each other.

I tell him I don't understand.

He tells me It doesn't matter, because it got the bad out.

And he's right, it did.

We drink. He picks up the breadknife.

Cut, he says.

We sit side by side and look at it. It's as long as a school ruler and has Woolworth's written on the handle.

The knife is dirty so I rub it on my shirt. A rook scraws. When we look again we can see ourselves in the blade.

Brothers, he says. Lips, hair, eye and eye.

He tells me we should make a promise, like in films when Red Indians turn blood brothers, but I don't want to cut myself, and I tell him so.

He says, Spit then. So I spit in my hand, and then he spits in his. The spit is slippy between us. It's funny. We drink.

They're trying to find you, he says, And they'll tell you that happy is only if you belong to them.

I think about happy. It doesn't take long. I tell him what I think.

That's the riddle, he says, It doesn't matter to them what you think, when they catch you they'll tell you it's bad to be alone.

Will they always be after me?

Yes, he says, The world is already made that way.

I feel sad now, and he sees it.

C'mon, he says, Follow me.

We walk through the wood to where the trees run out and the meadow starts. Somewhere a song thrush is singing. It sounds beautiful. As we leave the trees the sun hurts my eyes. We sit down in the long grass and lie on our backs. I shield my eyes with my arm. The sun feels good, sending little tickles over my skin. We drink. I can hear him breathing. A grasshopper is making a little crackly-creak sound.

Everything out here is stuck together, he says, Because everything needs everything else, or it dies.

I like the sound of his voice. It seems to fit between all the other sounds I can hear. The song thrush. The grasshopper. The little breezes that blow the grass. I ask him to say more things so I can listen. We drink.

Then he says, The grass doesn't think, the birds don't think, the flies don't think. But people do. And that's the riddle.

I don't understand and I tell him so.

Thinking makes rules, he says, But if you tell them no, they throw you out but keep you in at the same time.

This riddle is hard. I still don't get it. We drink, then I ask him to say more so I can understand.

He says, We didn't ask to be with them. They told us we were. We didn't have a choice. And when we said no, they said we were guilty.

I tell him this must be true because I am guilty, that being guilty makes me feel bad, that I've always felt bad so I must have been guilty always.

Yes, he says, But what's true?

We drink, and then I see it's all gone. Everything looks different. The world bends through the empty bottle. To get more means to go back, and I can't go back. I throw it. Gone.

We look into the blade again and he tells me it's alright. He kisses me on the lips. His kiss is cold but it feels nice.

We stand up, walk slow back into the wood. I can't hear the grasshopper anymore, or the song thrush. The air is colder here, and the deeper we go, the darker it gets. I follow him to the dead baby tree.

I was winning, I tell him.

NO! he shouts, and he runs at the baby, kicks it in the head, sends it crashing through nettles to where neither of us can see it anymore. **NO!** he shouts, and he stabs the knife into the tree, hard. I watch him as he carves lines of bark out, the lines becoming letters, the letters becoming words. I see it, and understand. We lie down in a prickly nest of flattened nettles. We look into the blade.

Let's finish the game, he says, and he kisses me, his tongue cold as it strokes my cheek. I look up at the carved marks, the glisten of the yellowing insides, the barkless spaces bare where sap slow weeps from the words.

Everything always goes forward, he whispers, Never back.

I close my eyes as his kisses sting my face. He kisses harder, his tongue prodding sharp, the hot wetness now running across my cheeks, down behind my ears, my neck, and it hurts, but I don't want him to stop. In me, I tell him, and his tongue is in my mouth, cold as it burns, deeper, twisting, and I taste the blood, the burning, and the fire is on me, in me, deeper, twisting, until I cough the sharp snake out, open my eyes as his tongue kisses my throat cold open, the rook scraws, an angry breath shakes the leaves with the sound of a river, and I am alone, at last, and falling, the dark woods blacken around the burning words as every light draws in, a pale moth that flickers as a hand reaches out, and I kick it away, not wanting, not needing no God as the words burn red on the flaming tree above, telling them all, for no one

BILLY

WOZ

ERE.